PATH *of* BEASTS

THE KEEPERS

Museum of Thieves
City of Lies
Path of Beasts

LIAN TANNER

THE KEEPERS

PATH of BEASTS

ALLEN&UNWIN

This paperback edition first published in 2013

Allen & Unwin
83 Alexander Street
Crows Nest NSW 2065
Australia
Phone: (61 2) 8425 0100
Email: info@allenandunwin.com
Web: www.allenandunwin.com

A Cataloguing-in-Publication entry is available from
the National Library of Australia
www.trove.nla.gov.au

ISBN 978 1 74331 166 0

Cover and text design by Design by Committee
Cover and text illustration by Sebastian Ciaffaglione
Set in 12 pt Adobe Caslon by Midland Typesetters, Australia
Printed in Australia by SOS Print + Media Group

10 9 8 7 6 5

For Jesse, Maddii and Seb,
with love

CONTENTS

CONTENTS

Who can walk the Beast Road?
There must be three.
Two mortal enemies
with one between them
who is both friend and enemy,
native and stranger.

Where does the Beast Road go?
To a timeless place
from which no one
has ever returned.

What does the Beast Road hold?
Terror for those who hurry.
Death for those who linger.
But for Furuuna
it holds salvation.

These are the words of an old Furuuna
song. Before Goldie Roth, the last person to
walk the Beast Road was Herro Dan's father,
accompanied by two of his brothers. The three
men were not mortal enemies - far from it - but
their country was being overrun by the invaders
from Merne and they were desperate.

Dan, who was six years old at the time, was
to remember their departure for the rest of his
life.

None of them ever returned.

THE CAPTIVE CITY

It was night-time when the three children entered the city of Jewel. Ragged and filthy, they clung to the shadows, their feet making no sound on the cobbled paths.

They had been gone for weeks, torn away from home without the chance to say goodbye, and they were bursting with impatience to see their parents. But they carried secrets with them – secrets that would get them killed if they were caught by the

Goldie Roth

wrong people. And so they stopped and listened at every corner.

They saw no one, but the hair on the backs of their necks prickled and their faces were pale with tension. This was not the city they had left behind. Fear hung over the streets, as thick as fog. The light of the watergas lamps seemed to tremble as it spilled across the deserted footpaths. The houses, with their locked doors and tightly drawn curtains, held their breath.

The children crept deeper and deeper into the city, until at last they came to the Bridge of Beasts, where it crossed the Grand Canal. They paused there, watching for any sign of movement. Then they slipped across the bridge one by one.

They were close to their homes now, and eager to press on. But the last few weeks had taught them the value of caution, and they paused again.

It was just as well they did. Somewhere nearby a boot struck the cobblestones. Immediately, Goldie gave a hand signal and all three children pressed into the shadows at the end of the bridge. Toadspit wrapped his fingers around the hilt of the sword that he carried at his side. His younger sister Bonnie gripped her longbow. But Goldie shook her head fiercely at them, and they did not move again.

The five men who came swaggering up the middle

of the boulevard were clearly soldiers, although their uniforms and haversacks seemed to be made up of bits and pieces from a dozen different armies. They carried rifles slung across their chests, and their eyes and teeth gleamed in the gaslight. They looked as if they owned the city and everything in it.

Goldie had been expecting something like this, but still it was a shock to see such men on the streets of Jewel. She found her hand straying towards the sword on Toadspit's hip. Her breath quickened . . .

No! She jerked her hand back. The wolf-sark, the battle madness that she carried so unwillingly inside her, lay just below the surface. If she drew that sword she would be lost. She had almost killed someone last time the wolf-sark took hold of her. She would not risk it happening again.

She swallowed her anger and prayed that the soldiers would pass quickly.

But the soldiers seemed to have no intention of passing. One of them, a tall man with red side-whiskers that curled almost to his chin, leaned his rifle against the canal fence and took biscuits and a water canteen from his haversack. His companions copied him.

Toadspit touched Goldie's hand, tapping out a question in the quick, subtle movements of fingertalk. '*Go or stay?*'

Goldie chewed her lip. She and Toadspit could easily slip away without being seen. If they *really* wanted to, they could probably steal the biscuits out of the soldiers' hands and leave them wondering where their supper had gone. But Bonnie had not had the same training and might well be spotted.

'*Stay*,' Goldie signed.

The men lounged against the fence, throwing biscuits at each other and guffawing at the tops of their voices, as if they wanted everyone in the surrounding houses to hear them and tremble. They reminded Goldie of the soldiers she and Toadspit had encountered deep inside the Museum of Dunt, behind the Dirty Gate. *Those* soldiers were the remnants of an ancient war that only survived within the museum. They carried pikes and swords and old-fashioned muskets, and spoke in the accents of Old Merne.

But these men were modern, and their scrappy uniforms suggested that they were mercenaries, whose loyalty could be bought and sold. Goldie wondered what they had done with the city's militia. And where was the Grand Protector? *She* would never have allowed mercenaries on the streets of Jewel—

Goldie's thoughts were interrupted by the sound of a street-rig clattering over cobblestones. The mercenaries hastily shovelled food and drinks back into their haversacks and grabbed their rifles.

'What sort of idiot drives around after curfew?' growled the red-haired man. 'Anyone'd think they *want* to be stuck in the House of Repentance!'

'They're coming this way,' said one of his companions, strutting out into the middle of the road.

Spoked wheels rattled towards him. An engine roared, and headlights pierced the shadows that surrounded the children. Goldie dared not look at her friends, but she could feel Bonnie as tense as a wire beside her, and Toadspit, balanced on the balls of his feet, ready to run. If the mercenaries turned around now . . .

But the men were strung across the boulevard, blocking the path of the approaching street-rig. For a moment, Goldie thought it wasn't going to stop. It rumbled towards the soldiers at a steady pace, bathing them in light. Its horn blared twice. An angry voice shouted something incoherent. The mercenaries raised their rifles and took careful aim at the cabin behind the lights.

With a squeal of brakes, the street-rig skidded to a halt. The engine died. The shout came again, but this time Goldie heard it clearly.

'How dare you? How *dare* you? Remove yourselves from our path immediately!'

The mercenaries didn't budge. 'Out of the rig,' said the red-haired man in a bored tone. 'Come on, make it quick.'

There was a mutter of voices and, to Goldie's relief, the headlights snapped off. By the time her eyes had adjusted, two people were stepping down from the street-rig – two people wearing the heavy black robes and black boxy hats of the Blessed Guardians.

A shiver of loathing ran through Goldie. It was more than six months since the Blessed Guardians had been banished from the city. The Grand Protector had put them on trial first, for treason and cruelty. Then she had thrown every single one of them out of Jewel, with a warning never to return.

But here they were, back again.

Goldie touched Toadspit's hand. '*Leave now, while they're busy,*' she signed.

Toadspit nodded, and murmured in his sister's ear. But before they could move, the two Guardians swept past the mercenaries and marched straight towards the end of the bridge.

'Hey!' shouted the red-haired man, striding after them with his side-whiskers bristling. 'Where do you think you're going? There's supposed to be no one on the streets at night. That's our orders.'

The Blessed Guardians stopped, not five paces from

6

where the children crouched. One of them, a man with very pale skin, raised his eyebrows. 'The curfew doesn't apply to *us*, you fool!' he said, in a high, grating voice. 'Go and carry out your orders somewhere else.'

He turned to his companion, as if the mercenaries had already gone, and waved his hand at the canal. 'This place will do as well as anywhere. It is tidal here, and the levees are open. The – ah – rubbish will be swept out to sea before morning.'

'But what if it is not?' said the second Guardian, a woman, in worried tones. 'If someone sees it, it could cause trouble.'

Goldie's heart pounded against her ribs, and her fingers crept to the blue bird brooch that was pinned inside her collar. The Guardians had only to turn their heads, and she and her friends would be discovered.

'If someone *sees* it,' said the pale man, 'we will simply convince them that they did *not* see it.' He laughed. 'And if they persist in their error, well then, I believe there are still plenty of empty cells in the House of Repentance.'

Behind him, the mercenaries muttered to each other. The red-haired man clearly resented being called a fool and, when the Guardians turned to walk back to their street-rig, he blocked their path.

'The way *I* understand it,' he said, 'no one on the streets means *no one* on the streets. Nothing in our orders about making an exception for people in funny hats.'

His friends sniggered. The pale man sighed, and spoke slowly, as if he was dealing with very small children. 'Listen carefully. I am Guardian Kindness, and this—' he nodded to the woman at his side '—is Guardian Meek. We are here on the Fugleman's business. Remember the Fugleman?' His voice was sarcastic. 'He is our leader. He is also the Lord High Protector of this city. Which means that, while you are in his employ, he is *your* leader as well.'

Goldie felt Bonnie's cold hand slip into hers, and knew that they were all wondering the same thing. If the Fugleman, the worst traitor in the history of Jewel, was truly in charge, and calling himself Protector, what had happened to the real Protector?

'It would not be wise,' continued Guardian Kindness, 'to hinder us. In fact, you would do better to help. We have a certain parcel that we need to dispose of. Please get it out of the rig and bring it here.'

The red-haired man snorted. 'You want us to do your work for you? I don't think so!' He began to walk away. The other mercenaries followed.

'You *will* bring it here, if you know what's good for you. We are the servants of the Seven Gods and they will not be kind to those who oppose us.'

Something in Guardian Kindness's high voice made Goldie's skin crawl. She flicked her fingers to ward off the attentions of the Seven Gods. So did the red-haired man. But he kept walking.

The youngest of the mercenaries, however, hesitated. 'What sort of parcel?'

'It is just some rubbish that we wish to dispose of,' said Guardian Meek quickly. 'It won't take a minute to throw it in the canal. A strong fellow like you—'

'Leave it!' snapped the red-haired man, over his shoulder. 'It's their business, not ours. We're not taking orders from *them*!'

'It is apparent,' said Guardian Kindness, 'that you do not understand your proper place—'

He was interrupted by the very ordinary sound of a man clearing his throat. It had an immediate effect. The Blessed Guardians snapped to attention. A chill ran up Goldie's spine. She heard the hiss of Toadspit's indrawn breath, and felt Bonnie's nails dig into her hand.

The door of the street-rig swung open. An elegant boot appeared, followed by an immaculate trouser leg. A cloak, blacker than the blackest of nights, fell around that leg in perfect folds. A sword glittered in the lamplight.

It was the Fugleman.

A PARCEL OF RUBBISH

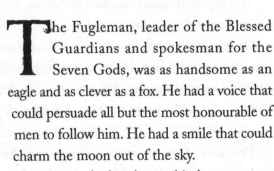

The Fugleman, leader of the Blessed Guardians and spokesman for the Seven Gods, was as handsome as an eagle and as clever as a fox. He had a voice that could persuade all but the most honourable of men to follow him. He had a smile that could charm the moon out of the sky.

But beneath the charm, his heart was as black as his cloak.

At the sight of her old enemy, anger rose up inside Goldie like a blast furnace. A bitter taste filled her mouth and, deep in the cellars of her mind, the voice of a long-dead

The Fugleman

warrior princess whispered, *Kill him now, where he stands.*

Once again, Goldie's hand strayed towards the sword.

No! She shuddered and pulled it back. There would be no killing, not if she could help it.

The Fugleman gestured towards the street-rig. 'The parcel of rubbish,' he murmured. 'Into the canal, please, gentlemen.'

This time the red-haired man did as he was told. Goldie saw him pause briefly at the open door of the rig, as if he was surprised at what he saw there. Then he beckoned to the youngest of his companions. 'Grab the other end.'

The younger man showed even more surprise, but he covered it up quickly, and scrambled into the rig to grab hold of a long, heavy parcel wrapped in hessian. Between them, the two men dragged it out the door and carried it to the gate in the canal fence.

The Guardians watched in silence. The Fugleman took a silver toothpick from his breast pocket and began to clean his teeth. Bonnie's nails bit so hard into Goldie's hand that she thought they would draw blood.

The younger mercenary opened the canal gate, then stopped. Goldie thought she heard a sound come from the parcel. A groan? A half-strangled breath?

The mercenary looked as if he was going to say something, but the redhead scowled at him and muttered, 'Heave ho.'

With a mighty swing, the two men threw the parcel into the canal. There was a splash and a gurgle. The taste in Goldie's mouth was so sour that she could hardly swallow.

The mercenaries wiped their hands on their trouser legs, their faces expressionless. The two Blessed Guardians hung back politely while the Fugleman climbed into the street-rig, then they followed him, slamming the doors behind them. The engine hiccuped. The spoked wheels turned. The rig rumbled back the way it had come.

The youngest mercenary cleared his throat. 'That parcel,' he began. 'I think—'

'No, you don't,' growled the redhead. 'You don't think anything at all. You just follow orders like the rest of us. Come on. We've got work to do.'

And the five of them marched away without a backward glance.

As soon as they had gone, the children slipped out of the shadows. 'Did you *see?*' whispered Bonnie. 'It was—'

She put her hand over her mouth, her eyes huge. Toadspit nodded grimly. Goldie unlatched the canal gate and they ran down the stone steps.

The lamplight barely carried this far. Goldie scanned the surface of the water, but all she could make out was a ripple of movement, as if the tide was just past the turn. The stones around her stank of salt and slime and gutted fish.

'There!' said Toadspit. 'Under the bridge!'

A narrow towpath ran along the canal just above the high-tide mark. The children edged down it – and there was the parcel with one end sticking up out of the water, snagged on a projecting iron bolt. The current lapped against it, trying to drag it past the bridge and the open levees, out into the bay.

'We'll have to float it back to the steps,' whispered Bonnie.

'No,' said Goldie. 'It's safer here. If the mercenaries come back, or the Guardians, the bridge will hide us.'

As she spoke, she unhooked the hessian from the iron bolt. 'Grab hold,' she whispered. 'It's heavy.'

It took them several tries to haul the parcel out of the canal onto the wet stone. It flopped awkwardly, and their hands were clumsy with the cold. Goldie could hear Bonnie's teeth chattering.

At last the parcel lay at their feet. The hessian was bound with rope, and the knots were tight. As Toadspit unfolded his knife and began to slice through them, Goldie wished that she could walk away, just go home to Ma and Pa and not have to see what the Fugleman had been so keen to get rid of in the middle of the night.

But the voice in the back of her mind whispered, *A warrior does not walk away.*

With the rope gone, Toadspit slit the hessian at one end and pulled it back. Goldie heard the sharp hiss of her own breath—

—a whimper from Bonnie—

—Toadspit's groan.

The body that lay on the narrow path, bloodstained and limp, was that of the Grand Protector.

BOW, SWORD AND WOLF-SARK

For a moment all three children were so shocked that they could not move. Goldie had to make herself breathe. She remembered the sound that she had heard – that she had *thought* she heard. She put her hand on the Protector's throat and felt a feeble pulse.

'She's alive,' she whispered. 'Just.'

Toadspit leaped to his feet, his face as pale as candlewax in

Toadspit

the darkness. 'I'll go and get Sinew.' He dropped his sword belt to the ground and was gone almost before he finished speaking.

Goldie sat back on her haunches and gathered her scattered wits, trying not to look at the Protector's frozen face.

'She's bleeding,' said Bonnie. 'There, on her chest.'

Goldie's heart jolted. 'We'd better try to stop it. See if you can find where it's coming from.'

Neither she nor Bonnie had a scrap of clean cloth on them, and the Protector's own clothes were sodden and filthy. Goldie fumbled in the crevices of the bridge and dragged out a handful of spider webs.

She was folding them into a wad when Bonnie said, in a small voice, 'Goldie? She's wearing a padded vest under her blouse. It buckles at the side and I can't undo it. I'm scared I'll hurt her!'

Goldie fumbled with the buckles, wishing she had more light. It was probably the vest, she thought, that had saved the Protector from whoever had attacked her. She wondered if the Fugleman had done this dreadful thing himself, and how many other people he had killed or tried to kill since he had returned to Jewel.

The buckles gave way at last, revealing a stab wound. Goldie pressed the spider webs against it, trying to stop the bleeding. The skin beneath her fingers was as cold as winter stone.

'Lie down next to her,' she said to Bonnie. 'Put your arms around her.'

Bonnie's mouth fell open. 'Put my arms around the *Protector?*'

Goldie almost laughed. Her head felt too light, as if she had a fever. 'Body heat,' she said. 'We've got to warm her up. Like this.'

She lay down on the narrow path, as close to the Protector as she could while still keeping pressure on the wound.

Bonnie gulped, and copied her. 'This feels weird!'

'I know. Think about something else.'

Bonnie was silent for a moment. Then she said, 'I'm going to think about when we were in ancient Merne. When I was Uschi, the Young Margravine of Spit. And you can think about when you were Princess Frisia!'

'Yes,' said Goldie reluctantly. 'I can think about Princess Frisia.'

Frisia, warrior princess of Merne, had been dead for five hundred years. And yet a part of her still lived.

The wolf-sark, or battle madness, was hers. So was the warlike voice that whispered in the back of Goldie's mind. The bow that Bonnie carried, Toadspit's sword – they all belonged to Princess Frisia.

Goldie lay beside the Protector, pressing on the wad of spider webs and thinking about the bizarre events of the last few weeks. The voyage to the city of Spoke. The Festival of Lies. The Big Lie that had saved the children from certain death by whisking them back five hundred years to the court of ancient Merne.

Even now Goldie wasn't sure if they had truly been in Merne, or if it was just an illusion. All she knew was that, when the Big Lie had ended and the children had came back to modern-day Spoke, Princess Frisia's bow and sword had come with them.

But the princess's weapons were not the only things to come out of the Lie. Deep inside Goldie, the royal wolf-sark smouldered, like coals waiting for the bellows. The princess's knowledge of war was there too, along with her memories and the echo of her voice whispering bloodthirsty strategies and instructions.

Goldie hadn't told anyone about the wolf-sark and the voice, not even Toadspit. The whole thing was too strange and frightening. With a shudder she remembered the uncontrollable rage that had taken hold of her on board the *Piglet*. She remembered the red mist that had descended upon her, and how she had raised the heavy sword and sliced it through the air towards Mouse, a small, terrified boy who had done nothing to deserve her anger . . .

She had barely stopped herself in time. She still wasn't sure how she had done it, or whether she could do it again. So although the sword and the bow were really hers, she did not want them.

She didn't want the princess's voice in the back of her mind either. But she had promised herself that she would not give up her city to the Fugleman without a fight, and for that she was going to need Frisia's knowledge of war and strategy.

Goldie clenched her fists, then forced them to relax. There was nothing to fear from those bloodthirsty whispers, she told herself. Unlike the Fugleman, there was a limit to the weapons she would use. No matter what happened, no matter how strongly the princess urged her, she would have nothing to do with the wolf-sark. Or with killing.

Nothing whatsoever.

The first Goldie knew of Toadspit's return was when she heard a soft yap, and a little white dog darted towards her from the direction of the canal steps.

'Broo!' she said, sitting up carefully so as not to dislodge the spider webs from the Protector's wound, and her heart thumped with joy and relief.

But instead of jumping up and licking her face as he had always done in the past, Broo stopped a few paces away and tipped his head to one side, as if he wasn't sure who she was. Goldie held out her free hand; he sniffed it and shuffled backwards. His curly tail drooped.

'Broo, what's wrong? It's me!' whispered Goldie, but by then the little dog had hurled himself at Bonnie and was licking *her* face instead.

Goldie bit her lip. 'Sinew?' she whispered, wondering if he too had forgotten her.

But to her relief, the tall, awkward-looking man hurrying down the steps beside Toadspit bent over and wrapped his arms around her in a quick hug. 'Morg flew in yesterday,' he said. 'So we knew you wouldn't be far behind. Welcome home!'

He hugged Bonnie too. Then he folded his long legs and squatted next to the Protector, his face serious. 'What happened?'

Broo sniffed the Protector's foot, and whined softly.

'She's been stabbed,' said Goldie. 'But she's got a padded vest—'

'Good,' said Sinew. 'I gave it to her some time ago, but I wasn't sure if she'd wear it.' He checked the wound, then put his ear against the Protector's mouth.

'Is she still breathing?' whispered Toadspit, strapping on his sword belt.

'Just.' Sinew took off his cloak and wrapped it around the unconscious woman. 'That bleeding seems to have settled down a bit, but we'd better get her up to the museum as quickly as possible. Bonnie, you walk with me and keep pressure on the wound. It'll be awkward, but I'm sure you can manage. Like this.'

He showed Bonnie where to put her hand. Then, with a grunt of effort, he hoisted the Protector up into his arms. 'Toadspit, Goldie, you go ahead and make sure the way is clear. Take Broo with you. There are mercenaries everywhere and we don't want to run into them.'

It was not the sort of homecoming that Goldie had been hoping for. As she slipped through the gate at the top of the steps, with Toadspit at her side and Broo trotting a few paces in front of them, she thought longingly of Ma and Pa, and wondered when she would see them. One thing was clear – it would not be tonight.

The two children and the dog wound their way through the shadowy streets of the Old Quarter, keeping a wary eye out for mercenaries. At the same time, Goldie found herself studying her surroundings in a way that she had never done before. The building on the other side of the road, for example – it overlooked three canals, and would make a good observation post. As for that plaza they had just passed, the statues and trees around its edges would easily conceal a dozen men—

She stopped, realising that she was thinking like Princess Frisia. Jewel was her home, and she was treating it as if it was a battlefield.

But it IS a battlefield, she reminded herself. *And if I want to beat the Fugleman I NEED to think like Frisia.*

All the same, the ease with which she had slipped into it made her shiver.

'What's the matter?' whispered Toadspit.

'Nothing,' said Goldie. Broo peered up at her and wagged his tail uncertainly, as if he wanted to comfort her, but wasn't sure how to go about it.

They were nearly halfway up Old Arsenal Hill when the little dog stiffened, and a warning growl rumbled in his throat.

'What's wrong, Broo?' whispered Toadspit.

Broo growled again, and the hair on his back stood up. A shadow skittered past him, as furtive as a rat.

'Did you see that?' said Goldie. 'What was it?'

'I don't know! Broo, leave it! Leave it!'

But Broo took no notice. A dreadful snarl burst from his chest and, before Toadspit could stop him, he launched himself at the prowling shadow.

With a twist too quick for the eye to catch, the shadow sprang into the air and landed on the little dog's back – where it curdled into the shape of a grey-spotted cat. Its claws, as sharp as the new moon, raked Broo's flesh. He screamed.

And, to Goldie's horror, the silence of the city erupted into chaos.

MORTAL ENEMIES

If Broo had been an ordinary dog, the fight would have been over within seconds. The grey-spotted cat, which Goldie had last seen on board the *Piglet*, had killed far bigger opponents in its time.

But there was nothing ordinary about Broo. He was a brizzlehound, the last of his kind, and a creature of surprising talents. One moment he was small and white and screaming with pain; the next he was as black as tar and

Broo

as big as a bull, and the scream became a bellow that echoed up and down the street.

The cat clung to his back, its claws raking his massive head. Drops of blood spattered Goldie's face. 'Stop it, cat!' she cried.

'Leave him alone!' shouted Toadspit.

The cat took not the slightest bit of notice. It fastened its teeth into Broo's ear. Broo threw himself to the ground, and the cat leaped free just in time.

Both children grabbed at it, but it danced away. The brizzlehound surged to his feet, roaring.

'Stop it, both of you!' cried Goldie. 'The mercenaries will hear you! What's the *matter* with you?'

'This CRRRREATURE is descended from an IDLECAT!' growled Broo. 'We are MORRRRTAL ENEMIES!'

The cat glared at him. 'Hhhhhound!' it spat, then it flew at him again, its claws bloody in the lamplight. Broo's massive jaws snapped. The cat leaped to one side, and Broo dived after it, bellowing with rage.

Goldie remembered the Protector and glanced back the way they had come. But there was no sign of Sinew and Bonnie. They must have taken another road as soon as the battle began.

She looked at the fighting animals. 'We need a bucket of water.'

'There's no time,' said Toadspit. 'The mercenaries'll be here any minute. We'll have to try to drag them apart.'

But the fighting was so ferocious that they could not get close. A whistle sounded, no more than three blocks away. The cat lashed at Broo's nose with its claws. Broo jumped aside, then rammed the cat with his shoulder. It flew through the air and sprang back, undaunted.

Toadspit and Goldie screamed at the two creatures, begging them to stop. When that didn't work, they threw stones. But the brizzlehound and the cat fought on, tearing the night apart with their fury.

Above the uproar, Goldie heard the tramp of approaching feet. 'Broo!' she shouted in despair. 'They're coming! They'll catch you!'

'They'll shoot you!' groaned Toadspit.

Neither of them noticed the small white-haired boy until he trotted past them. 'Mouse!' gasped Goldie.

Mouse smiled over his shoulder. Then, with a wordless cry, he jumped right into the middle of the fray.

Goldie had seen the little boy in action before, had seen his inborn love of wild creatures and his talent for taming the untameable. But even she was astonished by how instantly the fighting stopped.

The cat still hissed. The hair on Broo's back still

bristled, and both animals shook with rage. But they stood apart, with Mouse humming between them, and made no further move to kill each other.

Behind Goldie, the whistle blasted a second warning. A deep voice shouted, 'Curfew patrol! Stay where you are!'

'Quick!' said Goldie, grabbing Mouse's hand. And the children and Broo ran into the darkness. The cat hesitated for just a moment, then followed them.

Several miles away, on board the *Piglet*, a boy with tow-coloured hair and a thin weasel face was gloating over his good fortune.

'You is mine,' he whispered, gazing around the little fishing boat.

He still didn't quite believe it. Right up to the last minute, as the *Piglet* slipped into this disused harbour, Pounce had been sure that Goldie, Toadspit and Bonnie would try to take the boat for themselves.

He'd been ready. He had all sorts of tricks up his sleeve, tricks he'd learned on the streets of Spoke. He knew how to double-cross, did Pounce, and how to triple-cross too, and be the one who came away laughing.

But in the end he hadn't needed any of it. The three snotties had slipped over the side onto the rotting jetty, and disappeared into the night without a fuss.

Pounce's friend Mouse had gone extra-quiet after they left. The little boy had sat in a dark corner of the deck with his white mice running up and down his jacket and that nasty old cat watching over him like some sort of demon granny.

Gave Pounce the creeps, that cat. So he was glad when it too had leaped over the rail and slunk away. That'd left just the pair of them, Pounce and Mouse. Plus dumb old Smudge to do the heavy work.

Pounce admired his new possession one last time, then stuck his head down the hatch and shouted, 'You finished there yet, Smudge?'

He heard footsteps, and the big man appeared directly below him. 'I just gotta get one of them gas lines cleaned, then I'm done.'

'Can't ya leave it till later?'

Smudge looked shocked. 'Can't 'ave dirty gas lines, Pounce!'

'Well, 'urry up.'

'Where we goin'?'

'Dunno yet.' Pounce pulled his threadbare coat tighter. 'Somewhere warm, with lots of food. South, I reckon.'

Smudge's eyebrows drew together, and he shook his head. 'Can't go south. Cord never goes south, 'cos of the slavers. Old Lady Skint's on the prowl, that's what Cord says. She's bought a new slave ship, and we gotta stay outta her way.'

'Listen, matey,' said Pounce. 'Cord's gone. The sharks took 'im, and good riddance too. So what 'e says don't count no more.'

'But I don't wanna be a slave!'

'Course ya don't. And ya won't be, 'cos I'll look after ya. *I'm* captain now.' He stuck his narrow chest out. 'Cap'n Pounce! And you is my crew. You and Mousie.'

He grinned and looked over his shoulder. 'Hey, Mousie! This is yer captain callin'. Where ya hidin'?'

''E ain't hidin',' said Smudge. ''E's gorn.'

Pounce turned back, quick as a flash. 'Course 'e ain't gone! Don't be an idjit, Smudge, I won't 'ave idjits on me boat!'

But Smudge was nodding vigorously. 'I seen 'im, Cap'n, before I come down to do the gas lines. 'E popped over that rail as quiet as a ghostie, just after the cat. I reckon 'e's followed them three snotties. 'E must like 'em, eh?'

Pounce felt as if his head had fallen off his shoulders. He muttered fiercely, ''E likes *me*, that's who 'e likes. No one else.'

29

But even before the words were out of his mouth, he was scrabbling beneath the upturned bucket where he had hidden Cord's pistol. Because the truth was, Mouse *did* like the Jewel snotties. He liked that nasty old cat too. And going after them was just the sort of thing the little white-haired boy would do.

'It'd serve 'im right if I sailed away and left 'im behind,' he muttered.

'Ya can't do that, Pounce. 'E's ya friend!'

'Some friend,' said Pounce bitterly. He tucked the pistol into his belt. 'You wait 'ere, Smudge. Don't move an inch. And don't go thinkin' that you can run away with me boat. I'm the captain, remember?'

Smudge nodded. ''Ow long ya gunna be, Cap'n?'

'Not long,' said Pounce. 'With a bit of luck I'll grab Mousie and be back before ya know it.' He bared his teeth at Smudge. 'And if the *Piglet's* not 'ere, I'll come after ya. And when I catch ya, you'll wish that Old Lady Skint *had* got ya, 'cos she'd be as sweet as puddin' compared to me!'

A FINE WARRIOR

By the time the children reached the Museum of Dunt, with the cat slinking behind them, the Protector had been put to bed and Herro Dan was ladling thick pea soup into bowls, ready for the latecomers. His old brown face was grim.

'How could the Fugleman treat his own sister with such viciousness?' he muttered. 'First he starves her, then he stabs her, then he chucks her in the canal like a bucket of scraps!' He shook his head. 'That man ain't got no heart!'

The Cat

'All he cares about is power and money,' said Olga Ciavolga, sawing ferociously at a loaf of fresh bread. Her grey hair crackled and her eyes flashed with anger. 'He will tear this city to pieces if we do not find a way to stop him.'

'Sto-o-o-o-op hi-i-i-i-im,' croaked a harsh voice.

Goldie looked up and saw the familiar black feathers of Morg, the slaughterbird, perched in the rafters. She breathed in the comforting smell of soup. Around her, the museum dozed, its dusty corridors and strange shifting rooms as dear to her as her own home.

I'm back, she thought and despite everything that was worrying and out of joint she felt a slow surge of happiness. *I'm Fifth Keeper of the Museum of Dunt, and I'm back where I belong.*

'Will she be all right?' said Bonnie, through a mouthful of bread. 'The Protector, I mean.'

'Hopefully she will mend,' said Sinew, who was crouched beside the cast-iron stove, feeding it with small logs. 'As long as that wound doesn't get infected. We'll have to watch her carefully for the next few days.'

The stove crunched and mumbled as the new wood caught fire. Mouse edged closer to the warmth.

'What *I* want to know,' said Toadspit, leaning back in his chair, 'is how we're going to stop the Fugleman. It was hard enough before, when it was just him and his Blessed Guardians. But now he's got mercenaries as well!'

In the back of Goldie's mind, the princess's voice whispered, *Divide his forces.*

'We'll have to divide his forces,' said Goldie. And then she bit her tongue, because she had spoken without thinking, and everyone was suddenly looking at her, even Broo and the cat, who had been glaring at each other from opposite ends of the table.

Goldie tried to catch up with her thoughts, which were partly hers and partly Princess Frisia's. In the depths of her mind, lessons in military strategy collided with a tall, red-haired mercenary and his companions. Behind her eyes, the armies of ancient Merne rubbed up against two Blessed Guardians called Kindness and Meek.

And then, with a click like the cocking of a rifle, it all came together. Goldie picked up a crust of bread and tore it in two. 'The Blessed Guardians—' she held up one piece of bread '—and the mercenaries—' she held up the other piece '—already dislike each other. We saw that tonight. We must work on that dislike, drive a wedge between them. Make them *loathe* each other. If we can do that, we're halfway to beating them already.'

She popped both scraps of bread into her mouth –

and stopped. The three adult keepers were staring at her as if they had never seen her before.

'What?' she said.

Toadspit grinned. 'You sounded exactly like Princess Frisia.'

'Like *who*?' said Olga Ciavolga.

'I did not!' Goldie reddened, wondering what had given her away.

'You did,' said Bonnie. 'Sort of bossy and clever.'

'What are you talking about?' said Olga Ciavolga.

Toadspit laughed. '*Very* bossy—'

'Answer me!' Olga Ciavolga banged her fist on the table so hard that everyone jumped. 'What do you know about Princess Frisia? Why are you saying these things?'

'But we told you about the Big Lie,' said Goldie. Then she stopped in confusion. *We HAVEN'T told them!* she realised. *We were so pleased to get back safely, and so worried about the Protector . . . They don't know any of it!*

In the end, it was Toadspit who began the story. He described how Bonnie had been snatched off the streets of Jewel by two men working for the mysterious Harrow, and how he and Goldie had followed them and stowed away on the *Piglet*. When he got to the part where he too had been captured and drugged into unconsciousness, Goldie took over.

With a shiver she described the voyage to Spoke, and the search for her friends in a strange city. And how Mouse had befriended her and told her fortune.

On the other side of the table, Mouse smiled his sweet smile, and Herro Dan shook his hand and gave him a second bowl of soup. Sinew picked up his harp and played a lonely string of notes, with a bright chord of friendship at the end.

The story was a complicated one, and Goldie had to backtrack several times to make sure she had left nothing out. But at last she came to the part where she had rescued her friends, only to have Guardian Hope trap them all in a disused sewer—

'Guardian Hope?' said Sinew, looking up from his harp with a frown. 'The very same Guardian Hope we know and love? Are you *sure* it was her?'

Goldie rolled her eyes at the thought of anyone loving Guardian Hope, and nodded.

Bonnie wriggled in her chair. 'She was going to drown us! She had orders from Harrow, because we knew too much. But Goldie saved us by telling a Big Lie, and that's how we ended up in—'

'Hang on,' said Herro Dan, holding up his hand. 'Back up a bit, lass. What did you know that was important enough to kill you for?'

'The true identity of Harrow,' said Toadspit.

And he told them.

Olga Ciavolga's eyes narrowed to furious slits. Sinew played a sequence of notes that made the hair on Goldie's neck stand up.

'Well, that makes sense at last,' said Herro Dan through gritted teeth. 'Keep goin', Bonnie. You were sayin' that Goldie saved you.'

By the time Bonnie had finished explaining about the Big Lie and the sword and the bow, and how Guardian Hope was probably dead at last, Mouse was yawning and the cat had tucked itself into a warm spot next to the stove. Its eyes were closed, but its ears followed Broo as he leaned towards Goldie, his nostrils flaring.

'A warrior princess?' rumbled the brizzlehound. 'That is why I did not know you earlier. You look like a friend, but you smell like a stranger.'

Goldie's cheeks burned. She hated holding things back from her fellow keepers and for a moment she thought that perhaps she would just tell them and get it over with. She sat forward in her chair—

But before she could speak, Herro Dan rubbed his chin and said, 'I've heard of all sorts of things comin' out of a Big Lie. Leftover smells, a sword, a bow – *that's* nothin' to worry about. But every now and again someone comes out the other end as mad as a quignog. They've got another life still stuck inside 'em and it tears

36

'em apart. You can never trust 'em again. I'm glad that didn't happen to you young 'uns.'

Goldie sat back, feeling sick. If she tried to tell them about Princess Frisia and the wolf-sark now, they'd think she was mad. As mad as a quignog! They wouldn't trust her any more, and who could blame them – she hardly trusted herself. They might even decide that she could no longer be Fifth Keeper!

Mouse was watching her. *He* knew there was something wrong. She avoided his eyes and said to the brizzlehound, 'That's all it is, Broo, a leftover smell. I'm me. I'm not a princess any more. I'm just me.'

'Well, *I* wish you were still Frisia,' said Bonnie. 'When she fought the Graf von Nagel, she shot an arrow right through his heart. If you were the princess you could shoot the Fugleman!'

'Or I could challenge him to a duel,' said Toadspit. His hand caressed the hilt of his sword. 'And kill him.'

Olga Ciavolga shook her head. 'Think carefully before you get blood on your hands, all of you. It does not wash off easily. I was there at that final battle with von Nagel, and I tell you, I would not wish to go there again.'

Goldie stared at Olga Ciavolga in astonishment. She had always known that the senior keepers of the Museum of Dunt were far older than they looked.

But the battle with von Nagel was *five hundred years ago*!

'You were *there*?' breathed Toadspit. 'In a proper battle? Will you tell us about it?'

'No, I will not,' said Olga Ciavolga shortly.

Goldie leaned forward again, her heart thumping. 'Did you know Princess Frisia, Olga Ciavolga? What was she like?'

For a moment the old woman said nothing. Then she heaved a sigh. 'She was self-centred and ruthless. Not a nice person.'

'Oh,' said Goldie, wishing she hadn't asked.

'You're not bein' fair,' said Herro Dan. 'The girl had her strengths.'

Olga Ciavolga inclined her head. 'I suppose she did. She was a fine warrior.'

'What happened to her?' asked Toadspit, excitement shining in his eyes.

'She died on the battlefield.' And with that, Olga Ciavolga pressed her lips together and would say nothing more, no matter how much Toadspit begged.

But when Goldie yawned and stood up, still clutching her secrets, the old woman followed her out of the kitchen.

At first they walked in silence through the dusty rooms, past suits of armour, stuffed birds, gilt-framed paintings and an endless line of whirring, ticking clocks. But then Olga Ciavolga stopped and said, 'You did well in Spoke. I am proud of you, child. You did well tonight too, and tomorrow after you have seen your parents we will discuss exactly how we should go about dividing our enemies. But for now, tell me. The bow, the sword, the scent of a princess. Were these the only things to come out of the Big Lie?'

Her eyes were so sharp that Goldie felt transparent. Nonetheless, she nodded. 'That's all. There was nothing else.'

The clock behind her hiccuped in protest, then fell silent. Olga Ciavolga said, 'Indeed. Goodnight, then.'

'Goodnight,' said Goldie. And she walked away, knowing that the old woman stood and watched her go.

Meanwhile, down by the docks, in one of Jewel's many warehouses, Pounce was building himself a hidey-hole. He had thought of going back to the *Piglet* to sleep, but it was too far away and he was too tired and crabby. As he dragged a battered old crate into a corner and patched it with cardboard to keep out the cold, he muttered to himself.

'How am I s'posed to find 'im in a strange city, eh? How am I s'posed to know where to look? 'E could be anywhere. I could spend the rest of me life searchin' for 'im!'

He climbed into the crate to inspect it, then scrambled out again. The cardboard wasn't enough. He needed something warmer.

'I bet Mousie's sorry now that 'e took off,' he mumbled. 'I bet 'e's hidin' in a doorway somewhere, wishin' he was back with 'is old mate Pounce.'

He shivered, only partly from the cold, and peered around the warehouse. It was filled with boxes, piled one on top of the other and as easy to crack open as an oyster. Pounce ignored them. He squeezed his thin body out the window he had entered earlier, and broke into the next building but one. There, after a bit of hunting, he found a bale of brand new black woollen robes.

'Mm, not bad,' he said. He took a dozen of the robes, resealed the bale so that it looked untouched, and headed back to what he was already beginning to think of as his own warehouse. Before long, his hidey-hole was as warm and squishy as a nest of rats. He snuggled down in the black robes, whispering reassurances to himself.

'I bet I find 'im tomorrow. Or the day after, at the latest. No need to worry. Everythin's gunna turn out all right.'

The trouble was, Pounce's whole life up until now
had taught him that things *didn't* turn out all right.
In fact, they usually went as badly as they possibly could,
and then took a turn for the worse.

What if he couldn't find Mouse tomorrow or the day
after? Or what if he *could* find him and the little boy
didn't want to be his friend any more? What if Mouse
was sick of boats and sewers and not knowing where
his next meal was coming from, and had run away from
Pounce forever?

'No,' said Pounce quickly. 'He made a mistake, that's
all. Or— Or maybe Goldie and Toadspit stole 'im away
somehow, while me back was turned! Yeah, I bet that's
what 'appened!'

He grinned viciously and took the pistol from his
belt. 'Well, they ain't gunna keep 'im. I'll grab 'im back
from under their noses. And if they try to stop me, I'll
shoot 'em!'

A yawn took hold of him. 'Don't worry, Mousie,'
he murmured, as he fell towards sleep, still clutching
the pistol. 'I'm comin' to save ya. 'Cos you and me is
friends, and we gotta stick together. We don't care about
no one else, do we? It's just Pounce and Mouse. Always
'as been, always will be. Everyone else is . . . *yaaaaawn*
. . . trouble.'

REUNION . . . AND PARTING

Early next morning, Toadspit, Bonnie and Goldie muffled their faces with scarves and winter hats and went down into the city.

The streets were not as quiet as they had been the night before, but the fear was still there. People hurried to the markets or to their jobs, peering nervously over their shoulders and falling silent whenever they saw a squad of

Mouse

mercenaries.

'Look how scared everyone is,' whispered Bonnie. 'Isn't it horrible!'

'We'd better copy them,' said Toadspit. And although they were almost bursting with excitement at the thought of seeing their parents at last, the children hunched their shoulders and peeped anxiously from under their hats until they looked as timid as everyone else.

When they came to the Fallen Bridge, which was not fallen at all, but spanned Gunboat Canal in a graceful arc of bluestone, they separated. Toadspit and Bonnie hurried towards their house, and Goldie continued along Misery Street, which led to the Plaza of the Forlorn.

Now that she was alone, her excitement had turned to worry. The last time she had seen Pa, he had been suffering from dreadful nightmares, and Ma had had a hacking cough that showed no sign of getting better. Goldie had only been gone for a few weeks, but a lot could have happened in that time.

She slipped in the front door of her apartment, her feet making no sound on the tiled floor. 'Pa?' she called softly. 'Ma?'

There was a cry from her parents' bedroom, and Ma came flying out with her hand over her mouth. When she saw Goldie she stopped and jammed her eyes shut, as if she didn't dare look.

'Are you— Are you real?' she whispered. Her eyelids fluttered. 'I've dreamed about you so many times, and woken with my heart in tatters. I'm not sure that I can bear to do it again.'

'Ma,' said Goldie, hurrying towards her. 'It's me! Look! It's really me!'

But it was not until Ma was folded in a bear hug that she could be persuaded to open her eyes. Then she began to cry. 'Oh, my lovely girl, how we missed you! Are you all right? Where have you *been*? That vile Fugleman—'

She stopped, and glanced at the wall of the adjoining apartment. 'Frow Edel,' she mouthed. 'I think she sometimes listens to us!'

She put her lips closer to Goldie's ear. 'The Fugleman said you were in Spoke. Only of course he didn't know that it was you and Toadspit and Bonnie; the Protector made sure of that. So what he said was, the *missing children* were in Spoke. Only then something went wrong, and he said that the missing children were probably—' her voice broke '—probably *dead*, and that it was the Protector's fault! I didn't believe a word of it. Not a word! But still— Oh, my sweet!'

Tears flooded down her face, and down Goldie's face too. 'You've shrunk, Ma,' she whispered. 'Your cough's not worse, is it?'

'No, my cough's the same as ever. And your Pa is no better and no worse.'

Goldie held her mother at arm's length. 'But you *have* shrunk.'

'No, dearling, you've grown. You're getting more like my sister Praise every day.' Ma touched the little blue bird that was pinned inside Goldie's collar. 'You know, I thought you had disappeared, just like she did so long ago, and it broke my heart. But here you are. And you've still got Praise's brooch! I thought you might have lost it, after all that has happened.'

'I'll never lose it,' whispered Goldie. 'It gives me courage.'

Ma hiccuped a laugh. 'Courage? Dear me, that's something you never lacked! Oh, I wish your pa was here! He's gone to the markets – he should be back any minute. Now tell me *exactly* what happened to you. No, better wait until Pa arrives. Just tell me a little bit. How's Bonnie? And Toadspit? Are they safely home too?'

It was impossible not to start telling the story. Goldie had just reached the point where Toadspit was captured, when the front door opened and Pa stood, frozen with shock, on the threshold.

There were more tears then, and more explanations. Pa had shrunk a little too, and there were new lines on his forehead, but his chest was still broad and comforting and his eyes were growing happier by the moment.

When Ma had made hot chocolate, and Pa had fossicked in the shopping baskets and brought out a teacake, Goldie started again at the beginning of her story. Her voice was no more than a murmur, but when she came to the part about Harrow, she lowered it even further.

'There are two important things you should know about him,' she whispered. 'First, he was behind the bomb that exploded in Jewel last year.'

Ma gasped. That bomb had killed one child and wounded several others, and the city's militia had never found out who was responsible.

'And second—' Goldie paused dramatically. '*Harrow is really the Fugleman!*'

Total silence greeted her words. Ma and Pa stared at her, then at each other. Goldie began to worry that they might not believe her. 'I promise you—'

'I knew it!' Ma thumped her fist into the palm of her hand. 'I knew he was rotten! Didn't I say so? The scoundrel! The treacherous, lying—'

'Ssshhh!' said Pa. 'Sssssshhhhh!' But at the same time, he was nodding. 'We've been hearing such stories,' he whispered to Goldie. 'The most ridiculous one is that it was the Protector who set off the bomb last year, in league with the militia. According to some people, the Fugleman was forced to hire the mercenaries and take over the city in order to stop her!' He snorted. 'You wouldn't think that anyone could believe such nonsense, but they do.'

'Frow Edel told me just yesterday,' whispered Ma, 'that all the old stories about the Fugleman were lies, put about by his enemies. She thinks he's a wonderful man and so forgiving of those who have tried to harm him.' She rolled her eyes. 'The woman is an idiot.'

'And there are far too many like her,' whispered Pa. 'Those of us who have been in the House of Repentance know better than to trust the Fugleman. But others—'

'They long for a return to safety and stability,' said Ma. 'And he promises it.'

Goldie knew how persuasive the Fugleman could be, so she wasn't surprised that people were once again falling for his lies. But she *was* surprised when Pa folded his arms and said, 'We can't let him get away with this.'

'Now that we know the truth, we must tell people,' agreed Ma.

'No!' said Goldie quickly. 'It's too dangerous.'

Pa raised his eyebrows. 'I never thought I would hear you say such a thing.' He turned to Ma. 'Are you sure this is our daughter, and not an impostor?'

Goldie blushed. 'I mean— I thought you could come back to the museum with me. You'll be safer there.'

'While you do what?' said Pa.

'Well—'

'Exactly,' said Ma. 'Are *you* going to sit with your hands folded while Jewel is overrun with lies and cruelty? Of course not! So why should we?'

Goldie racked her brains for a way to dissuade them. 'You might be imprisoned again!'

Pa's eyes were sober and perhaps a little frightened, but he smiled quietly. 'We survived the House of Repentance once, dearling. If necessary, we will survive it a second time.'

There was little more to be said. Pa pulled out his pocket watch and reminded Goldie that she was due to meet Toadspit and Bonnie soon. Ma wrapped the remains of the teacake in waxed paper, with instructions to make sure that Herro Dan, Olga Ciavolga and Sinew got at least one slice each.

Then it was time to go. Goldie hugged her parents, her heart almost bursting with love and pride and worry. They hugged her back. 'Take care, sweeting!' they whispered. 'And we'll see you in a few days.'

But as she slipped out of the apartment, Goldie knew that there was a good chance she would *not* see her parents in a few days. In fact, if things went wrong, he might never see them again.

Field Marshal Brace

A MAGNIFICENT
CONTRAPTION

When the children met, three hours after they had parted, all of them had the marks of tears on their cheeks.

'They won't listen!' said Bonnie. 'We told them they should come back to the museum with us, but they said they've got work to do here. They're going around to visit your parents. They're really angry about the Fugleman!'

'Good,' said Goldie, glad that Ma and Pa wouldn't be facing danger alone.

In the back of her mind, the warrior princess stirred. *It is time to find out more about the invaders. To learn their strengths and weaknesses.*

Goldie hesitated, remembering Herro Dan's words of the night before. What if he was right? What if it tore her apart, having this other life stuck inside her?

No, she told herself, she wouldn't let it! She would use Frisia's knowledge of war to fight the Fugleman, but that was all. She wouldn't go mad. She wouldn't betray anyone's trust. There was nothing to fear.

Aloud, she said, 'Let's go back to the museum a different way. We need to see as much as we can in daylight. Then we can work out what we're going to do.'

They followed the Grand Canal all the way to the House of Repentance. The last time Goldie had seen that notorious prison, it had been deserted. But now a dozen or more black-clad figures patrolled the front courtyard, their robes thrown back so that everyone could see the heavy brass punishment chains wound around their waists.

High above them, at the top of the steps, the boards had been stripped from the windows, and the façade of the building gleamed white from hours of scrubbing. And on the newly repaired roof, two flags – that of the Fugleman and that of the Grand Protector – flew on a single mast.

As the children scurried past, hunching their shoulders like whipped puppies, a squad of mercenaries marched up the boulevard. Their faces were wooden and their eyes were as flat as the buttons on their ragged coats. The only scrap of feeling in them seemed to be for their rifles, which they cradled across their chests like babies.

When they drew level with the House of Repentance, the mercenaries came to a clattering halt. The Blessed Guardians stopped their pacing and hurried forward to stand beside them. A hush fell over the courtyard.

'They're waiting for something,' whispered Goldie.

'Listen!' Toadspit had the keenest ears of the three children. He nodded towards the west. 'Whatever it is, it's on its way.'

A moment later Goldie heard it too, a low grinding sound, like a thousand cobblestones rubbing together. As it grew louder, the people who had been hurrying past with their heads averted stopped and looked around nervously. A crowd formed and the children slipped into the middle of it.

They could hear shouts now, and a hissing, clanking sound. The ground beneath their feet began to shake. Then, with a particularly loud grumble, an enormous tractor hove into sight at the far end of the boulevard, accompanied by another squad of soldiers.

'It's pulling something,' said Bonnie.

Toadspit squinted. 'What is it?'

'I don't know,' said Goldie.

She was lying. She *did* know. Or at least she thought she did. Princess Frisia had seen something like this, five hundred years ago.

Goldie hoped desperately that the princess was wrong.

As the *thing* drew closer, the tractor groaned under its burden. The onlookers groaned too; by now, even the most short-sighted among them could see what had been dragged into the heart of Jewel. They could see the great iron wheels, nearly twice as tall as a man, and the iron carriage. They could see the nuts and bolts, and the name 'FROW CARRION' inset between them in huge iron letters.

But most of all, they could see the long iron barrel, with its gaping black mouth.

Goldie watched it with a sense of horror that echoed through the centuries. Princess Frisia was not wrong. It was a great gun. And it was bigger than any great gun that the princess had ever seen.

Deep inside the House of Repentance, the Fugleman was demonstrating his sword skills to Field Marshal Brace, the leader of the mercenaries. He was a little rusty, so he didn't try anything too elaborate. He merely cut and thrust to show off the strength of his arm, then launched into a series of soft parries.

'It is a great pity,' he said, as he trod gracefully back and forth across the floor of his office, 'that the city has been subdued so easily. I was hoping for someone to test my blade on.'

'Mmmph,' said Brace, who was a man of few words.

The Fugleman drove his imaginary opponent in a circle around the desk. 'But,' he said, 'we will soon move on Spoke. The people there will fight harder for their freedom.'

'You know the city of Spoke well?'

'As well as I know this sword. Not only that, but one of my Guardians is there as we speak, preparing the ground for our arrival.'

The Fugleman sliced at his invisible opponent's neck, wondering when Guardian Hope – or Flense, as she was called in Spoke – would arrive back in Jewel.

As agreed, there had been no messages between them since his release from the House of Repentance; he did not want his enemies stumbling upon the fact that the Fugleman of Jewel was also the master-criminal Harrow. But it should not be long now before Hope completed the jobs he had entrusted to her, and returned home.

He finished off his imaginary opponent with a stab to the heart, and smiled. It would be interesting, he thought, to hear about the death of the children . . .

'There was a ruckus on Old Arsenal Hill last night after curfew,' said the field marshal, tipping back his chair and scratching at his moustache. 'There may still be pockets of resistance here.'

'I doubt it,' said the Fugleman. He wiped his forehead with a kerchief. 'I have come to believe that Jewel does not know the meaning of the word.'

Brace grimaced, but said nothing. He was a pompous

little man, thought the Fugleman. His face was as plump and soft as a yeast bun, and he was ridiculously proud of that silly moustache. No one would have guessed that he was a soldier – not until they looked into the grey puddles of his eyes and saw what lay beneath the surface.

The sound of the great gun arriving outside the House of Repentance was a welcome distraction. The Fugleman led the way to the top of the steps, and both men watched as the gun was drawn up, with a deal of shouting and scraping, into the middle of the courtyard.

'A magnificent contraption,' said the Fugleman. He glanced sideways at his companion. 'Though I was beginning to wonder if it would ever arrive.'

Brace grunted. 'I gave my word, did I not? Rules of war. A soldier does not break his word.'

The Fugleman laughed, thinking that the field marshal had made a joke. 'Look at the crowds!' he murmured. 'How fascinated they are. How they fear it!'

Up close, the gun was even more impressive. It smelled of gas and black powder, and its huge iron sides were pitted with the wounds of war. The Fugleman liked it. Oh yes, he liked it *very* much.

But the frightened whispers from the crowd were

growing louder, and he could see the doubtful glances that were coming his way. He let it all go on for just long enough, then he swung around (with an elegant swirl of his cloak) and cried, 'Do not be afraid! This mighty weapon—' he stroked Frow Carrion's flank '—this *magnificent* weapon is here to protect our city from slavers and other such scum. It may look like a monster, but it is our friend.'

He smiled his charming smile. When people began to smile back, he bent down and murmured to the field marshal, 'They'll believe any lie if it is big enough. And if it fits in with their pathetic desire for safety.'

The field marshal inspected his black leather gloves and glared at three children who had crept too close. 'When will my men get their money?'

'I'll send a handcart with the first payment in silver thalers tonight, two hours after curfew.'

'To the barracks?'

'Of course.' The Fugleman adjusted the folds of his cloak, and gazed thoughtfully at the crowd. 'You know, Field Marshal, I do not believe for a moment that you are right about the resistance. But if by some unlikely chance you *are*, it will come from a single quarter: the Museum of Dunt. Its keepers are the only people in the city who would dare stand against me.'

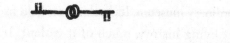

He patted the barrel of the great gun. 'But now I am ready for them. The moment there is a whiff of trouble I will batter the museum to the ground, and destroy everything and everyone within it!'

Frow Carrion

FIRST STRIKE

'He's mad!' said Toadspit, as the children hurried back up the hill. 'How could he even think of doing such a thing? Doesn't he realise what would happen?'

Goldie shivered. The Museum of Dunt was no ordinary museum. Its back rooms held five hundred years of living history, much of it violent. If the Fugleman attacked it with his great gun, that violence would burst out onto the streets of Jewel, bringing death and destruction to everyone in the city.

'Does this mean we can't fight him after all?' asked Bonnie.

Toadspit and Goldie looked at each other. Neither of them was prepared to give up, but the threat of the great gun was so terrible that they could not immediately see a way around it.

They continued on in silence, each of them sunk in their own thoughts. Goldie stared at the cobblestones, thinking about the money that was to be delivered tonight, two hours after curfew. It was the perfect opportunity to stir up trouble, and she did not want to waste it.

But when she said so, Toadspit scowled. 'And then sit back while Frow Carrion blasts the museum to smithereens?'

In the back of Goldie's mind, Princess Frisia whispered, *Warfare is based on*—

'—on trickery and deception,' murmured Goldie. 'Yes, I know.' It was one of the first lessons the princess had ever learned. But what did it have to do with the Fugleman and his threats?

The children hurried around a corner into a cul de sac, and there in front of them was the museum, an ugly little stone building that gave no hint of the wonders and dangers it contained.

Trickery and deception . . .

And suddenly the whole thing was laid out inside Goldie like a campaign map. 'Of course!' she said, as she led the way down the cul de sac. 'What we have to do is convince the Fugleman that any attacks are coming from somewhere else!'

Toadspit chewed his lip. 'I suppose that'd do it. But how—'

'We lay red herrings,' said Goldie. 'Things that point away from the museum. And at the same time, we make the museum look as if it has lost its power and become weak and helpless.'

She grinned at Toadspit. 'If we can carry that off, we'll be free to do whatever we like! You and me, Herro Dan and Sinew and Olga Ciavolga—'

'And me,' said Bonnie quickly.

'I've got another job for you,' said Goldie. 'Have you ever met the Fugleman? Does he know what you look like?'

Bonnie wrinkled her nose. 'I don't think so. Guardian Hope does—'

'Guardian Hope's dead. We don't have to worry about her,' interrupted Toadspit.

'—and the Fugleman has seen my description,' said Bonnie. 'He saw *all* our descriptions when he was pretending to send out messages searching for us. But I don't think he's ever seen me.'

'Good. Then you can be the Museum of Dunt's first and only line of defence,' said Goldie, as the three children trotted up the steps. 'Or maybe you and the cat—'

She broke off. Mouse was waiting for them just inside the front door, gesturing at the walls with a dozen unspoken questions.

When the children had left the museum earlier that morning, it had been quiet, with no sign of the wildness that lurked in every corner. But now that wildness was stirring. The air crackled, as if there was lightning not far away. The rooms *shifted*. Somewhere nearby, Sinew played his harp, plucking out the notes of the First Song.

Goldie and Toadspit threw off their hats and scarves, laid their hands on the nearest wall and began to sing the same sliding notes that Sinew played. '*Ho oh oh-oh*,' they sang. '*Mm mm oh oh oh-oh oh.*'

Wild music surged up from the centre of the earth and poured through them. Bonnie clenched her fists. She was not a keeper and could not feel the *shifting* or hear the wild music. But she had learned many of the museum's secrets from her brother, and she said, 'It's the great gun, isn't it? The museum doesn't like being threatened!'

Toadspit nodded and kept singing. Mouse signalled another question.

'It's because of all the wildness,' explained Bonnie. 'Jewel used to be a very dangerous place. But people got sick of their children being eaten by idlecats and dying of horrible diseases, so they drove all the dangerous things out of the city. Or rather they thought they did, but really all those things ended up here in the museum. Nice things like brizzlehounds and slaughterbirds, and nasty things too, like plague and famine and war. Only *those* bits are locked away behind the Dirty Gate, deep in the back rooms of the museum, so they can't hurt anyone.'

'*Ho oh oh-oh*,' sang Goldie. The wild music churned through her bones and would not settle. She sang louder. Mouse listened to Bonnie with his eyes half-closed and his fingers wiggling in time with the First Song.

'Toadspit says you can't keep wildness in one place, and that's why the rooms shift all the time,' continued Bonnie. 'The trouble is, if anything threatens the museum or its keepers, the shifting gets worse. Like now. And the keepers have to calm the museum down by singing to it. Because if the shifting gets *really* bad, all the wars and plague and stuff will break out from behind the Dirty Gate!'

She bit her lip. 'It'd be the end of Jewel. And of us too, probably.'

Mouse patted her arm. Then, to Goldie's surprise, he put his hand on the wall and began to hum a rough approximation of the First Song, as if he could calm the Museum of Dunt in the same way that he had calmed Broo and the cat.

And perhaps he could, because the museum began to settle almost immediately. The wild music was still there, but now it rumbled along beside them, like a huge beast that has agreed to be tamed – for a while at least. '*HO OH OH-OH,*' sang the museum. '*MM MM OH OH OH-OH OH.*'

Fifteen minutes later, the children met up with the older keepers in the room called Rough Tom. This was not one of the wildest rooms in the museum, but it *was* one of the strangest. Half a dozen enormous sailing ships lay on their sides in the middle of the floor, as if a tide had brought them there and left them stranded. The air smelled of mud and salt water.

The news about the great gun drew a groan from Sinew's harp strings and turned Herro Dan pale. Olga Ciavolga merely nodded, as if nothing the Fugleman did could surprise her.

Toadspit repeated his question. 'Doesn't he know what would happen if he attacked us?'

'He knows,' said Olga Ciavolga, 'but he does not care. All he wants is destruction. The city, the Protector, everything.'

Goldie thought of the limp body that she and her friends had dragged from the canal. 'Has the Protector woken up yet?'

'Not yet,' said Olga Ciavolga. 'She has a slight fever, which worries me. I wish she would regain consciousness—'

'You know, I'm not sure you're right about the Fugleman,' Sinew interrupted her. 'This city is his base. He's not going to want to see it flattened.'

'So why is he threatening us?' asked Bonnie. 'He'll get killed too if everything breaks out from behind the Dirty Gate, won't he?'

Sinew nodded. 'Which makes me think that he doesn't really understand what the museum is.'

'Oh, come on, Sinew,' said Toadspit. 'He's been in the

war rooms! Of course he—'

'He knows a *bit* of it,' said Sinew. 'He stole a book from the Protector's office last year – a book about the Dirty Gate. That's how he learned about the war rooms. But you know what he's like; clever – brilliant even – but he has little patience. I suspect he read just enough of the book and no more, and as a result he has no idea of the museum's true power. He's picked up a twig and mistaken it for the whole forest.'

'Then shouldn't we tell him how dangerous—' began Bonnie.

'*No!*' cried Herro Dan and Olga Ciavolga together.

'I shudder to think what he would do with such knowledge,' said the old woman. 'He cannot be trusted in any way. It is bad enough that he has discovered a small part of the truth.'

'Besides, he wouldn't believe us,' said Goldie. 'He'd think we were trying to fool him.'

'Trouble is,' said Herro Dan, 'whether he knows what he's doin' or not, the museum's growin' restless again. Which means we daren't leave it alone, not even to fight him.'

At the old man's words, the stranded ships moaned as if the tide was coming in. The smell of the sea grew stronger.

'But if we don't fight the Fugleman, the museum will

get even worse!' said Goldie. 'We can't just give in!'

Olga Ciavolga raised an eyebrow. 'Did Dan say anything about giving in?'

'No,' said Goldie, reddening, 'but if we can't leave the museum—'

'*We* can still fight, Goldie,' interrupted Toadspit. 'You and me.' He looked hopefully at the other keepers. 'You don't need us so much now. Mouse can take our place. Did you hear him singing?'

Mouse had been leaning against Sinew's legs, listening to the conversation. His face was drawn, as if he was missing Pounce now that the excitement of the *shifting* was over. But at Toadspit's words his eyes brightened.

'Hmm,' said Herro Dan. 'We hadn't thought of takin' another keeper. But yes, I *did* hear him— Was that your idea to try him out, Sinew?'

'Don't look at me!' The corner of Sinew's mouth twitched. '*I* thought the boy was happily playing with his mice in the corner, like any normal seven-year-old. Next thing I know, he's out in the front hall, humming the First Song.'

'The museum seemed to like him—'

'*Like* him?' Sinew winked at Mouse. 'From what I heard, he could probably make the whole place sit up and dance if he chose!'

Mouse laughed. Goldie felt a twinge of jealousy, but it did not last for long. 'Good,' she said. 'That leaves Toadspit and me free to fight the Fugleman.'

'And me!' said Bonnie.

Olga Ciavolga cleared her throat. A silence fell over Rough Tom, as if everyone was thinking about how ridiculous it was to send three children against a man who had a mercenary army at his beck and call.

'We can beat him,' said Goldie, hating the note of uncertainty in her voice.

'Of course you can.' Sinew smiled at her. 'And the rest of us will help whenever we get the chance. If you need anything, just tell us.'

'Guns,' said Toadspit. 'That's what we *really* need!'

In the back of Goldie's mind, Princess Frisia whispered approval. 'No,' said Goldie quickly. 'We fight with trickery, not bloodshed. We're not going to kill anyone.'

Toadspit rolled his eyes but said nothing. The stranded ships moaned again, and their tattered rigging whispered a song of anticipation, as if the incoming tide was almost upon them.

Under Goldie's instructions, the children made their

preparations for the night's work. Then, as the day wore on, they rested.

The Museum of Dunt *shifted* and turned around them, stirred up by the Fugleman's threats. Rough Tom changed places with the Lady's Mile. The black waters of Old Scratch swirled and hissed in their subterranean chamber.

Herro Dan and Olga Ciavolga roamed the restless spaces, soothing them with the First Song. Sinew sat in the office, playing the same song on his harp and watching Mouse, who hummed as he tore up old gazettes and dropped them into a baby's bath, where his pet mice paddled them into nests and burrows. Broo and the cat lay on either side of the little boy, pointedly ignoring each other.

Curfew began at seven o'clock. At six, the children woke and ate, and put the things they had prepared into three old haversacks. Goldie watched as Bonnie strung her bow and strapped a leather guard to her left arm.

'Are you sure you want to come?' she said.

Bonnie looked up, worried. 'You're not going to say I can't, are you?'

Goldie was tempted. It would be dangerous out on the streets once curfew began, and Bonnie had never learned the skills of Concealment that the two older children knew.

But for Goldie's plan to work, they needed someone skilled with a bow. If Bonnie didn't come, Goldie would have to do it. And pulling the bow was like drawing the sword – it woke the wolf-sark that crouched inside her, and when the wolf-sark was roused, no one around her was safe.

For just a moment Herro Dan's words seemed to hang in the air in front of her. *As mad as a quignog . . .*

Goldie forced a smile. 'Of course you can come. We couldn't do it without you.'

The barracks, which should have housed the city's militia, but which now sheltered the mercenaries, were on Deathblow Canal, twelve blocks from the Treasury. A person bringing money from one to the other by handcart was likely to follow the shortest route, which went via Coffin Plaza and Needlework Bridge.

By eight o'clock, Goldie, Toadspit and Bonnie were tucked into a dark doorway at the far edge of Coffin Plaza, with the haversacks at their feet. Their faces and hands were blackened with soot, and they had gone over the plan half a dozen times to make sure they each knew what to do.

Goldie wasn't sure when the handcart would come. Had the Fugleman meant that it would leave the Treasury two hours after curfew? Or was that when it would arrive at the barracks?

She heard the blast of a Guardian's whistle some-where to the north, and stiffened. But there was no further sound, and after a while she leaned back against the door and flexed her fingers and toes so they would not go to sleep.

The children had been waiting for half an hour or more when Toadspit's hand touched Goldie's, and he tapped out a message in fingertalk. *'Coming. Two plus handcart.'*

Immediately, Goldie slowed her breathing. Both she and Toadspit were experts at Imitation of Nothingness, one of the Three Methods of Concealment. They could hide themselves so well in a crowd, or in a patch of dappled shade, that not one person in ten thousand could see them. On a night like this, it was as easy as falling asleep.

I am nothing, thought Goldie, as the edges of her mind frayed and drifted outwards. *I am the fur on a moth's wing . . .*

She could sense Bonnie beside her, as tense as her own bowstring. And Toadspit, his heart beating with a fierce courage. She could feel a nest of sparrows shuffling their wings sleepily in the eaves above her head, and a colony of ants beneath her feet, and a thousand other tiny lives that had made their homes in and around the plaza.

I am nothing. I am a spider dreaming . . .

As the handcart trundled into the plaza, Goldie and Toadspit stepped out of the doorway and crept unseen across the cobblestones.

One of the Guardians pushing the cart was complaining loudly. 'I must confess, Colleague Kindness,' she said, 'that I hardly knew how to react when His Honour gave us our orders. A *handcart*? Could we not have had a rig for the delivery?'

'His Honour moves in mysterious ways, Colleague Meek,' replied Guardian Kindness in his cold, high voice.

Goldie swallowed, and wrapped her hand around Auntie Praise's brooch. These were the same two Guardians who had thrown the Protector into the Grand Canal!

In the back of her mind, Frisia whispered, *Kill them now. They deserve no better.*

'Mysterious, indeed,' said Guardian Meek. Her words rang around the plaza, and she quickly added, 'I am not criticising him, you understand.'

'Of course you are not. It is a reasonable question. Why a handcart?'

'Have you a theory on the matter, Kindness? I have racked my brains, but am no closer to understanding it.'

If she focused very carefully, Goldie could just see

the shadow that was Toadspit. He was moving towards Guardian Meek, so Goldie slipped up behind Kindness. Despite the danger of the situation, and the bloodthirsty whispers in the back of her mind, it was hard not to laugh. The Guardians were so engrossed in their complaints that the children could have danced a jig around them and not been noticed.

Goldie slipped her hand into her pocket and took out a folding knife. When she opened it, the wolf-sark inside her pricked up its ears and growled, and she held her breath. But the knife was so small that it hardly counted as a weapon, and after that first rumble, the battle-rage subsided.

'As a matter of fact, I *do* have a theory,' said Guardian Kindness. 'I believe that His Honour is putting the mercenaries in their place. They are little more than ruffians – *useful* ruffians, mind, but ruffians all the same – and they do not *deserve* to have their wages delivered in a street-rig like civilised people. A handcart is good enough for them. And if you and I must suffer for it, then so be it.'

Goldie kept pace with the cart. *I am nothing. I am the soft breath of a sleeping city* . . .

Her hand slid beneath the Guardian's robe, as smooth as butter. She felt the cold links of the punishment chains, and a bunch of keys. And, hanging on a cord next to the keys, a whistle.

She held the cord steady. Then, with one quick movement, she sliced through it, and caught the whistle as it fell.

'I think you are right,' said Guardian Meek, smirking. 'It is a subtle insult. A little *too* subtle, do you think, for such crude minds?'

'Perhaps we will say something when we arrive, to drive the message home,' said Guardian Kindness. 'Here, this is our direction.'

They turned out of the plaza onto Rough Rind Street. As the houses drew in around them, Goldie drifted back to the doorway and touched Bonnie's arm.

'Is that you, Goldie? Did you get it?' breathed Bonnie.

'Yes,' Goldie whispered in her ear, and picked up one of the haversacks. A moment later, Toadspit joined them, letting the Nothingness slip away just far enough to show them a second whistle. He picked up his haversack, nudged Bonnie and whispered, 'Your turn now, pipsqueak. Come on. Make sure they don't see you.'

This time the children crept after the Guardians together, keeping to the shadows. Bonnie was not as silent as the other two, but she was quiet enough for their purpose, and the man and woman ahead of them heard nothing.

The handcart passed a corner that the children had scouted earlier, and trundled towards a pool of light cast by a street lamp. As the Guardians stepped into the light, Bonnie fitted an arrow to her bow, aimed carefully, and loosed it.

The Guardians were talking so loudly that they didn't hear the soft *thunk* of the bowstring. But they couldn't miss the arrow that flew past their elbows and buried itself in the wooden handcart.

With a squawk of alarm, they dived behind the cart, fumbling for their whistles and trying to see where the arrow had come from. But Bonnie had ducked back around the corner, and Goldie and Toadspit were still Concealed. The narrow street appeared to be empty.

Goldie crept closer until she could hear the Guardians whispering to each other.

'My whistle is gone! Quickly, blow the alarm, Meek!'

'Yes, yes, I am already— Wait! Mine is gone too! What is happening? Are we under attack? Who is it? What do they want?'

'The money, of course. But they won't get it. We will shout for help. One of our colleagues is sure to hear us. Come now, we must shout together.'

'But perhaps if we shout they will attack more ferociously! We don't know how many of them there are.'

Goldie pressed herself against the wall of the nearest house, and took a stone from her haversack.

'It will be one or two renegades, that's all,' whispered Guardian Kindness. 'Once they realise we are not going to hand over the money, they will crumble like biscuits. You'll see.'

Goldie tossed the stone underarm. It sailed in a high arc over the handcart and crashed against a door several paces beyond the Guardians. Their heads jerked and, in that moment when they were looking the other way, Bonnie stepped around the corner, loosed another arrow and disappeared again.

The second arrow thudded into the side of the cart. Guardian Meek yelped. 'We are surrounded! They can pick us off whenever they choose. And see! There is a message tied to this arrow! What does it say?'

Guardian Kindness's pale hand reached from behind the cart and tore the paper from the shaft of the arrow. '*Wrap your cloaks around your heads and lie face down on the ground.*' He snorted. 'What nonsense is this?'

'There's more! Read the rest of it!'

'*Do not make a sound or the next arrow goes through your heart.*'

'I told you that we must not shout,' whispered Guardian Meek. 'Perhaps if we do as they say, they will not kill us.'

'We are not giving in, Colleague,' hissed Guardian Kindness angrily. 'Think of what His Honour would say if we lost the payment!'

'His Honour is not lying here with his life in jeopardy! If he was, he would do what I am about to do. We can get the money back later, and take our revenge at the same time!'

And with a cry of 'Don't shoot!', Guardian Meek threw herself out from behind the cart and lay face down on the cobblestones with her cloak wrapped around her head.

Guardian Kindness swore under his breath. Then, with a grunt of disgust, he crawled from his hiding place, covered his face with his cloak and joined his colleague on the ground.

Goldie checked to make sure that neither of them was looking, then she let the Nothingness slide away, and waved to her friends.

Toadspit became visible again, and he and Bonnie ran towards the Guardians.

'Don't hurt us!' mumbled Guardian Meek into her cloak. 'Please don't hurt us!'

The children said nothing. Bonnie pressed the tip of an arrow to Guardian Meek's neck while the other two took ropes, blindfolds and gags from their haversacks.

When Guardian Kindness was trussed so firmly that he could not move or see or speak, they did the same to his colleague.

Kill them and leave no witnesses, whispered Frisia, in the back of Goldie's mind.

Quickly, the children loaded the first payment, which consisted of four bags of coin, into their haversacks. Bonnie collected her arrows and, before they hurried away, Goldie pinned a note to the back of Guardian Meek's robe, where it would not be missed.

She had thought very carefully about the wording on that note. It was the first step in her campaign to convince the Fugleman that there was indeed resistance in the city – resistance that had nothing to do with the museum.

But more than that, it was an irritation, a play on words and a challenge. It was time to let the Fugleman know that his secret identity was a secret no longer.

'The Hidden Rock will blunt the Harrow.'

THE PROMISE

Despite the dangers of being out after curfew, and the weight of coins they carried, the children could not contain their glee. As they trotted through the dark streets of the Old Quarter, Bonnie imitated – very quietly – Guardian Meek's terrified squawk. Toadspit hissed, 'We are not giving in, Colleague!' and pretended to fall flat on his face.

Goldie laughed under her breath, trying not to think about Princess Frisia's bloodthirsty whispers. But they lingered in the back of her mind, as if a

Pounce

part of her was still in ancient Merne, where death and violence were commonplace.

Kill them and leave no witnesses.

Too late, she realised that there was someone behind her. She felt something press between her shoulderblades, and a familiar voice said, 'What've yez done with Mousie?'

Bonnie spun around, beaming. 'Pounce! Where did you come from? Guess what we did! Look at all the money we've got!'

Goldie and Toadspit turned more slowly. 'I was wondering when you'd show up,' said Toadspit.

'Well, 'ere I am.' Pounce scowled and took a couple of steps backwards so that they could see the pistol in his hand. 'Money, is it? Good. Gimme one of them bags.'

Bonnie's smile faded. 'Pounce, it's *us*!'

'I don't care if it's Bald Thoke's granny,' said Pounce. 'Give us the money or I'll shoot ya in the gizzards.'

Goldie shrugged. What did it matter if they gave away one of the bags? At least the mercenaries wouldn't get it.

But Toadspit didn't like to be threatened. Especially not by Pounce. 'No,' he said.

Goldie stared at him. 'Toadspit—'

'It's the spoils of war, and we're keeping it.'

'But he'll *shoot* you!' squeaked Bonnie.

'If he does,' said Toadspit, 'he'll never see Mouse again.'

'Course I will,' sneered Pounce. 'I don't need you lot.' But there was an uneasiness in his eyes that hadn't been there a moment ago.

'If he *doesn't* shoot me,' continued Toadspit, 'we'll take him to the museum. I'm sure Mouse would be pleased to see him.'

Pounce glared, but it was clear that Toadspit had won. Goldie leaned towards Bonnie and whispered, 'We are not giving in, Colleague!' and they both laughed shakily.

After that, the night became almost normal again. Pounce stuck the pistol in his belt and swaggered along beside the other children, forgetting his threats. But when they turned into the cul de sac and walked up the steps of the museum and under the stone arch, he stiffened, and a wary look crossed his thin face, as if he could feel the museum's restlessness and did not know what to make of it.

He's a thief, thought Goldie. *Of course he can feel it.*

The cat met them outside the office, bumping against Goldie's legs and curling its tail into a question mark. 'Hoooow?' it said.

'Is that scruffy old bag of bones still around?' said Pounce. 'I thought someone woulda turned it into a sandwich by now.'

'They'd better not try,' said Bonnie.

Goldie stroked the cat's arched back. 'It went well,' she whispered. 'We got the money, and they didn't see us.'

Although it was late, the light in the office was still on. As Toadspit pushed the door open, Goldie heard Sinew say, 'Mouse, would you please wait until I have read the day's gazette before you dissect it? There is barely a scrap of news left!'

Mouse giggled. Then he saw Pounce and sprang to his feet with a wordless cry of joy.

Pounce flushed and muttered, 'Don't go all soft on me, yer little idjit.' But at the same time he hugged his friend tightly, and whispered something in his ear that Goldie couldn't catch.

Sinew was sitting at the desk, holding a gazette that was more holes than paper. 'How did it go?' he said, ignoring Pounce and raising an eyebrow at Goldie.

Goldie dropped her haversack on the floor beside the cat. 'It was good.'

'It wasn't *good*,' said Bonnie. 'It was perfect!'

'I wish you had let me come with you,' rumbled a gravelly voice. 'It is a long time since I tasted a Blessed Guardian.' And Broo stepped from behind the door, his eyes glowing like rubies.

Pounce's mouth fell open. 'Bloomin' 'eck, it's the

Black Ox!' And he jumped backwards, dragging Mouse with one hand and fumbling for his pistol with the other.

But the pistol was not in his belt. He took his eyes off Broo for long enough to glare at Toadspit. 'I shoulda known I couldn't trust ya,' he said bitterly. Then he swung back to the brizzlehound, his skinny body as tight as a wire. 'I won't let ya take Mouse, ya nasty old Black Ox. And *I* won't go easy, neither!'

Goldie had never imagined that anyone might mistake Broo for the dreaded Black Ox, who was sent by the Seven Gods to carry away evildoers. In the back of her mind, the warrior princess stirred. *Trickery and deception* . . .

'Pounce,' she said, 'he's not the Black Ox. He's a brizzlehound.'

'Sure 'e is. And I'm Bald Thoke's favourite pussy-cat.'

Broo cocked his head to one side. 'You are not a cat,' he rumbled. 'You are a boy.' The great black nostrils flared, and a growl erupted from the enormous chest. 'You are the boy who BETRRRRRAYED my friends in Spoke!'

'Broo,' said Sinew quickly, but the brizzlehound was already advancing on Pounce, his lips drawn back from his teeth in a snarl.

Mouse whistled. A dozen white mice swarmed down his arm and leaped onto Pounce's shoulders.

Broo's ears flicked back and forth. 'I have no argument with *you*, small people,' he growled to the mice. 'You had best get out of the way, or I might eat you by mistake.'

The cat pushed past Bonnie. 'Eat mooouuses?' it wailed, its tail thrashing. 'Noooooo!'

Goldie held her breath. Mouse pulled away from Pounce's nerveless fingers, put his hand on the brizzlehound's shoulder and crooned.

Broo gave a great *huff* of disgust. 'I suppose if he is *your* friend, I cannot kill him after all.' And he turned his back and sat on his haunches.

Through all this, Pounce had stood as if frozen. Now he too sat down, his legs no longer able to hold him. 'Yer a wonder, Mousie, you are,' he whispered. 'Ya tamed the Black Ox!'

'He's *not* the Black Ox,' said Goldie, but Pounce just shook his head and stared at his friend, awestruck. The white mice nibbled his ears in a friendly fashion, then dived across the floor and disappeared into the baby's bath. The cat curled up beside them with one eye fixed suspiciously on Broo.

Sinew leaned back in his chair, pretending to mop his forehead with his sleeve. As he did so, the museum *shifted*. Pounce squawked and tried to drag Mouse under the desk, but the little boy pulled away from him. Sinew grabbed his harp. Goldie and Toadspit stroked the walls of the office and sang.

The wild music boiled around them, but as soon as Mouse joined in with his own odd version of the First Song, the music seemed to pause and listen. By the time it quietened, Pounce had recovered from his fright and was whispering urgently to his friend.

Sinew mopped his forehead again. 'One thing you can say about this place, it's never dull . . .'

Toadspit laughed, and heaved his haversack of coins up onto the desk. 'Look what we've got. The Hidden Rock has made its first strike!'

Goldie lugged her haversack up to the desk too. But first she took out a fistful of coins and gave them to Pounce.

'Is that all?' He sniffed ungraciously, and shoved the coins in his pocket. Then he scrambled to his feet, keeping as far away from Broo as he could, and held out his hand to Toadspit. 'Thanks for keepin' me gun nice and safe, I don't think. I'll 'ave it back now. Mousie and me's gotta go.'

Reluctantly Toadspit gave up the pistol. As soon as Pounce's fingers wrapped around it, his old swagger returned. 'Come on, Mouse. Grab yer pets. Smudge'll be wonderin' where we's got to.'

He was out the door before he realised that his friend wasn't following him. Goldie saw him stiffen. But when he turned around, he was smiling. 'We got a whole ocean to explore, Mousie. Wotcha waitin' for?'

Mouse's hands danced in his own odd version of fingertalk.

'What's he saying?' asked Goldie.

Pounce ignored her. 'Stay 'ere? In this creepy place?' He laughed. 'Not a chance.'

'Good,' growled Broo over his shoulder. 'I do not want you here.' His voice sank to a mutter. 'I do not want that cat here either.'

The white-haired boy's hands moved again. He pointed towards the mice.

'Course they like it,' said Pounce, with a disdainful expression. 'That's 'cos it's a dump, and they like dumps. But we got a boat now, Mousie! We can go wherever we want. We can go where it's warm! Wouldn't that be good?'

Mouse shook his head. He was standing very straight and firm, and for the first time it struck Goldie that she was not the only one who had been changed by the Big Lie. In ancient Merne, Mouse had become Ser Wilm, a young knight in his early twenties. Watching the little boy now, Goldie could see the shadow of that knight. Mouse might be only seven, but he was older and wiser than his years.

Sinew cleared his throat. 'Pounce, you're welcome to stay. There's plenty of room in this – er – dump.'

'Nah,' said Pounce. 'I ain't stayin'.' He turned his back on everyone except his friend, and lowered his voice. 'Listen, Mousie. I won't say nothin' about the Black Ox jumpin' out of corners when ya don't expect it, 'cos that don't seem to bother ya. But there's a war goin' on 'ere, between this lot and Harrow.'

The cat's ears twitched. Mouse nodded.

'So let me tell ya who's gunna win. Harrow, that's who. He always wins, ya know that. Which means the only sensible thing for you and me to do is get outta here. Wars ain't good for snotties, they's always the first ones to get stomped on.'

'He's right,' said Sinew from behind the desk. 'This isn't a safe place, Mouse. You might be better off on the high seas.'

Mouse's hands flashed angrily. Pounce snorted. 'Look at 'em, Mousie! What hope 'ave they got? They ain't even got guns!'

Once again the smaller boy's hands flashed. Pounce sighed. 'I reckon ya might change yer mind when things get nasty, so I'm willin' to 'ang around for a few days. Not 'ere, I'm not stupid. I'll be in the city, keepin' outta trouble. You'll find me quick enough if ya need me.'

Mouse smiled. Goldie stepped in front of the door, blocking Pounce's exit. 'You mustn't tell the Fugleman – that's Harrow – that we're the ones who stole the money tonight,' she said. 'And you mustn't tell him anything about the museum.'

Broo growled, his eyes glowing a brilliant red. 'He will not tell.'

'Nah,' said Pounce quickly. 'I won't.'

Toadspit grunted his disbelief.

'Do you promise?' said Goldie.

'I said, didn't I?'

Mouse lifted one of his tiny pets out of the baby's bath and held it up. Pounce rolled his eyes, but he put a finger on the white mouse's head and said, 'I promise on the 'eads of Mousie's mousies that I won't tell Harrow nothin' at all. There, that good enough for yez? Now let me out.'

Goldie stepped away from the door. She thought Pounce would probably keep his promise, for a while at least. But he would break it in an instant if he had to. If things got bad for him or for Mouse, Pounce would go straight to the Fugleman.

FIRST AND ONLY
LINE OF DEFENCE

Just after dawn the next morning, Bonnie and the cat took up their station on the steps of the museum. Bonnie wore a suit of armour cobbled together from flattened-out tins, and carried a wooden sword. The cat wore armour too, made of silver paper and string. Tied to its neck with pink ribbon was a sign that said, 'BeWaRe!!!! FieRCe IDle-Cat!!!!!!'

Bonnie nearly fell over laughing

Bonnie Hahn

when she saw herself in the mirror. 'Will it work, do you think?' she said to Toadspit. 'Will we fool them?'

Her brother cracked his knuckles. 'I hope so.'

'If we don't,' said Goldie, 'we're in big trouble.'

The cat craned its head to look at its 'BeWaRe' sign. 'Prrrroud,' it murmured, which set Bonnie to laughing again.

But when a number of street-rigs pulled up at the end of the cul de sac, a few minutes before midday, she stopped thinking it was funny and felt the full weight of the responsibility that lay upon her shoulders.

'They're here!' she whispered to the cat. 'Remember, don't say anything and don't scratch anyone. You're just a harmless little pussy-cat.'

'Harrooooow?' murmured the cat.

'Yes, I can't see him yet, but he'll be there somewhere. He's the Fugleman. Now shhhh!'

Her first sight of the visitors came in the form of half a dozen mercenaries. They threw themselves into the cul de sac, their backs pressed against the stone walls, their rifles aimed at the museum. When they saw Bonnie and the cat, they stopped. One of them shook his head in disbelief, and Bonnie heard him mutter to his companions, 'You sure we're in the right place?'

'Could be a trap,' said another man. 'Keep your guard up.'

Bonnie's legs were trembling, but she did her best to stand firm as the mercenaries sidled down the dead-end street towards her.

'What's that blocking the doorway? A sofa?' The man who had shaken his head snorted with quiet laughter. 'You *sure* we're in the right place?'

'*Two* sofas,' said the soldier behind him.

'And a cat, don't forget the cat.'

'Oooh, I'm scared.'

Still, they did not lower their rifles. They were no more than ten paces away now, and Bonnie felt as if she might fall over out of sheer fright. She closed her eyes and pretended that she was back in Care, with fetters around her ankles and Guardian Bliss trying to bully her into submission.

Her shoulders went back. Her chin went up. She opened her eyes and cried out, 'Halt!'

To her amazement, the soldiers stopped. *They* were surprised too – they looked at each other and snickered.

'I am the guard of the museum, and I won't let you past!' said Bonnie. 'Put down your guns, or I'll set my idle-cat onto you!'

She said it as fiercely as she could, knowing that it would not sound fierce to men like these. The mercenaries stared at her open-mouthed – then burst out laughing.

Bonnie stamped her foot. 'Don't laugh at me! I *will* set the cat on you. I will!' She waved her wooden sword in the air. 'Attack them, puss! Don't show any mercy! Attack!'

By now, the soldiers were laughing helplessly. But what happened next made them roar with delight. The cat – the *wonderful* cat – rolled onto its back and began to purr.

There was a shout from the mouth of the cul de sac. 'Is there a problem in there?'

The soldiers quickly straightened up, wiping their hands across their eyes. 'Sir?' called one of them. 'Field Marshal? You might want to look at this. You too, Your Honour. There's – ah – no apparent danger.' He winked at his companions and they snorted silently.

The Fugleman and the field marshal strode down the little street in a flurry of robes and polished silver. Behind them came a phalanx of Blessed Guardians and mercenaries, jostling each other for position. The six soldiers stepped back smartly so their superiors could see Bonnie and the cat.

Bonnie could not bring herself to look the Fugleman in the eye. This was the man who had given the order that she, her brother and Goldie be killed, so that they couldn't betray his secrets. Not only that, he had tried to murder the Protector, and nearly succeeded.

But what made Bonnie *really* angry was the knowledge that, in his guise as Harrow, this man had once set a trained fighting dog onto the cat, just for fun. The cat had won the fight, and killed the dog in the process, but that was not the point. It had been sheer cruelty, and Bonnie could not forgive the Fugleman for it.

She wished that she had her bow and arrow, and that she and the cat were real guards, not fake ones. But if the Fugleman saw her bow, he would know who had taken the money. For the sake of the museum, she must not get this wrong.

'Stop!' she cried, waving her wooden sword in the field marshal's face, and hoping the Fugleman wouldn't remember the cat. 'Or I'll run you through!'

The field marshal was as amazed as his soldiers had been. He barked with laughter. 'Is this your dreaded museum?' he said to the Fugleman. 'Guarded by a little girl and a cat?'

'It's . . . not what I expected,' murmured the Fugleman, staring over Bonnie's head at the sofas. 'Perhaps it's a diversion.'

'Perhaps,' said the field marshal, 'our wages were stolen by children and felines.' The cat dabbled at the hem of his trousers with a playful paw. The soldiers laughed.

'I don't think so,' said the Fugleman with a thin smile. He raised his voice. 'Guardian Kindness, are you there?'

There was a bustle in the crowd at the foot of the steps, and Guardian Kindness stepped forward, his pale face expressionless. 'There were twelve men at least, Your Honour, as I reported this morning when we—' his nostrils flared '—when we were found at last, and released from our bonds. The men were very strong. We did our best to resist, but they overpowered us. There were certainly no children among them.'

'Hmm,' said the Fugleman, not yet convinced.

The field marshal nudged the cat with his toe, then turned away and began to descend the steps. 'Waste your own time here if you wish,' he said over his shoulder. 'But while you are playing children's games, my men and I will be searching for this Hidden Rock. I'll wager it's members of the militia who escaped the round-up.'

Bonnie saw a muscle in the Fugleman's cheek twitch at the insult of *children's games*. He took one last look at the museum, then followed the field marshal down the steps. 'If it *is* the militia,' he said in a cold voice, 'we will execute them. Make an example of them. Perhaps we will execute their families as well. *And* their pets.'

Bonnie stared at the back of his head, horrified. If she could have, she would have shot him, right there and then. But without her bow she could do nothing. Except perhaps frighten him with something nasty—

'Watch out for plague!' she called.

'*What?*' The Fugleman and the field marshal swung around so quickly that Bonnie found herself cowering backwards.

She swallowed. 'I— I heard there's plague in the city.'

There was a hum of alarmed voices. 'Nonsense,' snapped the Fugleman. 'There hasn't been plague in Jewel for centuries. The girl is talking rubbish.'

Despite his words, the mercenaries peered around nervously. The Blessed Guardians picked up the hems of their robes and began to trot back down the alleyway.

Anger flickered across the Fugleman's face, but was quickly replaced by a smile of immense charm. 'Of course, what we *should* be talking about,' he said, clapping the field marshal on the back in a brotherly fashion, 'is getting your men's wages paid. Would tonight suit you? I will send the coin by street-rig this time, and increase security. There will be no further trouble, I guarantee it.'

Bonnie grinned at the cat and whispered, 'That's what *he* thinks.'

With the Fugleman's gaze turned away from the museum – for now at least – the rooms began to settle. Goldie and Toadspit, who were busy planning the second strike, could feel it like a sweetening of the air. The moans of the ships in Rough Tom subsided to whispers, and the waters of Old Scratch calmed. Even the Protector seemed to fall into a more natural sleep, and Olga Ciavolga reported that, although she had still not woken, her fever was gone and the patient had swallowed a little water.

By late afternoon, things were quiet enough that Sinew could lay aside his harp for an hour or so and hurry down into the city to talk to some of his contacts. When he came back, he called the children into the kitchen and placed a sheet of paper on the table in front of them.

'It seems,' he said, 'that you have some secret allies.'

The paper looked a bit like the front page of the *New Evening Gazette*, except that the print was rougher and the columns were crooked, and there were no black and white engravings to make it more interesting.

But what was there was interesting enough.

FUGLEMAN LIES! screamed the first headline in enormous letters.

THE TRUTH ABOUT THE BOMB! shouted the second, smaller headline beneath it.

Goldie read the page with growing disbelief. In precise words it told the story of the bomb that had exploded in Jewel last year, and how the Fugleman had been behind it, and what he had gained from it.

The signature at the bottom said, *The Hidden Rock*.

'But who wrote this?' said Goldie, looking up at Sinew. 'Who printed it?'

Toadspit scowled. 'No one knows all this stuff, apart from us.'

'Your parents do.' Sinew smiled at the expression on the children's faces. 'They said they wanted to tell people the truth, didn't they? Well, they have been very quick off the mark, and ingenious with it. These bulletins were stuck to lampposts all over the city. The mercenaries and the Blessed Guardians were pulling them down almost as fast as they went up, but a lot of people read them before they were destroyed.'

Goldie could hardly imagine it. Ma and Pa doing something like this? 'But how did they know about the Hidden Rock?'

'Yes,' said Bonnie, 'we didn't tell them. We hadn't even thought of calling ourselves the Hidden Rock when we saw them!'

Sinew laughed. 'People have been whispering the name all over the city since early morning. Perhaps your parents heard them and decided to add it to the bottom of their gazette at the last minute. However it happened, it's there now, and people are taking notice.'

The children looked at each other, their eyes wide. 'We've started something,' said Toadspit.

Bonnie did a little dance, her absurd armour jangling like a bunch of keys. 'The Hidden Rock's famous!'

'Yes,' said Goldie with great satisfaction. 'And after tonight it will be even more famous!'

SECOND STRIKE

The Shark was an ancient street-rig with globular headlights and a canvas canopy. Herro Dan drove it around the museum when his arthritis was bad, and Goldie was used to the sound of its horn echoing plaintively through the wide corridors.

But now she was driving it herself, and she was nowhere near the corridors of the museum. Instead, she was in the Old Quarter, in the lane that spilled onto Rough Rind Street, waiting in

Broo

the dark for the Blessed Guardians to deliver the mercenaries' pay.

She had driven the Shark down here twenty minutes before curfew, clutching the steering wheel and trying to remember what Herro Dan had taught her. The Shark bumped through the dark streets, its iron wheels muffled with rope and blankets. There were very few people out this late and Goldie did not think that anyone had seen her.

It hadn't been easy to persuade Toadspit that the Blessed Guardians would take exactly the same route as they had taken the night before. 'They're not stupid,' he said, when she explained her plan.

'No,' said Goldie. 'But they'll be out to catch the people who call themselves the Hidden Rock. So they'll *act* as if they're stupid, and hope that we fall into the trap.'

'She is right,' growled Broo. He seemed to have got used to Goldie smelling like a stranger, and he sat next to her with his single white ear pricked and his skin twitching with excitement. 'They will want revenge for last night. They will pretend to be helpless, like a spider that plays dead until its prey is close enough to kill.'

On the other side of Goldie, the cat cleaned its paws and took no apparent notice of the discussion. But when they started to talk about signals, it raised its head and said, 'Yoooowl. Looooooudly.'

'Good,' said Goldie. 'Now, here's what we're going to do . . .'

The lane off Rough Rind Street was cold and dark. Goldie pulled her scarf up around her nose, and ran through Herro Dan's instructions in her head.

The brake – a simple lever beside her left hand – was on, and the gearstick was disengaged. A small pilot light burned on the dashboard. When the time came, she must switch the pilot light downwards, take off the brake and throw the gearstick forward. If everything went as it had during practice, the Shark would rumble to life.

And then . . .

In the back of her mind, Frisia murmured, *And then you will kill them.*

The princess's voice was louder than usual, and for a moment Goldie thought she could see trees and rocks all around her, and a narrow path, and men leaping out of ambush with swords and old-fashioned pikes—

She shook her head. 'I'm not going to kill any-one,' she whispered. 'We're not fighting that sort of war.'

But the picture lingered, full of death and horror, and Goldie knew that this was one of the princess's memories, and that it was a part of *her* now, whether she liked it or not.

As mad as a quignog . . .

'I'm not mad,' she whispered. 'I'm not!'

Still, it was a relief when the unmistakable sound of a street-rig cut through her thoughts. She put her hand on the lever that controlled the pilot light. An eerie wail rose on the night air. 'Nnnnnooooooow!'

With a flick of the wrist, Goldie tipped the pilot light upside down. Then she released the brake and shoved at the gearstick.

There was a soft *whump* somewhere under her feet, like the sound of a gas lamp catching. The Shark's engine gurgled. 'Come on!' whispered Goldie. And to her relief, the iron wheels creaked, and the ancient machine lurched out into Rough Rind Street.

Headlights were already pouring around the corner. With her heart thumping, Goldie guided the Shark forward until it was blocking the street, then she threw on the brake, disengaged the gears and scrambled out of the driver's seat.

She was barely in time. Wheels rattled on the cobblestones. A horn blared. Goldie crouched behind the iron wheels and jammed her eyes shut so that the headlights wouldn't blind her.

She heard a street-rig screech to a halt, and a shout of warning from Guardian Kindness. 'It's a trap, Colleagues! Take your positions! Chains at the ready!'

The headlights snapped off. A dozen chains rattled, then there was silence. Goldie held her breath . . .

One of the Guardians hissed, 'Do we advance, Colleague?'

'No, wait for them to make the first move—' Guardian Kindness broke off with a gasp as a howl of despair rose somewhere behind him.

Goldie gasped too, even though she had been expecting it. The cry was so desolate, so full of fear and pain and regret that it curdled her blood.

'What was *that*?' whispered another Guardian.

'A— A trick,' came Guardian Kindness's uncertain answer. 'Nothing but a—'

Again he broke off. Because this time the howl had words. 'No! No! Not the Black Ox! Forgive me, Great Wooden! I promise I'll never— *Aaaaargh!*'

Goldie peeped out from behind the Shark, frantically flicking the fingers of both hands.

'The Black Ox?' cried one of the Guardians.

'Impossible!' cried another.

'No, no, look!' cried a third, pointing back the way they had come.

Down the street towards them galloped a monstrous sight. It was huge and black and powerful, and its fiery eyes burned with rage. Its horns were twice as wide as a man's outstretched arms. Its hooves struck sparks from the cobblestones.

And on its back— Goldie shivered. On its back was a boy, his clothes bloody and torn, his face a mask of terror. As the great beast plunged down the street, he screamed for help.

'Please don't let the Black Ox take me! I'm sorry for what I did! Pleeeeeeeease!'

His cries were joined by an unearthly wail that made Goldie clap her hands over her ears. If she hadn't known better, she would have thought that the Seven Gods themselves were descending on that narrow street.

The Blessed Guardians obviously thought so. They picked up their robes and pelted past the Shark without a second look, their prayers flying in all directions.

'Great Wooden, *please*, I'm a Guardian, I'm *Blessed*!'

'I regret my sins! Save me!'

'Oh Seven Gods, I didn't mean to do it, it was an accident! Forgive me! Keep your creature away from me!'

Up the street they ran, crying out their penitence. Not once did they look back. Not once did they dare confront the terrifying spectre of the Black Ox.

If they had, they would have seen it laughing.

'Huh huh huh,' panted Broo. 'That was almost as much fun as chasing a slommerkin. I would like to do it again, but not now. These iron shoes hurt my paws.'

He peered towards the Shark. 'Did I make a good Black Ox?'

A feline shadow strutted past him. 'Coooow,' it murmured.

Broo stiffened. 'I was *not* a cow! I was an ox—'

Goldie slipped from her hiding place and put her arms around his neck. 'You were wonderful, Broo. You were all wonderful, all three of you. You even scared me!'

'We'd better not hang around,' said Toadspit, sliding from the brizzlehound's back.

He and Goldie removed Broo's shoes and horns, then loaded the sacks of money into the Shark, while the animals kept watch at opposite ends of the street.

The last thing Goldie did before they set off on the dangerous drive back to the museum was leave a note on the bonnet of the Guardians' street-rig, weighed down with a stone.

'*The Hidden Rock will CRACK the Harrow.*'

THE FORTUNE

It was barely dawn when Field Marshal Brace marched into the Fugleman's office. 'That's two payments gone,' he snapped, his moustache bristling. 'Don't bother with excuses. What I want to know is, was the money there in the first place?'

The Fugleman's fist curled around the note he had been reading. He forced a smile. 'Delightful to see you, too, Field Marshal. Have you had breakfast? Or do soldiers not bother with such trivial things?'

Toadspit

The field marshal prodded him in the chest with a gloved finger. 'There's a rumour going round that there's no money in the Treasury. That your Guardians have salted it away for their own use. That's why it keeps disappearing. It's a cover-up. You were never going to pay us in the first place—'

The Fugleman gritted his teeth and pushed the field marshal's finger aside as politely as possible. But despite his best efforts, some of his anger spilled into his voice. 'Jewel is *not* a poor city, Brace. And my Guardians would not *dare* to steal from the Treasury. The payment was on its way, exactly as we agreed. But—' he opened his fist to reveal the note '—it was waylaid.'

'The Hidden Rock?' Something crackled in the back of the field marshal's eyes. 'Are your Blessed Guardians imbeciles, to be tricked twice by the same people?'

The Fugleman smiled again, showing his teeth this time. 'I am beginning to think that they must be. But then, so are your men. They are supposed to be patrolling the streets, but these people come and go as if there were no curfew.'

'Hmph,' grunted the field marshal, and he took a step backwards and began to smooth his moustache thoughtfully. After a moment he said, 'They know about your other life as Harrow.'

'They do indeed. Which is a great inconvenience. It makes me think that perhaps they have friends outside Jewel.'

'Mm-hmph.'

'As for the money, there is plenty in the Treasury, and I will personally oversee the next payment.'

'Today.'

'No, there is something else that needs to be done today.'

'My men will not—'

'Your men, Brace, will receive their due payment tomorrow morning, plus a generous bonus. Send a squad to the Treasury to collect it, if you like. That will have the double benefit of keeping the money safe, and stopping these rumours.'

The field marshal nodded slowly. 'And the *something else* that needs to be done today?'

'Ah, yes.' This time the Fugleman's smile was genuine. 'Let us show these rebels what happens when I am crossed . . .'

⧘—◍—⧘

Everyone except the Protector was at breakfast that morning. 'Her colour is much better,' said Olga Ciavolga in answer to a question from Bonnie. 'But she has not yet eaten.' She smiled faintly. 'Unlike our other guests.'

'Gue-e-e-ests,' croaked Morg, balancing on the back of Toadspit's chair. 'Gue-e-e-e-ests.'

Mouse, who was sitting next to Sinew, looked up from his third serving of porridge and beamed. The cat licked its whiskers graciously, as if it was doing them all a favour by cleaning their plates. The mice in the baby's bath rustled.

At the other end of the table, Goldie was trying not to think about madness. She had dreamed the night before that she was still in ancient Merne. Now the dream came back to her in such vivid detail that she felt as if she was standing right there—

—*in the library in front of her father, King Ferdrek V, and promising that she would kill Graf von Nagel and bring back his head in a sack*—

With an effort, Goldie dragged herself back to the present, where Bonnie was asking Mouse if he would tell the Protector's fortune. 'Then we'd know if she's going to be all right.'

The little boy made a circle with his finger – a circle that included everyone in the kitchen.

Goldie was feeling oddly dislocated, as if a part of her was still there in that centuries-old library. She did her best to ignore it and said, 'Mouse wants to tell *all* our fortunes.'

Sinew pushed his empty bowl towards the cat and leaned forward, his long face alight with interest. 'I've been wanting to see this. I had my fortune told by a goat once, but none of its predictions came true.' He grinned. 'Particularly not the one about bearing fifteen children and my husband running off with another woman.'

Herro Dan snorted with laughter. Then he turned to Mouse and said, 'We'd be honoured, lad. Might give us some guidance for the days ahead. The Fugleman won't take these attacks lyin' down, and it'd be good to stay a step or two in front of him.'

Mouse smiled and whistled. Immediately, the rustling in the baby's bath became more purposeful, and it was not long before the mice emerged with their scraps of paper and laid them on the kitchen table. The older keepers watched with great interest while Mouse threw all but five of the scraps back, then rearranged the ones that were left.

'What does it say?' asked Goldie.

'It's like a code, yes?' said Sinew. 'Well then, I think it might be about you. This first one says, *of gold*.'

Goldie jumped from her chair and peered over Mouse's shoulder. 'And the second one says, *this journey will*. I must be going somewhere!'

In his basket by the stove, little white Broo yelped, as

if he was dreaming. The cat strolled down the tabletop and dabbled at the third bit of paper with its paw.

'I was getting to that one,' said Goldie. 'It says, *last chance to win.*' She wrinkled her nose. 'So wherever I'm going, it's got something to do with beating the Fugleman!'

'Yes, but where are you going?' said Toadspit.

'I don't know. The next bit of paper just has one word, *beast*, and the last one is a picture of a road.'

Goldie saw Herro Dan stiffen – for the briefest of moments, no more. Broo yelped again, and woke up, his little ears twitching as if he had barely escaped from a nightmare.

'Do you know what it means, Herro Dan?' said Goldie. 'Beast? Road?'

The old man's face was as innocent as sunlight. He shook his head. 'Nope.'

He's lying, thought Goldie.

—And deep inside her, in an ancient library, a king's daughter raised her head in disbelief. LYING? To ME?

Sinew tapped his fingernail on the table. 'I'm sure I've heard of something called the Beast Road. Wasn't it you who mentioned it, Dan? Years ago?'

Broo climbed out of his basket and gazed up at the old man, his head tipped to one side. Herro Dan smiled. 'Wish I could help you. But I've never heard of it.'

'And if Dan has not heard of it,' said Olga Ciavolga firmly, 'then it does not exist. The fortune must mean something else.'

'E-e-e-e-e-else,' muttered Morg.

Goldie felt the strangest sensation, as if something was trying to drag her out of the present and into the past; as if she was *shifting*, the way the museum did . . .

'Herro Dan,' she said, doing her best to sound normal. 'Are you *sure* you've never heard of it?'

'I'm sure,' said Herro Dan, as innocent as ever.

—And suddenly her whole body was buzzing with royal pride and anger. She felt hot and cold, clear-headed and dizzy. The old man had lied to her. Twice! To HER, the crown princess of Merne!

She would not tolerate it.

'You MUST tell me about the Beast Road!' she said. 'I order you to tell me! I COMMAND you!'

And then she was back in the kitchen, and everyone at the table was white with shock. Toadspit's mouth hung open. Sinew's hand rested, frozen, on the strings of his harp. Even the cat looked surprised.

Morg was the first to find her voice. 'Comma-a-a-a-and,' she cawed in mocking tones.

Herro Dan glanced worriedly at Olga Ciavolga, then back at Goldie. 'Now, lass—'

But Goldie was in control of herself once again, and she could not bear to stay in the room for a moment longer. Not with her friends staring at her as if she had turned into a monster. 'I— I'm sorry!' she whispered. 'I didn't mean it! It was—'

She could think of no excuse except the truth, and if she told them that she would lose everything – their trust, their love and her position as Fifth Keeper. And so, without another word, she ran out of the room.

Pounce had kept his promise so far. He hadn't been near Harrow, hadn't said a word to anyone about what he knew. Instead, he'd spent most of his time begging.

He didn't need to, of course, not with the money that Goldie had given him. But begging gave him a feel for the mood of a city. He could tell whether people were happy or sad, stirred up or solid.

And this morning, as he sat outside a pie shop with his hand outstretched and a pitiful look on his face, Pounce could see that the black-robed Guardians and the mercenaries striding past were well and truly stirred up.

He would've bet the shirt on his back that it was something to do with Goldie and Toadspit, and the war they were waging against Harrow. All yesterday and first thing this morning he'd heard whispers about 'The Hidden Rock'. No one seemed to know who it was. No one except Pounce.

'Blessings on ya, Frow,' he muttered to an old lady, as she tucked a pastry into his hand.

'Watch out for the soldiers, lad,' she whispered. 'There they go, the brutes!' And she hurried off.

Pounce looked up in time to see a squad of mercenaries marching towards the centre of the city with a purposeful look on their faces and an open-topped rig rattling behind them.

'Oho!' he whispered to himself. 'I reckon Harrow's decided to fight back, even if 'e can't see what 'e's fightin' against.'

He followed the mercenaries at a distance, chewing on his pastry. Most of the people who had been on the streets earlier had disappeared and Pounce could see no more than a dozen adults, hurrying along with their heads bent and their snotties clutched tight against their sides.

He didn't blame them for being scared. There was something nasty in the air this morning, something that made him slide into the shadows whenever one of the mercenaries looked in his direction.

The street spilled into a plaza, and the line of men stamped to a halt. There were more people here, crossing the plaza as quickly as they could, trying not to look at the mercenaries or make themselves noticeable.

The open-topped rig pulled around until it blocked the way it had come.

'Oho!' whispered Pounce again, glad that he had had the sense to stay well back, and glad too, for once, that Mouse was tucked up safely in the museum.

He peered past the rig, the pastry forgotten. The mercenaries had broken into small groups and were hurrying to block the entrances of the other three streets that joined the plaza. No one except Pounce seemed to have realised what was happening. He gnawed his bottom lip and glared at the citizens of Jewel.

'Soft idjits!' he muttered. 'Open yer eyes, why don't ya?'

They didn't hear him, of course. But their eyes were opened soon enough. When they tried to leave the plaza, the mercenaries blocked their way and would not let them pass.

Most people immediately scuttled off to the next street, and then the next one, darting around like fish in a bucket. Pounce groaned. And when the mercenaries began to snatch the snotties from their parents and carry them off to the rig, he groaned louder.

'Bite 'em!' he whispered. 'Kick 'em in the shins! Take 'em by surprise, then run fer yer life!'

But although the snotties screamed and cried, they didn't know the street-fighting tricks that Pounce knew, and they were quickly chained to the seats of the rig.

Their parents were so shocked that they hardly protested. Men and women stood frozen, with their hands outstretched and their mouths open, as if someone had given them the evil eye and they could not move or speak.

'What's wrong with yez?' muttered Pounce. 'If anyone tried this sorta nonsense in Spoke there'd be blood on the streets by now!'

But there was to be no blood on the streets of Jewel. It wasn't until the rig drove away, with the snotties wailing and the mercenaries marching beside them, that the spell was broken. Even then the parents hardly made a sound. They ran after the rig, crying silently and holding each other upright. Some of them staggered, as if the road was crumbling beneath their feet.

Pounce couldn't bear it. He shoved the last bit of pastry in his mouth and hurried away, shaking his head and muttering, 'Poor soft idjits. They need someone to 'elp 'em. Someone who knows 'ow to fight. Now, if it was *me* up against them mercenaries—'

He realised what he was saying, and laughed at himself. Who was the soft one now? Of *course* they needed someone to help them. But it wouldn't be Pounce.

'Nah,' he said. '*I'm* not stupid enough to go against Harrow. Not me.'

He looked over his shoulder at the weeping parents and felt an unfamiliar pain in his chest. 'Not me,' he said. But this time his voice was less certain. 'Nah, not me.'

A FEW CAREFULLY
PLACED RUMOURS

The Fugleman

'Princess Frisia's memories have been inside me all along,' whispered Goldie. '*And* her voice. But this time it was different. I was *there*. I was back in ancient Merne. I was Frisia!'

It was a relief to confess her secret to someone, even if that someone was unconscious and couldn't hear her. The rightful Protector of the city of Jewel lay in a narrow bed, with only her head and one arm showing above the quilt. Olga Ciavolga was right – the Protector's colour was better. But her eyes were closed, her hair was lank and her face was far too thin.

'Maybe Herro Dan was right, after all,' whispered Goldie. 'Maybe I'm going mad. Maybe I'll find myself, one dark night, slitting throats and cutting off ears, and thinking it a perfectly normal thing to do!'

She shuddered at the thought. As if in response, the Protector's breathing grew quick and shallow.

Goldie felt a pang of sympathy. 'I wish you'd wake up,' she whispered, and she squeezed the Protector's limp fingers.

The fingers squeezed back. Goldie jumped, but there was no further movement from the woman in the bed – except for a faint smile that lay across her face like a blessing.

Goldie sighed, knowing that she could hide away no longer. She must tell Olga Ciavolga that the Protector was showing signs of waking. She must apologise properly to Herro Dan, and invent some excuse for her rudeness.

And she must talk to Toadspit about the third strike.

She found Toadspit in the room called Stony Heart, practising his swordplay. Bonnie and the cat were watching him, surrounded by suits of armour and skeletons. Above their heads, an iron mantrap ground its teeth in uneasy sleep.

Goldie had known that Toadspit was keeping up his practice, but this was the first time she had seen it. She stopped just inside the door and watched curiously as he stepped back and forth between the skeletons, his shoes thumping on the floor, his face a scowl of concentration.

Lunge, strike, parry. Sidestep. Lunge, strike, strike. Block. Counter strike.

The moves were so familiar that Goldie could feel them in her bones, and in the muscles of her legs and arms. As if she was still Princess Frisia . . .

'Is that Graf von Nagel you're fighting?' said Bonnie. 'Did you kill him? Hooraaaaay! We win!'

Toadspit grinned over his shoulder. Then he saw Goldie and his face became a sudden, careful mask.

But before he could say anything, Sinew loped into the room, his eyes gleaming, his harp strings singing a triplet of notes. 'You were right, Goldie! The Protector is awake at last! And—' His tone was that of someone reporting a great military victory. 'And she has eaten some soup!'

'Hooray!' said Bonnie. 'Is she going to help us fight the Fugleman?'

'I expect so,' said Sinew in his normal voice. But perhaps we should give her a little more time to recover. After all, she didn't actually hold the soup spoon herself. She might have trouble with armed combat for a few days yet.'

Toadspit laughed. Sinew played another triplet on the harp. 'But that's not the only news,' he said. 'Broo has killed a rat in the Tench.'

Bonnie pulled a face.

'Diseased?' asked Toadspit.

'I don't think so,' said Sinew. 'The museum has been quieter since the Fugleman started hunting elsewhere for the Hidden Rock—'

'Harrooooow,' muttered the cat in disgusted tones.

'—but it has given me an idea. Yesterday, Bonnie warned the mercenaries and the Guardians about plague.'

'They were scared,' said Bonnie, beaming at Goldie. 'The Fugleman said it wasn't true, but everyone got really jumpy all of a sudden.'

'And a few carefully placed rumours,' said Sinew, 'should make them even jumpier. So I'm going down to the city again—'

'Can I go with you?' Bonnie interrupted him.

'Aren't you and the cat supposed to be guarding the front door?' asked Toadspit. 'In case the Fugleman comes back?'

119

'He won't come back. We've been out there since breakfast and no one's been near us. I'm bored. So's the cat. Aren't you, cat?'

'Noooo,' said the cat.

'Yes, you are! We want to do something different! Something interesting!'

'Unfortunately,' said Sinew, 'your brother is right—'

'Her brother is *always* right,' said Toadspit.

Bonnie hit him.

'We really do need you on the front door,' said Goldie, speaking for the first time. 'I know it's boring, but it's important. The Fugleman might come back today or tomorrow or next week, and the museum has to look as silly and helpless as possible.'

'That's me, is it?' Bonnie put her hands on her hips. 'Silly and helpless?'

'No, but—'

'So from now on you and Toadspit get to do all the interesting stuff while I stand out the front of the museum looking silly? It's not fair!'

'Of course it's not,' said Sinew gently. 'None of it is fair, Bonnie. But at times like this we each do what we must.' He pulled a wry face. 'I suspect that before this is over we'll all be very sick of *interesting stuff*. Even you.'

Bonnie sniffed, unconvinced. 'Come on, cat,' she said. 'Let's go and be silly and helpless while the *important* people here get on with saving the world.'

'Prrrroud,' murmured the cat. And, with its nose in the air, it followed Bonnie out to the front steps.

Sinew left not long after, trailing a string of notes behind him. Goldie eyed Toadspit. Now that they were alone, she was sure he would confront her over what had happened at breakfast.

But instead he said, 'You realise the next payment will be so closely guarded that we won't get near it?'

Goldie nodded, relieved. 'If I was the Fugleman, I'd break the pattern now. He wants to catch the Hidden Rock, but it's even more important that the mercenaries get paid.'

In the back of her mind, Frisia began to whisper. Goldie felt an awful slipping sensation, and suddenly she was—

—standing on a hill overlooking a battlefield, with her father the king beside her, discussing strategy. 'If the enemy changes direction,' said the king, 'then you must change direction also, and reach his destination before him.'

Below them, six thousand fighting men wheeled and turned in answer to the trumpets—

And then Goldie was back in the museum with her legs shivering like wind-blown grass.

It's happened again, she thought, and her stomach churned. She tried to remember what she had been saying a moment ago. 'So— So— So we'll break the pattern too. We— We're going to need Morg's help. Where *is* Morg? Do you think she's strong enough to carry a grappling iron? She wouldn't have to carry it far; maybe we could find a small one.'

She knew she was gabbling, but she couldn't help it; she was so afraid that Toadspit would realise the truth. 'Where can we get some lead?' she said. 'Perhaps there'll be some in Early Settlers, let's go and see.'

Fortunately for Goldie, there was a lot to do before the third strike, and Toadspit was soon distracted. The two children scoured the back rooms of the museum for the things they needed, watching out for rats all the while. But Sinew had been right when he said that things were quiet, and they saw nothing out of the ordinary.

There was one *shift*, which came just as they were melting lead piping in a tin over a fire, and pouring it into moulds. But the rooms settled quickly, although a few of the moulds were ruined and had to be done again.

They saw Broo several times, dashing through the long corridors in his little dog shape, his white coat plastered with mud and a look of sheer joy on his face. By then, Goldie was so caught up in their preparations that she had let down her guard.

So when Toadspit said, innocently, 'I've never seen Broo hate another creature as much as he hates that cat', she merely nodded and murmured, 'Mm, mortal enemies.'

The innocence vanished from Toadspit's voice. 'Like Princess Frisia and Graf von Nagel?'

Goldie went very still. 'Why did you say that?'

'No reason.'

'You must've had a reason!'

'Maybe,' said Toadspit, turning to stare at her, 'I was wondering why you never talk about what happened in ancient Merne. Bonnie's always going on about it—'

'Bonnie's ten.'

'—and I talk about it a bit too. But you *never* do, and when—'

'There's a lot of other things happening, in case you hadn't noticed! Like our city being overrun! And a war to be fought!'

'—and when someone mentions it, you act as if you've been ambushed. Like now.'

Goldie blinked at him with her mouth open. 'Um—' she said, feeling *exactly* as if she had been ambushed.

She wished she could tell him. But she couldn't. For Toadspit the world of Merne had passed like a dose of fever. He had come out of it a trained swordsman and, like Bonnie, he remembered everything that had happened there. But he didn't have someone else's life still stuck inside him, threatening to drive him mad.

If she told him, he'd never trust her again.

'Um—' she said. 'Do you know the symptoms of plague?'

'*What?*'

'It's just— We should know what to look out for. In case that rat *was* diseased.'

Toadspit glared at her. 'I thought we were friends. I thought, after everything that's happened—'

'Boils,' said Goldie desperately. 'Don't people get boils? In their armpits?'

She could see the anger and disappointment on Toadspit's face, and she thought he might walk away. Instead, he gritted his teeth and rattled out, 'It's not boils, it's swellings. Buboes, they're called. Neck, armpits, groin, that's where you get them. You get a fever too, and vomiting, and according to Herro Dan you feel really tired and want to sleep a lot. Oh yes, and you get black patches on your skin, from the bleeding underneath. There, does that satisfy you?' He scowled. 'I'm going to see if Sinew's back yet.'

'Wait!' Goldie called after him. 'I'll come with you. We need to ask him about the Treasury.'

Sinew was back, but only just. He and Herro Dan had their heads together in the office. Mouse was listening to them, his small body tense and unhappy.

'What's the matter?' said Goldie. 'What's happened?'

Sinew turned a bleak face towards her. 'The mercenaries are grabbing children off the streets and putting them in the House of Repentance. Word is that it's in retaliation for the thefts. The Fugleman doesn't know who took the money, so he's punishing the whole city.'

In the back of Goldie's mind, Frisia cursed and called for her sword—

'This changes everything,' said Toadspit. 'We'll have to stop. No more Hidden Rock.'

'What?' said Goldie, struggling to pull her thoughts together. 'No!'

Herro Dan cocked an eyebrow at her.

'If we stop,' she said, 'the Fugleman has won. He'll be able to do anything he likes and no one will dare go against him, not ever! Don't you see? We have to beat him!'

'But what about the children?' said Toadspit. 'The ones in the House of Repentance? What if something even worse happens to them because of us?'

Goldie shook her head helplessly, wishing that there were no hard decisions to be made. 'I don't know. I just know that we have to make this third strike tonight.'

With a sigh, Herro Dan sat down at the desk. 'It's a bad choice either way. Whatever we do, someone's gunna suffer. But—' He smiled sadly at Goldie. 'I agree with you, lass.'

'You *do*?'

The old man nodded. 'The Fugleman's half-mad with power, and someone has to stop him. Reckon it's up to us.'

'All the same,' said Sinew, 'Toadspit's right. Innocent lives could be lost.'

Innocent lives are the price of war, whispered Frisia in the back of Goldie's mind. *Battles are not won by soft hearts.*

But it seemed to Goldie that, if she was willing to sacrifice other people to gain victory, she was no better than the Fugleman. 'We'll do our best to save them,' she said.

And that seemed to satisfy both Sinew and Toadspit, for now at least.

THIRD STRIKE

Even in peaceful times, the Treasury was the most carefully guarded building in Jewel, with half a dozen militia stationed, day and night, outside its front doors. Now of course the militia were either dead or imprisoned, but the Treasury was watched more closely than ever.

'We don't want to go in blind,' Goldie said to Sinew. 'Toadspit thought you might know where the vaults are. And the best way to get in.'

Morg

Sinew pulled a thoughtful face. 'Yes, we used to have the original plans for most of the public buildings in Jewel. Let me see, where did I put them . . .' He ran his fingers over his harp strings to help him think.

'Aha!' he said, a moment later, and he strode towards the kitchen, with the two children trotting behind him.

The plans were sealed inside a breadbox, which was in turn stowed at the back of one of the kitchen cupboards between a sack of carrots and a cast-iron mincer.

'Perfect filing system!' said Sinew, emerging from the depths of the cupboard with a carrot in his top pocket. '*I* can find them, but no one else can.'

He brushed the spider webs out of his hair, and stripped the wax from the lid of the breadbox. 'I've never actually used these,' he said, leafing through the plans until he found the ones he wanted. 'But I keep them just in case. It can be amazingly useful to know where the bathroom is in a strange building.'

His jokes couldn't conceal the worry in his eyes. 'Sinew, we'll be all right,' said Toadspit.

'Of course you will.' Sinew smiled. 'I don't doubt it for a moment.' And he unfolded the plans.

Whoever had designed the Treasury, so long ago, had been very conscious of security. The stone walls were impossible to climb. The back door was so well barred from the inside that not even the cleverest thief could open it. There were no windows.

'But,' said Sinew, 'you know what Jewel is like in summer. Any place without windows would quickly turn into an oven. The builders realised this, even if the planners didn't.'

He ran a finger across the paper, following the faded lines of ink. 'This is the roof that was supposed to be built. And *this*—' He touched a faint pencil line that made a series of notches in the ink. 'This is what *was* built. See the hidden vents? They channel the air in and out of the building and make it one of the most pleasant places in the city.'

Goldie stared at him. 'You think we can get in through the vents? But won't they be blocked?'

'I don't think so. You see, the men who built the Treasury were in a difficult position. At the time, the city was under the rule of the first Grand Protector, a stubborn and vindictive man. He ordered the builders to follow his plans exactly, for the sake of security. I gather they tried to explain about the need for some sort of air flow, but he wouldn't listen. And so, for the sake of their own skins, they made their changes secretly, without telling a soul. The only evidence they left was a few pencil marks. And these plans – um – disappeared—' Sinew looked slightly embarrassed '—before anyone else could see them.'

It was those faded pencil lines that Goldie thought of later that night, as she and Toadspit crouched in the darkness. Across the road, four Blessed Guardians stood on one side of the Treasury portico, with the beginnings of a fog licking their ankles. On the other side of the portico stood four mercenaries. Two of each group surveyed the street, in the time-honoured manner of those who guarded this important building. The others watched the group opposite. The tension between them was so strong that Goldie could almost touch it.

Without a word, she and Toadspit retreated to the corner, where Morg was perched on their haversacks. They picked up the heavy bags and, with the slaughterbird flying ahead of them, slipped down the street that ran alongside the Treasury.

Away from the portico, with its carved frieze, the Treasury was like a fortress. The fog was rising, and Goldie stared up at the forbidding walls, her blood alight with fear and excitement.

'That's where the ledge is, along there,' Toadspit whispered, pointing upwards. He took a rope from his haversack, tied it to a small grappling iron and held it out to the slaughterbird. 'Morg, remember what we practised? Take this and hook it over the ledge. Make sure it's nice and firm. We don't want it to fall off when we're halfway up.'

He weighed the grappling iron in his hand and looked at Goldie, suddenly uncertain. 'The wall's higher than I thought. I'm not sure she can manage it.'

But Morg was already strutting towards him, blinking her wrinkled eyelids. 'U-u-u-u-up,' she muttered. She flexed her claws twice, and hunched her back. The tips of her feathers shivered. Then, with a thrust of her powerful wings, she launched herself into the air, snatched the grappling iron out of Toadspit's hands, and began to fight her way upwards.

The children watched, their heads tipped back, their mouths open.

'It's too high,' whispered Toadspit. 'She's not going to make it. Look, she's dropping! No, wait! She's trying to catch an updraft!'

The fog in the side street curled and twisted with the movement of the air, and Morg curled and twisted with it, her great wings beating desperately, the grappling iron dragging her down like an anchor.

Goldie dug her fingernails into her palms and whispered under her breath, 'Come on, Morg! You can do it! Come *on*!'

At last the slaughterbird found the current of air she was looking for. It carried her down the street, away from the children, but at the same time it pushed up under her wings like an extra muscle. Goldie and Toadspit ran after her, hauling the haversacks with them.

'Can you see her?'

'No. But she went up near here somewhere. Listen! I heard something!' Toadspit stood very still, his hand on Goldie's shoulder. There was a whisper of sound, and the rope dropped in front of them, hanging from the top of the wall to the bottom.

'Quick,' said Goldie. 'You go first.'

She kept watch while Toadspit shinned up the rope. When she felt his signal, she tied one of the haversacks to the end of the rope and tugged. It slid smoothly upwards. The rope came down again, and she tied the other haversack on and sent that one up too.

Then it was her turn. She gripped the rope with both hands, and jumped, wrapping her legs around it and pinching it between her feet. The fog drifted past her, carrying the dank smell of the canals, and the silence of a cowed city. In the back of her mind, the world of ancient Merne beckoned.

Goldie gritted her teeth and began to work her way upwards.

It took the children nearly an hour to do what they had come to do. By the time they climbed back out of the air vents, the fog had the whole city in its grip, and did not look as if it would be easing soon.

Goldie stood on the roof with Jewel blanked out in every direction. Inside her, Frisia was whispering urgently, and before she knew it—

—*she was in the highlands of Merne with her father the king, hunting a party of von Nagel's men who had crossed the border from Halt-Bern. The fog had closed in an hour ago, as white as mare's milk and twice as thick.*

Frisia stood beside her father, surrounded by the smell of horses and wet earth. A hawk cried somewhere overhead, but she could see nothing.

'We can use this fog,' said the king. 'Soldiers are superstitious creatures on the whole and von Nagel's men do not know these hills the way we do. We will demoralise them, frighten them—'

'Goldie?' Someone touched her arm.

For a moment the smell of horses and the deep rumble of her father's voice lingered. 'Take your hand off me!' she snapped—

And then she was back in Jewel, with Toadspit staring at her and that dreadful weakness making her legs tremble.

'I— I mean,' she stammered, 'you surprised me. I was thinking. About the mercenaries. And the Guardians.'

She could see that Toadspit didn't believe her, but she ploughed on, because it was true, in an odd sort of way. And besides, she couldn't bear the expression on his face.

'If the fog lasts, we can use it to frighten them,' she said. 'We can ask Sinew to help us, and Olga Ciavolga.'

Toadspit nodded slowly. Goldie could almost see his mind working. 'We could get Broo too,' he said. And with that, his eyes began to gleam and the moment of danger was past.

They slid one after the other down the side of the building. Morg unhooked the grappling iron and dropped after them, spreading her wings at the last instant so that she landed with barely a thump.

The two haversacks looked no different from before. They were still astonishingly heavy, and Goldie was tempted to throw them into one of the canals and hurry back to the museum to sleep. But if the sacks were found, all their night's work would be undone, and so she slung one of them across her shoulders again and crept up the street with Toadspit beside her.

At the corner, she hesitated. Her arms and legs ached, and she was tired to the bone from living the lives of two people, five hundred years apart. What's more, it was clear that Frisia was growing stronger, and that frightened Goldie more than she would admit, even to herself.

Still, this was too good an opportunity to miss. She peered through the fog to the unseen spot where the Guardians and mercenaries eyed each other so untrustingly. She nudged Toadspit. 'It wouldn't take long . . .' she whispered.

It was one of those moments when Toadspit knew exactly what she was talking about. A grin spread across his face. '. . . and it'd make tomorrow so much better.'

They hid the haversacks behind a fence, with Morg guarding them once again. Then they gathered the fog around them, so they would not be seen – *I am nothing. I am dust on the streets. I am a cobblestone dreaming* – and drifted along the road to the Treasury portico.

The space between the mercenaries and the Guardians was like a war zone. Nothing crossed it except superior looks and insults. Goldie and Toadspit slid around the edge of it to where the mercenaries were slouched, their various caps pushed back on their foreheads.

Goldie chose the biggest man there, the one who sniggered angrily whenever his fellows growled something about 'black crows' or 'Blessed Cardigans'. She sidled right up to him, so close that if he had swung around quickly, she would have been lost.

I am nothing. I am a silent rifle from a long-forgotten battle . . .

The ache in her legs no longer mattered. This was what she had been trained for, and it made her feel more herself than she had for days.

She slid her hand into the mercenary's pocket, as slick as an eel. Her fingers touched a pipe, a handful of coins, a dry biscuit and something that felt like a hare's foot. She took the pipe, the coins and the hare's foot, and left the biscuit where it was. As she inched backwards, she saw a shadow drift away from a neighbouring soldier.

It was the easiest thing in the world to slide the coins and the hare's foot into the robe pocket of one of the Guardians. Goldie kept hold of the pipe. But just before she eased her way out from under the portico, she opened her fingers – and dropped it.

The clatter it made as it hit the bare stone was shockingly loud. The Blessed Guardians jumped and shouted. The mercenaries threw up their guns, their bodies tense with anticipation.

Despite the fog, it took the big mercenary no more than five seconds to see his pipe lying snugly at the foot of one of the Guardians. And another two seconds to recognise it.

'Hey, that's mine! What's it doin'—' He fumbled in his pockets. 'Where's my money? And my lucky charm?'

Anger darkened his face. 'I've been robbed! The stinkin' Cardigans have robbed me!'

'Don't be ridiculous,' cried one of the Guardians, but the mercenaries, already infuriated by another day of unpaid wages, did not listen. They descended on the Guardians and wrestled them to the ground. Then they searched them.

'Look, look!' cried the big mercenary, holding up the hare's foot. 'I was right! Stinkin' Cardigans!'

A second voice howled with outrage. 'And this one's got my knife, the treacherous crow! Let's teach 'em a lesson, lads!'

Goldie glided away, with the shadow that was Toadspit beside her. The sounds of violence made her feel sick, and she had to remind herself that this was what she had wanted. She was dividing the enemy's forces. She was fighting a war.

There will be no mercy, whispered Frisia in the back of her mind. *War is not the place for mercy.*

THE FUGLEMAN
MAKES AN OFFER

'There, you see?' said the Fugleman, smiling his most charming smile and raising his voice so that the squad of mercenaries could hear him. 'Did I not promise that you and your fellows would be paid this morning, without fail?'

The fog that had beset the Old Quarter overnight wrapped around his legs and drifted past the men in front of him. They scowled and made no move towards the bags of coin that had just been brought from the Treasury.

Field Marshal Brace

'What's the matter with them?' the Fugleman murmured to Field Marshal Brace, who stood at his elbow. 'They want their money, don't they?'

The field marshal smoothed the fingers of one of his leather gloves. 'There was trouble during the night.'

'I heard. My Guardians came running to me in the early hours of the morning, complaining of ill-treatment at the hands of your men.' The Fugleman waved his hand dismissively. 'These things happen.'

'Did they tell you how it started?'

'A false accusation of theft, I believe.'

'Hmm.' Brace studied his boots. 'My men are not convinced that this is a genuine payment.'

'*What?*' The Fugleman laughed. 'I oversaw the counting of the money myself yesterday afternoon, and these bags have been sitting in the Treasury waiting for your men ever since. If that is not genuine enough, I don't know what is!'

At the sound of his laughter, a rumble of discontent ran through the ranks of the mercenaries. Quickly, the Fugleman stripped all expression from his face. This was more serious than he had realised.

His stride, as he approached the bags of coin, had a military sharpness to it. His eyes were as cold as the fog. He beckoned to one of the front-rank soldiers. 'You,' he snapped.

The man stepped forward automatically. The Fugleman pointed to the nearest bag. 'Open it. Check the coins.'

The mercenary was as scruffy and uncouth as the rest of his squad, but he understood what was needed. He knelt beside the nearest bag and whipped the tie from its mouth. His fellows craned forward. The mercenary dug into the bag, raised his hand and let a fistful of silver coins run through his fingers.

The rumble of discontent became a murmur of satisfaction. The Fugleman nodded and turned away. Good. *That* was settled. Now they could get on with laying a trap for whoever was behind this Hidden Rock nonsense—

'Hang on,' said the mercenary.

There was something in his voice that made the Fugleman swing back so quickly that he almost lost his balance. No one noticed. They were all staring at the mercenary, who was dropping a second fistful of coins, and listening to the sound they made as they fell.

It was nothing at all like the clear bright *chink* of silver.

A growl rose from the gathered men, and they curled their lips like dogs that have seen their supper snatched from under their noses. Field Marshal Brace hurried forward.

'Settle down!' he snarled. 'We'll get this sorted out. Needle, check the other bags. The rest of you, shut up.'

The Fugleman watched, stunned, as the soldier took out his knife and scraped at the coins. The silver colour flaked off like the cheap paint it so clearly was. Beneath it, the coins were nothing but worthless lumps of lead.

The rage that erupted from the mercenaries then almost shook the ground. There were roars of *'Treachery!'* and *'Where's our money?'* and *'Just like last night!'*.

The Fugleman found himself unable to think. What in the name of Great Wooden was going on? The money had come straight from the Treasury! He would have bet the lives of half his Guardians that it was good silver! And yet—

The hair on the back of his neck rose. The Hidden Rock! It had to be!

With anger burning in his veins, he pushed his way through the furious crowd. 'There's treachery indeed,' he cried, 'but it's not mine! Look for a message! Do you hear me? *Look for a message!'*

No one took any notice of him. Small groups of men were already striding away into the fog, shouting over their shoulders to their fellows, 'I've had enough! There's no money here, not for us, anyway!'

Brace was trying to summon them back, with limited success. He scowled at the Fugleman, who had given up trying to get someone to do his bidding and was digging into the bags of coins for the note that he knew must be there.

'Yes!' cried the Fugleman at last, waving a strip of paper above his head. 'It's the Hidden Rock again! Wait! Come back! We have *all* been tricked!'

'What does it say?' asked Brace.

'It says—' The Fugleman ground his teeth. '*The Hidden Rock will SMASH the Harrow!*'

'Mmm,' muttered the field marshal. 'Mm-hm.'

'Is that all you can say?'

'Well, it's convenient, isn't it?' The field marshal gazed after his departing men. 'For you, I mean. Not to have to pay us.'

'*Convenient?* Are you *insane?* Look at what's happening! I'm losing a quarter of my forces!'

Brace cleared his throat. '*My* forces. And you can't expect them to stay without wages. Rules of war. Always pay your men promptly.'

'*I. Am. Doing. My. Best*—' The Fugleman thought his head might explode with fury. But he managed to stop himself before he said anything he might regret. He could not afford to lose Brace's support.

With a monstrous effort, he dragged his face into the

semblance of a smile. 'Come with me now,' he grated. 'Bring as many of your men as you wish. We will open the Treasury and pay them on the spot.'

'Mmm,' said the field marshal again. He nodded towards the remainder of his men, who were gathering in hostile groups. 'I'm not sure that it will be enough to keep them here. Once they lose trust . . .'

The Fugleman could not help himself. He snarled, 'I will *not* be hindered like this! Your men *will* stay, and between us we will deal with these rebels once and for all! Did they think we were bluffing yesterday when we imprisoned their children? Let us show them that we were not!'

Brace looked wary. 'I hope you're not suggesting that we execute those children. Rules of war, Fugleman—'

It was in fact *exactly* what the Fugleman had been about to suggest. But he shook his head. The most delicious idea was uncoiling inside him.

'There is no need for executions,' he said. He had himself under control now, and his voice was a soothing murmur. 'There are other ways of dealing with this. Have I told you about the allies I made while I was in exile? None of them as valuable as you, of course. But interesting. Oh yes, definitely interesting.'

'Allies?' said Brace, as if he couldn't care less. But there was a spark in his muddy eyes.

'One of them in particular.' With his smile firmly in place, the Fugleman threw back his head. 'Come, Brace, things are about to improve. Let us shower your men with silver thalers – *real* ones this time. Then I will send a message to my ally, making her an offer. One that will benefit us all.'

He winked at the field marshal. 'Except for the children, of course. And their parents. Oh yes, and the Hidden Rock. *They* won't like it one little bit!'

OMINOUS DAYS

espite the Fugleman's words, the days that followed were ominous ones for the mercenaries. The fog grew worse, and the men patrolling the city – those who had not deserted already – pulled their collars up around their necks and complained bitterly. They had been paid by this time, of course, and their pockets were heavy with silver, but the field marshal was right. Their trust was gone.

Goldie Roth

'Who knows if it's real,' grouched a large corporal, pulling out a coin and staring at it suspiciously.

'Could just be a better class of fake,' said one of his four companions.

'Yeah, I reckon those blokes who took off had the right idea. What sorta job's this? We're fightin' men, ain't we?'

'Course we are!'

'So where's the fightin'? Where's the war?'

'Not 'ere, that's for sure.'

They took out their water canteens and leaned against the nearest wall, with their rifles propped beside them. The fog was so thick that they couldn't see further than a few steps in any direction.

'Stinkin' city, stinkin' weather,' muttered the corporal. Then his face brightened and he dug in his haversack, saying, 'Ya know that pie shop down near the markets? I *persuaded* 'em to give us a bunch of pies, ha ha ha! Here we go, this'll gladden yer tonsils!'

He was handing out the fourth pie when it happened. Without the slightest warning, the fog seemed to split open, and something monstrous *roared* towards them. It was huge and black, and its eyes glowed as red as the fires of Great Wooden's forge. It sprang upon the mercenaries, tore the pie out of the corporal's fingers with its massive teeth . . . and was gone.

The five men stood gaping. 'What— What— What was *that*?'

The corporal swallowed. 'I dunno, but if it comes back—' With a shaking hand, he grabbed his rifle. Or at least, he *meant* to grab his rifle.

'Here,' he said, peering at the wall. 'Where's me gun? Which of you beggars took me gun?'

The fog swirled around him and his companions like a living thing. They stared at each other, and at the empty space where, just a moment before, their rifles had stood.

'Maybe that beast took 'em,' whispered one of the soldiers.

'What would a beast want with our rifles?'

'Listen!' hissed another man.

The sound, muffled by the fog, roused them from their shock. At the far end of the road, someone was throwing something into the waters of the canal.

Splash. Splash splash splash. Splash. Five times.

'Our rifles!'

They tore down the road with murder in their hearts. But by the time they reached the canal there was nothing to be seen – except for spreading rings where five objects had broken the surface of the water.

They were not fearful men, these mercenaries. They had fought in the bloodiest of wars, and were hardened to slaughter. They could face the might of a foreign army without flinching, and laugh at a hillside of corpses.

But they had two weaknesses. The first was a fear of disease, which could not be fought with guns and viciousness. The second was superstition.

Every one of them, even the corporal, carried a lucky charm of some sort. A hare's foot, a chipped coin, a stone with a hole through the middle. They dragged them from their pockets now, and rubbed them between their fingers.

'I don't like it,' muttered the corporal. 'There's somethin' nasty goin' on— Here, what's that?'

The sound of a harp was the last thing any of them had expected. It seemed to come from all around them, its notes curling like the fog, seeping into their heads, catching hold of their fear and dragging it into the light.

At first it was just music. But then a man began to sing. His voice was mocking. His song was one that they all knew – an old ballad about a foolish general who takes his army to an unearthly land . . .

'Where the demons were bad
And the witches were mad
And the men who had come there
Would ne'er see their loved ones again.'

148

The corporal knew he should say something. It wouldn't do to let his men think for too long about demons and witches. It wouldn't do to think too long about them himself!

But the beast with the red eyes (a *demon*?) and the inexplicable loss of the rifles (a *witch*?) had unnerved him.

As the song played out to its horrible conclusion, he drew closer to his fellows, wondering where the nearest war was, and if any of the armies involved were hiring men. And how long it would take him to get there from here.

The fog lasted for two weeks and, except for brief periods of sleep, Toadspit and Goldie kept up their attacks without ceasing. They stole biscuits from the soldiers' hands, charms from their pockets and rifles from their sides. They borrowed Olga Ciavolga's kerchief – the one that held the winds of the world tied in knots around its edges – and blew puddles into the mercenaries' faces and mud into their food.

Sinew came to help whenever he could be spared from the museum, with songs of betrayal and insidious whispers of plague. Broo stalked through the fog like something out of a nightmare. Morg flew over the soldiers' heads, dropping rocks that exploded with a sound like a pistol shot.

Meanwhile, in the sickroom, the Protector was slowly regaining her strength. She was sitting up by now and feeding herself, and chafing at her forced inactivity. Whenever they could, Goldie and Toadspit sat with her for a few minutes, and told her what they were doing, and asked her advice about what might most annoy the Fugleman.

Before long, they were able to report that they were not the only ones stirring up trouble. The Fugleman had overstepped himself when he had imprisoned so many children, and now even the most fearful citizens had turned away from him, and given their loyalty and admiration to the Hidden Rock instead. Stories of the Rock's exploits floated through the fog-bound streets like leaves on the wind, and the people of Jewel listened to them and laughed, and that laughter gave them the courage to create mischief of their own.

The men who had been hired to cook at the barracks doctored the mercenaries' porridge with a powder that caused vomiting. The women who did laundry for the House of Repentance secreted spiders and wasps in the Blessed Guardians' underwear. And although there was generally far more talk than action, it was not long before a small army of citizens was doing whatever it could to make life for both mercenaries and Blessed Guardians as miserable as possible.

Some people were caught, and swallowed up by the dungeons of the House of Repentance. But many more got away with their acts of rebellion, and grew bolder as a result.

When the Protector heard this, she was inspired. Under her instructions, a carefully disguised Goldie delivered a letter to the Blessed Guardians, apparently signed by Field Marshal Brace. The letter apologised for the violence of his men, and said that he had ordered them to be the Guardians' servants for the next few days, to make up for their actions.

'They will clean your boots and scrub your toilets—'

Toadspit delivered a similar message to the mercenaries. Only *that* one was signed by the Fugleman, and said that the Guardians would be the *mercenaries'* servants, to clean *their* boots and scrub *their* toilets.

The resulting battles between Guardians and mercenaries, each side believing they were in the right, were so fierce that Field Marshal Brace almost withdrew his men from the city in disgust. Only his agreement with the Fugleman – and a large bonus from the Treasury – kept him there.

Through all this, Goldie lived two lives. One in Jewel and one in ancient Merne. She did her best to hide it from those around her, but it was not easy. The warrior princess inside her was indeed growing stronger.

'I'm Goldie Roth, Fifth Keeper,' she whispered, whenever she was alone. 'I'm Goldie Roth, Fifth Keeper!'

The words sounded hollow and unconvincing. In the back of her mind a far more confident voice murmured, *I am the daughter of a warrior king . . .*

Toadspit watched her, but said nothing.

Goldie's troubles came to a head one afternoon in the Old Quarter. She and Toadspit were hurrying along Rotgut Canal when they heard someone shouting. The heavy fog made it almost impossible to tell where the sound came from, and the children turned in circles, wary of danger.

But when the danger came, there was no warning, not even the clank of punishment chains. Two Blessed Guardians loomed out of the fog and cannoned into Goldie.

She was knocked flat, and her elbow whacked against the cobblestones, sending a shaft of pain through her body. She gasped in agony and reacted like a warrior princess—

—*rolling to one side and scrambling to her feet. Her*

elbow was a distant fire and she knew that she would feel it after the battle. But now it counted for nothing.

She put her hand out for her sword. It was not there. Her bow was gone too, and so were her troops. There was no one in sight but her friend Harmut, the Young Margrave of Spit, and the two black-clad figures in front of her.

She had no idea who they were. But she knew they were the enemy, and that was enough.

I will kill them, *she thought.* I will kill them with my bare hands. *And she reached down inside herself for the only weapon she had left: the wolf-sark.*

She had done it before in the midst of battle, and she did it now. She IMAGINED her sword. She felt it slide out of its scabbard, felt the weight of it in her hand.

Immediately, the wolf-sark surged up, as hot as a forest fire in her belly. The red mist descended. The princess screamed a challenge. Then she fell into a fighting stance and advanced towards the enemy with death in her heart.

'Goldie?' said one of the black-clad figures. 'Goldie, what are you doing? It's me! It's Favour!'

There were not many people who could have called Goldie out of the wolf-sark. But Favour Berg was one of them. She had been Goldie's best friend since they were babies together and had stood beside her, in and out of trouble, with a quiet stubbornness that Goldie loved.

153

The two girls had not seen each other for several months, but Favour's familiar voice swept the red mist aside – swept *Frisia* aside – and left Goldie gasping with shock, her hands on her knees, her stomach heaving.

'Why did you scream like that?' said Favour, throwing her arms around her friend. 'Did I hurt you when I ran into you? Goldie? What's the matter?'

And then Toadspit was there, gently loosening Favour's arms so that Goldie could breathe. 'She's all right,' he said, putting himself between them. 'You just knocked the sense out of her for a bit. Give her time to recover. Where did you get the robes? Who was shouting? It sounded like mercenaries.'

Goldie had never been more grateful to Toadspit than she was at that moment. She was trembling uncontrollably and could not speak. She had nearly killed her best friend *with her bare hands*! If Favour had spoken just a moment later . . .

'The robes?' said Favour. 'The general found them, or at least that's what he says. *I* think he stole them. We've been throwing rotten eggs at the soldiers, pretending to be Guardians.' She tried to push past Toadspit. 'Goldie, I've been bursting to see you! We thought you were dead! Or rather *some* people thought so, but I knew you'd turn up. Are you sure you're all right?'

'Who's the general?' asked Toadspit.

'General Pounce, of course,' said Favour.

Goldie was so astonished that she almost stopped trembling. '*Pounce?*'

'We're part of his army,' said Favour's companion. 'He's been training us.'

'*Jube?*' said Goldie, astonished all over again at seeing one of her old classmates. 'Is— Is that you?'

Jube grinned and waggled his fingers. Then he took out his pocket watch and said, 'We'd better go, Favour. Your ma's expecting you.'

Favour threw her arms around Goldie again. 'Blessings, Goldie! I'm *so* glad to see you! We'll meet up properly soon! There's lots to talk about!'

'Yes,' said Goldie, and she clung to her friend. '*Yes!* Blessings, Favour! Take care! D-don't get caught!'

And then the black-clad figures were gone, leaving the two children from the museum alone.

There was a long silence. 'Goldie—' said Toadspit. He peered at her. 'It *is* Goldie, isn't it?'

Goldie stared at the ground, feeling sick. 'Yes.'

'But it wasn't a minute ago?'

Another silence. 'No.'

'Good,' said Toadspit.

'*Good?*' Goldie's head jerked up. 'I'm turning into a five-hundred-year-old warrior princess and you think it's *good?*'

155

'No, of course not,' said Toadspit tartly. 'I mean it's good that you told me. I've been worried. Everyone's been worried! Herro Dan and Olga Ciavolga asked me to keep an eye on you.'

'You're not going to tell them?'

'Why shouldn't I?'

'Just don't. Promise you won't!'

'But if they ask me—'

'*Don't tell them!*'

'All right, all right, I won't.' Toadspit paused. 'Is it getting worse? Herro Dan reckons it can drive people mad, but—'

'I *know* that, you don't have to remind me!' Now that her secret was exposed, the words poured out of Goldie in a desperate stream and she could not stop them. 'Didn't you see what happened back there? I almost killed Favour! I *would* have killed her, and not thought twice about it. I'm going mad and there's nothing I can—'

'Listen to me, Goldie!' Toadspit gripped her shoulders. 'No, stop! Listen! You're a keeper of the Museum of Dunt! You know all sorts of things that most people never learn. And you're brave and clever and – and – and if it wasn't for you, Jewel would've been a pile of rubble last year, and everyone we know would be either dead or enslaved!'

'But Herro Dan said—'

'That doesn't matter. Don't you see? *You're not just anyone!* You can beat this stuff! It doesn't have to drive *you* mad!'

There was yet another long silence while Goldie stared at him. At last she said, in a small voice, 'You really think so?'

'Yes! You just have to find a way to control it!'

It was amazing how those few words changed everything. Knowing that Toadspit believed in her; knowing that *he* didn't think she was going mad.

Goldie drew a shaky breath. 'Maybe— Maybe if I stopped listening to Frisia altogether . . . The trouble is, I need her. She knows so much about war.'

Toadspit's face was thoughtful, and it struck Goldie that the last few weeks had stripped him of much of his boyishness, and left him older and more focused.

'When we first came back from Spoke,' he said, 'and you insisted that we fight the Fugleman with trickery instead of bloodshed, I thought you were wrong. I wanted to fight properly, not just muck around like a bunch of children.'

'I know. Sometimes I wonder whether—'

'But you were right,' interrupted Toadspit. 'You just have to look at the mercenaries to see what real war does to you. I don't want to end up like them— Here, the fog's clearing at last. We'd better get back to the museum.'

The two children began to walk side by side along the canal path. 'But you're still practising with the sword?' said Goldie.

'Well, you never know when it might come in handy.' A sudden grin splashed across Toadspit's face. 'And besides, it's fun.'

Goldie glanced at him. 'I don't think Frisia knows much about fun. It's all war and strategy and stuff.'

'And that's why,' said Toadspit, slinging his arm across her shoulders as they walked, 'you mustn't let her take over. We need you, Goldie. We need you far more than we ever needed a warrior prin—'

He stopped. A familiar figure was loping down the path towards them.

'Sinew?' said Toadspit, dropping his arm.

Goldie's skin prickled with foreboding. Sinew was in his shirtsleeves, and she had never seen him so distraught. 'Are they with you?' he called, as soon as he was within earshot.

'Who?' said Toadspit.

Sinew drew up in front of them, breathless. 'They're not here? I feared as much. We didn't even realise they were gone, but now the museum is in turmoil – the war rooms and the plague rooms are on the move –

I must get back straight away – the cat is missing too—'

'What are you talking about?' demanded Toadspit, his face white.

'Great whistling pigs, isn't it obvious?' snapped Sinew. 'Mouse must have told a fortune. We found two scraps of paper – one said *a large hunting party* and the other said *Save me, friend!* But we did not find Mouse or Bonnie! They've disappeared. We think they've gone to look for Pounce!'

BLOOD-RED SAILS

ounce hadn't meant to get involved in the war against Harrow. Even now he wasn't sure how it had happened. Maybe he'd been bored. Maybe it was the sight of those weeping parents. Or maybe he was just a stupid idjit who didn't know how to keep his nose out of trouble.

Whatever the reason, he was having fun. He'd found himself a bunch of snotties who thought he was as clever as a six-legged cat. And so he was, compared to them. They didn't even know the hidey-holes in their own city!

Pounce

They soon learned, mind you, Pounce made sure of that. They learned how to do a snatch and grab too, and then scatter so that no one knew who to chase. So far none of them had been caught, which was a miracle, 'cos they weren't as quick as Pounce and he'd nearly been nabbed twice.

Still, he knew it couldn't last. Harrow always came out on top in the long run. So he wasn't surprised when, late in the afternoon, he saw a string of weeping snotties being marched towards the docks, all chained up like bears.

'Oho!' whispered Pounce to himself. 'They's the ones I saw gettin' pinched two weeks back. What's goin' on?'

A breeze had sprung up and the fog was fraying like an old singlet. Through the holes, Pounce spotted a dozen sour-faced Guardians. Behind them trailed the snotties' parents, who had been keeping vigil outside the House of Repentance. Their arms waved in odd, helpless patterns, as if they had forgotten how to use them properly. They opened and shut their mouths, and no sound came out, but every single one of them looked as if they were screaming inside.

Pounce swallowed. 'Poor sods,' he whispered. 'Glad I'm not one o' them!'

He was so busy watching the chained snotties and their poor broken parents that he didn't see the small troupe of mercenaries at the end of the procession. Didn't hear them either, creeping up behind him. He would've been snatched off the street like a hot pie if someone hadn't yelped a warning.

Pounce knew that wordless yelp. Knew it as well as the sound of his own breathing. He spun around just in time. Saw a hodge-podge uniform bending over him. Saw two hands reaching out to grab him. Heard the satisfied chuckle of a mercenary who thought he had a plump pigeon already in the bag.

But this pigeon wasn't ready to be caught. Pounce bit the nearest hand as hard as he could. The mercenary shouted with pain, and clenched his fist. The boy threw up one arm to protect himself. The mercenary grabbed his sleeve. Pounce ducked and jerked. There was a ripping sound and the sleeve – its seam carefully unpicked a few nights before – came away in the mercenary's hand.

Pounce danced up the street, laughing himself silly at the expression on the man's face and looking out for Mouse all the while. Because it was Mouse who'd yelped a warning, he was sure of it. The little snotty was round here somewhere, hiding in a doorway or behind a street-rig. He'd left the museum and its keepers, and come back to his old friend.

And wasn't Pounce glad! His feet felt as light as

goose feathers. He did a double skip, and stuck his tongue out at the mercenary, who was still glaring at him from a distance. His eyes scanned the street, looking for that tell-tale white hair.

'Come on, Mousie,' he whispered. 'I know you're 'ere somewhere.'

And then he saw him. Right back up the street, close to where Pounce had been a minute ago. Close to the mercenaries, who were snapping and snarling at each other, and looking around for another pigeon to make up for the one they'd lost. There was Mouse, creeping down the street behind their backs, with Bonnie beside him. Two small shadows, as frail as eggs next to those whopping great soldiers.

Pounce's gut felt as if someone'd tied it in a knot and stuck a knife through it. 'Careful now, Mousie,' he whispered. 'Take yer time! They ain't seen ya yet. Don't do nothin' that'll catch their eye!'

But the soldiers were on their mettle now. He could see it in the way they stood. He could see them remembering the warning yelp, and muttering to each other, and spreading out towards the shadows.

Towards Mouse and Bonnie.

The little boy's eyes found Pounce, and his face lit up like the first day of spring. He waved, thinking he was out of danger.

'No, Mousie!' groaned Pounce.

The mercenaries' heads snapped around, four of them, their eyes caught by that waving hand. Big lunks of men, all muscle and meanness, their bodies winding up to throw themselves at Pounce's white-haired boy.

Pounce screamed. 'Mouse! *Run!*'

Everyone in the street must've heard him. The mercenaries turned around just long enough to pinpoint him with their nasty eyes, then they leaped after Mouse, who was already skittering down the footpath with Bonnie by his side, quick as a hare.

But the soldiers were quicker. Pounce jigged up and down on the spot, watching four pairs of heavy boots gain on his friend.

'Run!' he groaned. '*Run!*'

The little boy was doing his best. So was Bonnie. They tore down the street, elbows pumping. As they ran, something broke away from them and flew at the mercenaries, all claws and teeth. It was the cat! The scruffy old cat that had come with them from Spoke! It ripped into the soldiers with a wail of fury, stopping three of them in their tracks as they tried to fight it off.

But the other man jumped past it, then turned around and laid into it with the butt of his rifle, shouting for back-up. Three more soldiers appeared out of nowhere, and took over the chase. The street rang with screams and wails. Pounce's heart clanged in his chest like a cracked bell.

'Run,' he whispered, in a voice that he didn't recognise. 'Mousie. Please. Run.'

The words were hardly out of his mouth when Bonnie stumbled and one of the mercenaries snatched her off the ground. Another man reached for Mouse. The little boy dived sideways. He doubled back. He skipped behind a street-rig, then up and over the top of it and down the other side.

But there were two grown men on his tail, and it was only a matter of time before they caught him. Pounce couldn't bear to watch. He closed his eyes.

That made it worse.

He opened them—

And saw Mouse surrounded. Trapped. All the air gone out of him as he stared up at his captors.

The air had gone out of Pounce too. He could hardly breathe. And when Mouse and Bonnie were chained to the other snotties and marched off, Pounce staggered after them, gasping like an old man. His arms waved helplessly. He opened and shut his mouth, and no sound came out. But inside, he was screaming.

He didn't think things could get any worse. But he was wrong. As the chained snotties approached the docks, a woman began to wail. It was a frightening sound, as high and desperate as a wounded dog, and it shook Pounce to the core.

A man's voice joined in, and another woman's. The mercenaries shouted at them, but they took no notice. All the parents were wailing now, and the snotties screamed and cried.

Pounce stared around, frightened out of his wits and not knowing why. He looked up, beyond the wharves, to the waters of the bay—

—and saw a ship. A fast barky, sleek and predatory as a hawk, curving across the waves towards them. Sailors were strung along its cross masts, rolling up the blood-red sails. Pounce could hear the throb of gas engines start up as it neared the wharf.

On the foredeck of the barky stood a massive old woman with long, frizzy black hair that whipped to one side in the sea breeze. She wore britches and a leather coat. As the ship came closer, Pounce thought he saw a pistol in her hand.

He knew straight away who she was. He had heard her described in hushed whispers by a score of sailors. He had seen engravings of her new ship, the *Silver Lining*, pasted all over Spoke, with the words 'WANTED FOR SLAVERY' stamped across them.

He heard himself whimper. He looked for Mouse's white head, and the tears poured down his face at the thought of what was coming.

Harrow had sold the children of Jewel to Old Lady Skint.

OLD LADY SKINT

Old Lady Skint

Old Lady Skint was as tall as the mercenaries who waited on the docks to greet her, and twice as wide. On her bosom, a tribe of beetles crawled back and forth, tethered by silken threads.

Pounce saw one of the mercenaries swallow and take a step backwards. Old Lady Skint smiled at him. Her lips stretched so tight that they looked as if they might split. Her teeth gleamed. Her chins wobbled. Her hard black eyes didn't change a jot.

'This the whole lot, or just the first instalment?' she said, tipping her chins towards the chained snotties.

'There's a few more to come,' said a mercenary. 'Fugleman said to bring 'em down over a couple of days. Make sure everyone in the city knows what's going on. He reckons they'll get the message better that way.'

Pounce was starting to regain his wits, and his thoughts were as dark as the darkest sewer. There was no way he was going to let this nasty old beetle-witch take Mouse away. He had to get the little snotty out somehow.

Trouble was, the old lady's crew – their faces tattooed with ferocious black stripes – were already hustling the children up the gangway onto the *Silver Lining*. Behind them, their parents wailed louder than ever.

'Idjits!' Pounce whispered savagely. 'No use cryin'. Ya should be *thinkin'*, like me!'

Trouble was, his thinking wasn't doing him any good. Didn't seem like the ship was going to leave straight away. But even if it stayed for a night or two, Pounce couldn't see any way of bringing Mouse off safely. Not with the chains and the mercenaries and that vicious-looking crew. Not without getting caught himself.

And what good would it do his friend if they were *both* tucked up in the hull of a slave ship with iron on their ankles?

No, he had to be cleverer than that. He had to forget about the crew, forget about the mercenaries, forget about the beetle-witch. And who was left, once you got rid of all them?

Harrow.

And what was Harrow always wanting more of, in Pounce's experience?

Information.

'I kept me promise, Mousie,' whispered Pounce, as he slipped away from the weeping mob and headed back down the wharf towards the city. 'I didn't go near Harrow. Didn't say nothin' to no one about them three snotties or the Hidden Rock. But things've changed. Ya can see that, can't ya? I gotta have somethin' to sell or he won't listen.'

He felt as if Mouse was there by his side, arguing with him. He bit his lip. 'Tell ya what. I won't say nothin' about Bonnie – about 'er bein' on the slave ship already. I'll just tell 'im about Goldie and Toadspit. Them two is big enough and ugly enough to take care of themselves.'

He ducked across a bridge, and ran along the Grand Canal, trying to ignore the hard twist of fear in his guts. Visiting Harrow was always a dodgy business. You never knew what sort of mood he'd be in. And while it was true that Pounce had good solid information to sell, there were also a few things that he meant to keep secret.

Like the part he had played in Cord's death. And the fact that the *Piglet* was tucked up in a nearby bay, ready to set sail for the Southern Archipelago. And, of course, the whole story of General Pounce and his army of snotties . . .

Harrow didn't like secrets. Or rather, he didn't like *other people's* secrets. They offended him.

And when Harrow was offended, you never knew what might happen.

'They probably just got bored and wandered off,' said Goldie, as she and Toadspit hurried across Lame Poet's Bridge. 'Sinew's worrying over nothing. We'll find them soon.'

Toadspit nodded, no more convinced by Goldie's words than she herself was. They had already scoured more than half the Old Quarter with no sign of the missing children. Now the streets around them were filling with men and women who stared towards the docks and whispered to each other with horror in their eyes.

When she saw those gathering crowds, Goldie felt as if a wire had snapped around her throat. Without another word to each other, she and Toadspit began to run.

They reached the docks in time to see Mouse and Bonnie marched up the gangway of a strange ship. It took them no more than a few seconds to discover who the ship belonged to, and what its trade was. The knowledge was like a blow to the belly. Toadspit slumped to the ground, as if he was wounded. Goldie crouched beside him, surrounded by wailing parents.

She wanted to comfort them. She wanted to say, 'It'll be all right, don't worry, we'll find a way out of this!' But the useless, lying words stuck in her throat, and she could not speak. If she had had a sword to hand at that moment, she would have drawn it, regardless of the consequences.

With a great effort, she swallowed her rage and despair. 'We need information,' she said to Toadspit. 'The more the better. Meet me back here in half an hour.'

Now that the breeze had swept the fog away, the day was bright and sunny. Normally, Concealment by Imitation of Nothingness would be impossible on a day like this. Unless there was a crowd.

Goldie found a corner where she would not be bumped, and closed her eyes. She slowed her breathing and let herself become a part of the wharf and the pilings and the bright sea air.

I am nothing. I am the smell of salt water . . .

As her mind drifted outwards, the grief of the crowd hit her like a claw hammer. She gasped and quickly pulled her thoughts back, and held them close so that she would not be overwhelmed. Then, with Nothingness wrapped around her like a cloak, she slid out of the corner and made her way towards Old Lady Skint.

The slaver, with her crew in attendance, was talking to two Blessed Guardians. On her bosom, half a dozen captive beetles tugged at their threads.

I am nothing. I am a forgotten dream of freedom . . .

Goldie edged closer, and realised that one of the black-clad figures was Guardian Kindness, and that he was arguing with Old Lady Skint.

'What you do not seem to understand,' he said, 'is that this is an honour. The Lord High Protector does not issue many invitations—'

'That's Harrow, is it?' interrupted Old Lady Skint. 'The Lord High whatsit?' She laughed, and her crew laughed with her. 'He always liked fancy titles, did Harrow. Why don't he just declare himself king and be done with it?'

'Ah— We don't actually *have* a king,' murmured Guardian Meek, who stood at Guardian Kindness's side. 'But my colleague and I will certainly pass your suggestion—'

'I need a reply!' snapped Guardian Kindness. 'Will you and your crew come to the Protectorate tonight or will you not? I warn you, it will be taken very badly if you do not appear. I cannot answer for the consequences.'

There was a murmur of anger from the sailors on either side of Goldie. The stripes on their faces twitched.

Old Lady Skint spat a glob of phlegm onto the wharf and smiled. 'I hope you're not threatenin' me, Guardian.'

'Not at all,' said Kindness, through gritted teeth.

'It's just a matter of catering,' said Meek quickly, peering at the sailors. 'How many desserts, that sort of thing . . .'

Her voice trailed off. One of Old Lady Skint's beetles had beheaded its neighbour and was steadily eating its way through the corpse.

'Mmm,' said the slaver captain, stroking the beetle's carapace with the tip of her finger. 'I suppose a banquet might be a nice change.'

She raised her voice. 'What about it, ratbags? Shall we say yes to their fancy food? Roast goat stuffed with skylarks?' One of her eyelids drooped in a wink. 'Jellied crows stuffed with their own self-importance?'

The sailors roared with laughter and nudged each other. Goldie slid away from their elbows, as silent as a memory. *I am nothing. Nothing!*

Old Lady Skint held up her hand for silence. 'Yeah, all right, we'll come. Or most of us will. It's tonight, you say? At the Protectorate?' She jerked a thumb at two of the sailors, one of whom had only half a nose. 'Mince and Jangle, you'll stay behind and keep watch. You and Double.'

The two men protested, but their captain cut them off. 'Don't worry, we'll bring you back some jellied crow.'

Guardian Kindness sniffed at the insult and said, 'Only three sailors to guard so many children? I would be careful if I were you. The Fugleman will not be happy if any of them escape.'

'Escape?' said the slaver captain, raising her eyebrows. 'From Old Lady Skint?' She turned to her crew and waved a fleshy hand as if she was conducting an orchestra. 'Is that gunna happen?'

'Nooooo!' bellowed the sailors.

The captain bowed in a mocking fashion. 'Thanks for that vote of confidence, ratbags. Now get back to work before I hang the lot of yez!'

And with that, the sailors moved away, chuckling, and Goldie was forced to move with them or risk being discovered.

Pounce wouldn't normally have gone anywhere near the House of Repentance. But today he didn't have a choice. He slid past the great gun and into the courtyard, where a score of Guardians stalked back and forth with their robes flapping and their heads together.

'Hey!' shouted Pounce. 'You lot!'

The conversations cut off like a tap. The Guardians glared at him.

'I wanna see Harr—' Pounce broke off. What was it they called him here? 'Um, that Foobleman bloke. I wanna see 'im.'

The Guardians couldn't have looked more disgusted if a gutter rat had reared up on its hind legs and spoken. 'You want to see the Fugleman?' drawled one of them. 'Well, I doubt *very* much that he wants to see you!'

And they laughed and turned their backs.

But Pounce wasn't to be put off so easily. 'I got some information for 'im! *Valuable* information.'

The Guardians scowled over their shoulders and rattled the chains around their waists. As if a few old chains were going to scare someone who'd grown up on the streets of Spoke!

Pounce skipped a bit closer, so he didn't have to shout. 'Course, yez don't *'ave* to take me to 'im,' he said, in a conversational tone. 'I can wait till 'e comes out. But when 'e asks me why it took so long to get this valuable information to 'im, I'll 'ave to tell 'im. "It was your pet crows," I'll say. "I told 'em 'ow important it was, but they thought they knew better."'

The Guardians stopped walking and looked at each other uncertainly.

'I wonder what 'e'll say to that.' Pounce grinned.

From there on, it was easy. Two of the Guardians swooped on him, and dragged him up the long steps and into the building. Pounce could have got away, but this was what he wanted, after all.

At least, he thought it was.

He kept his mouth shut until they dragged him into the richest room he'd ever seen. Carpet on the floor, as thick as grass. Big fat chairs all around the walls. Big fat shiny lights hanging from the ceiling. Pounce's mouth fell open and for once in his life he couldn't think of a single smart comment.

Harrow – the Foobleman – was sitting behind a desk, writing. He was all dressed in black and silver, like some sort of king, with a fancy sword laid out in front of him. When he saw Pounce, he looked down his nose in disgust.

'What is this?' he said.

The Guardians, who'd been as tough as old rope when it was just them and Pounce, bowed and smiled and bowed again for all they were worth.

'Beg pardon, Your Honour,' said one of them. 'This bit of scum says he has valuable information. He's probably lying, but we thought it best—'

The Foobleman raised an eyebrow.

The Guardian swallowed. 'Right. We'll take him to the cells and whip him, Your Honour. Yes, Your Honour. That's what we'll do, Your Honour.'

He began to back away, dragging Pounce with him. Pounce dug in his heels. 'Hey, Harrow,' he said. 'Remember me?'

One of the Guardians smacked him across the ear. 'You address him as *Your Honour*!'

'Yeah, all right,' said Pounce, rubbing his ear. 'Yer Honour?'

The Foobleman raised the other eyebrow.

'It's Pounce, Yer Honour. I done some jobs for ya in Spoke.'

'Ah. Yes, I remember.' The Foobleman waved at the Guardians to leave the two of them alone.

Pounce waited until they had gone. Then he took a step forward. 'Thing is,' he said, 'a friend of mine's been taken up by your mercenaries and given over to Old Lady Skint. 'E's only a little runt of a thing, won't fetch no more than half a thaler in the slave market. Prob'ly less. You'll prob'ly 'ave to pay someone to take 'im—'

The Foobleman held up a finger, stopping him. 'You want your friend back.'

'Yeah. That's it.'

'And what are you offering me in return?'

'Well—' began Pounce. And then he stopped. It should have been easy to hand over Goldie and Toadspit in exchange for Mouse. But he had promised to say nothing. He had promised on the heads of the white mice, which was the most sacred thing he and Mouse knew. Neither of them had ever broken a vow made like that.

The Foobleman tapped the hilt of his sword impatiently. Behind Pounce, the door opened.

'Beg pardon, Your Honour,' muttered one of the Guardians. 'You've got another visitor. It's—'

A hand shoved him to one side. A figure in a torn green cloak marched past him, right up to the Foobleman's desk. 'It's Guardian Hope reporting for duty, Your Honour!'

BETRAYAL

Half an hour after they had parted, Goldie and Toadspit met up again. They were desperate to tell each other what they had learned, but the thought of what might be happening to Bonnie and Mouse in the slave holds of the *Silver Lining* drove them back to the museum at a run, passing their information to each other in whispered fragments whenever they could catch their breath.

'Some of the slavers and the mercenaries know each other,'

Guardian Hope

hissed Toadspit. 'I heard them talking. The slavers wanted to know where they could get wine, and the mercenaries were warning them to watch out for plague. And demons!'

'There's a banquet tonight at the Protectorate. They're going to leave the ship with only three sailors on board! I don't know who Double is—'

'Double? She's Old Lady Skint's second-in-command—' By this stage they were running up Old Arsenal Hill. 'The sailors reckon she's sick,' continued Toadspit. 'She hasn't moved from her cabin since yesterday—'

'So *she* shouldn't be a problem. But the other two—'

'We could knock them out,' said Toadspit. 'Or take Broo with us, and he could hold them at bay while we get Bonnie and Mouse off.'

Goldie stopped at the entrance to the cul de sac. Frisia was whispering in the back of her mind again, and before she knew what was happening she found herself—

—in the highlands of Merne, with Harmut, the Young Margrave of Spit. They had lost five men last night, captured by the raiders from Halt-Bern, and Frisia was determined to get them back. Her plans were—

'Goldie,' said Harmut.

Frisia shook her head at the interruption. Her plans were—

'*Goldie! Wake up!*' said Harmut. And he slapped
her face.

'*How DARE you?*' she cried—

—and remembered who she was.

'Are you back?' said Toadspit fiercely.

'Yes,' said Goldie, wishing her legs would not tremble
so hard.

'Are you sure? Well don't do it again!'

'But Frisia had a plan for freeing her men! If I can
find out what it was—'

'I don't care about Frisia's plan,' cried Toadspit.
'We need a thief, not some mad warrior princess! We
need *you*!'

'But we can't rescue Bonnie and Mouse without
her—'

'Yes, we can! We have to! What if you go all weird in
the middle of something important? What if you start
killing people?'

Goldie thought of Favour, and her protests
evaporated.

'Come on,' said Toadspit, grabbing her arm and
pulling her into the cul de sac.

And then they *both* stopped, because the cat was
there before them, its fur clotted with blood, its claws
scrabbling at the cobblestones as it tried to take those
last few steps towards the museum.

'Cat!' cried Goldie, throwing herself down beside the poor battered creature. 'What happened?'

The cat hissed furiously at her, then fell in a heap.

'I'll fetch Olga Ciavolga,' said Toadspit, and he leaped up the steps of the museum.

Goldie knelt beside the cat. In the back of her mind, Princess Frisia was whispering about the wounds of battle, and—

—*she could feel the sweat on her forehead, and the bruises, and hear fighting somewhere in the distance*—

'No!' With an enormous effort, Goldie managed to drag herself back to the cul de sac. But ancient Merne was still there, no more than a fingertip away. And Princess Frisia was whispering again—

Goldie gasped, 'I'm Goldie Roth, Fifth Keeper!'

It was not enough. She could feel herself being pulled towards Merne, towards another life . . .

She shook her head. Toadspit was right. *This* was the life she wanted! She had fought for it; she had run away from home; she had risked everything to be who she was. And no warrior princess was going to take it from her!

She clutched the blue bird brooch and slowed her breath, as if she was about to Conceal herself. But instead of letting her mind drift outwards, she brought it inwards, until she could feel her heart beating, and the blood pulsing through her body, and her hopes and fears and dreams pulsing with it. *This is me*, she told herself. *This is who I am!*

She stayed like that and did not let herself think of anything else until Toadspit returned with Broo loping at his side and Olga Ciavolga no more than a second or two behind him.

'Let me see,' said the old woman, pushing Goldie out of the way and kneeling down in her place. 'Pff, you have been in the wars, cat!'

—she could feel the sweat on her forehead, and the bruises—

'No!' whispered Goldie. 'This is *me*!'

Broo lowered his great head and sniffed the cat's matted fur. 'Who has done this to you?'

'Ssss— Ssss— Sssssoldiers,' panted the cat.

A growl rumbled from the brizzlehound's chest. 'Soldiers? How DARRRRE they? You are MY enemy and they have no RRRRIGHT to touch you! Tell me where they are and I will EAT them!'

'Not now, Broo,' said Olga Ciavolga, putting her hand gently on the cat's ribs. The cat hissed and showed its claws.

'Do not be foolish,' said the old woman. 'You know that I am trying to help you.'

She picked the cat up as carefully as she could. It

squalled once with pain, then its eyes closed and there was nothing but the shallow rise and fall of its ribs to show that it still lived.

'Will it be all right?' asked Goldie.

'Cats are tough,' said Olga Ciavolga. 'And the descendants of idlecats are even tougher.'

As they hurried up the front steps, Goldie and Toadspit told the old woman what had happened to Bonnie and Mouse.

'SLAVERRRRRRS?' rumbled Broo. 'I will SHRRRRRED their bones! I will GRRRRIND them so small that the earth itself will forget they ever lived!'

'Griiiind,' whispered the cat approvingly, without opening its eyes.

'Hush,' said Olga Ciavolga. 'Preserve your strength, cat. I am taking you to the sickroom. We will meet Sinew and Dan there, and the Protector, and talk about what must be done.'

But before they could get anywhere near the sickroom, the museum *shifted*, and *shifted* again, and the spider webs above their heads heaved and jerked, and the waters of Old Scratch rose.

And deep in the heart of the museum, behind the Dirty Gate, the generals in the war rooms took out their maps and spoke of invasion, and the plague rooms rustled with the sound of a thousand rats, each of which carried a thousand fleas, which in turn carried a disease that Jewel had not seen for centuries.

There was a time, not long ago, when Blessed Guardian Hope had thought she would never see her home again. A time when she had been hunted through the streets of Spoke like a wild animal.

She still remembered that awful moment on the *Piglet* when she had been caught in a Big Lie for the second time in as many days. As the hounds snapped at her heels, she had thought she was lost. But somehow she had managed to keep running, right up until dawn when the Lie ended.

Ever since then, she had been longing to return to Jewel. But instead, she had remained in Spoke, carrying out her orders, sustained by the knowledge that Golden Roth and Toadspit Hahn were dead at last and that, one day soon, her reward would come.

Now that day was here, and she was determined that the Fugleman should know how brilliantly she had dealt with the brats.

She began her report in general terms. 'I have good news, Your Honour! Everything you required has been done – the bribes, the blackmail, the threats. Spoke is ripe for invasion!'

The Fugleman nodded, as if he had expected nothing less. Hope cleared her throat. 'Ah— I suppose Cord has told you about the children? It is old news, I know, but—'

'Cord has not yet returned to Jewel,' said the Fugleman.

A tremor of joy passed through Hope. 'Oh dear, such a pity!' she said, clasping her hands in front of her. 'I wonder where he could have got to? I told him to come straight here, but he has always been a little *unreliable*—'

'The children?' prompted the Fugleman.

'Ah yes, the children! Our coded messages did not permit me to tell you the identity of the two brats we stole. But now I can reveal it! One of them was a girl named Bonnie Hahn. The other was her brother Cautionary, who calls himself Toadspit.' Guardian Hope allowed herself the shadow of a smile. 'That name rings a bell, Your Honour, does it not? Imagine my delight when I discovered that the boy who had caused us so much trouble was in my power at last!'

The Fugleman raised an eyebrow, as if he wasn't particularly interested in her delight. Hope pressed on, knowing that the best was yet to come.

'Unfortunately, we – *ahem* – had a little trouble with them, as you know, Your Honour. Another child turned up and helped them escape. But I am here to report that we recaptured them. And now they are dead. Toadspit Hahn, Bonnie Hahn and—' she paused, savouring the moment '—and Golden Roth! All dead, thrown to the sharks on my orders!'

The Fugleman inspected her for a long moment. He did not seem nearly as surprised at the identity of the children – or as pleased to hear of their gruesome fate – as Hope had expected. 'Are you sure of this?' he said.

'Of course, Your Honour! Have I ever failed you?'

'Hmm,' said the Fugleman, pursing his lips.

That's when Hope noticed the boy. What was his name? Bounce? Pounce? He stepped forward, his face eager. 'What she's sayin', it's all rubbish, Yer Honour! Get me friend off Old Lady Skint's ship and I'll tell ya what *really* 'appened.'

The Fugleman leaned back in his chair. 'Very well, Pounce. Let us hear this information. *If* it is as good as you say, your friend will go free.'

'It's good, all right.' The boy grinned nastily at Hope. 'And 'ere's why. I don't know what 'appened to Bonnie, but Goldie and Toadspit ain't dead. They's alive and in Jewel. In fact—' Pounce hesitated, as if he was struggling with his conscience. Then his face hardened and he said,

'In fact, they is the ones what's been makin' trouble. A lot of that Hidden Rock stuff, that's them. They's livin' in a museum—'

Hope could not stay silent. 'Your Honour, I saw those children bound and helpless!' She sneered at Pounce. 'I suppose you're going to tell us that they managed to escape, and overpower Cord and Smudge? Pah! You weren't even there!'

The Fugleman steepled his fingers under his chin. 'She has a point, Pounce. You *weren't* there, were you? On the *Piglet*? You're not keeping *secrets* from me?'

'Nah,' said Pounce quickly, 'I got good contacts, that's all. Not like old Flense here, who's out of date as usual.'

Guardian Hope seethed at the insult. But at the same time she felt a flicker of doubt. After all, she hadn't actually *seen* the brats fed to the sharks . . .

'This is most enlightening,' said the Fugleman, tapping the hilt of his sword against his chin.

'So you'll let Mousie go? That's me friend. You could go and see Old Lady Skint right now—'

'Patience, boy, patience.' His Honour smiled. 'I don't suppose your sources know where Cord and Smudge have got to? They're supposed to be here by now, but they haven't arrived.'

There was something about that smile that reminded Hope of the hounds that had pursued her so relentlessly.

A bitter rage filled her heart. If Golden Roth *had* escaped ...

'Maybe they's scared,' said Pounce. ''Cos they let the snotties go. Maybe they can't face ya.'

'Hmm,' said the Fugleman. '*Most* enlightening. The trouble is—' He pushed his chair back and the smile disappeared. 'The trouble is, I don't believe you!'

He strode to the door and flung it open. 'Smudge!' he roared.

Hope sniggered angrily at the expression on Pounce's face. *Ha!* she thought. *You weren't expecting that!*

Smudge shuffled into the room, as big and stupid as ever. When he saw the boy, he shook his head sorrowfully. 'I waited, Cap'n, just like ya told me. But ya didn't come back. So I come lookin' for ya.'

Hope's brief moment of pleasure evaporated. 'I don't understand.' She turned to the Fugleman. 'Why is he calling the boy Captain? And if *he's* here, why isn't Cord? What *did* happen on board the *Piglet*—'

There was a shout from Smudge as Pounce made a dash for freedom. His Honour's sword whipped across the doorway, blocking the boy's exit.

'Not thinking of leaving us, are you, Pounce? I thought you wanted to go and see Old Lady Skint?' The Fugleman bared his teeth. 'And so you shall, boy. You can go this afternoon with the next load of children. In chains!' He nodded at one of the Guardians who hovered outside the door. 'Take him away! And find something useful for Smudge to do.'

As soon as they were gone, the Fugleman turned on Hope. 'You don't *understand*, Guardian? It is perfectly simple. Smudge has told me what happened on board the *Piglet*. To put it simply, it was a disaster. Cord, who should be alive, is dead. All three children, who should be dead, are alive! And now it seems that they are the ones who have been causing me so much trouble! You have failed me, Hope. I gave you a simple task to carry out and you failed miserably!'

If His Honour had said such terrible words to her six months ago, Blessed Guardian Hope would have cowered before him and begged for mercy. But her time in Spoke had changed her. While the Fugleman had been in the House of Repentance, pretending to be a humble prisoner, she had ruled an entire gang of vicious criminals. And when the Big Lie took her, she had risked her life, and nearly lost it!

She drew herself up, her chest swelling. 'I did everything you asked of me and more,' she snapped. 'And I will not stand here and be abused for Cord's failings!'

The Fugleman was not used to such plain speaking. His face darkened, and Hope felt the shadow of the dungeons pass over her. But she could not back down, not now. There was too much at stake.

'If the children are alive, as you say,' she continued quickly, 'then we must recapture them as soon as possible. Otherwise *any*one will think they can defy us. Fortunately, I have an idea.'

For a heart-stopping moment her future hung in the balance. Then His Honour laid his sword on his desk, wiped a spot from his sleeve and said, 'And this idea is—?'

Hope felt a thrill of righteousness. After twenty years of service, she had the Fugleman listening to her at last! Now all she had to do was come up with an idea for capturing the children before he changed his mind.

In the next breath she thought of – and discarded – half a dozen strategies. The brats would be warier than ever by now. What clever trick could she use to catch them?

The answer came to her like a gift from the Seven Gods. 'Pounce sounded very keen to win the release of his friend. May I use him?'

'If you must.'

Guardian Hope smiled malevolently. 'In that case, you can leave it to me, Your Honour. I will set a trap for those children that will see them enslaved for the rest of their lives. And this time *nothing* will go wrong!'

THE TRAP

That discussion in the sickroom was the darkest that Goldie had ever known. Not even Sinew could raise a smile. But by the time Olga Ciavolga had bandaged the cat's paw and strapped its broken ribs, the five keepers and the Protector had come up with a plan.

'Mind you, I don't like it,' murmured Herro Dan. 'Too many things could go wrong.' He chewed

Bonnie Hahn

his thumbnail and grimaced at Goldie and Toadspit. 'I wish more than anythin' that I could go with you.'

Olga Ciavolga nodded agreement, and so did Sinew. But then they had to break off to sing to the ever-more-restless rooms, and it was clear that the senior keepers could not be spared.

When the children had made their preparations, Olga Ciavolga sent them to get some sleep, so they would be fresh for the night's rescue. But Goldie could not sleep. The museum was seething, its rooms *shifting* every few minutes, and she knew that the three older keepers were struggling to keep control. One of the ships in Rough Tom had already fallen apart, cracked open like a nut. The tree in the Vacant Block dropped limbs on anyone who ventured near it. The Dirty Gate creaked and groaned as if it might swing open at any moment and loose a myriad of horrors on an unsuspecting city.

Goldie's mind seethed too, running over and over their plans for the night ahead until she felt like screaming. It was almost a relief when she heard Morg flap heavily past her door, crying, 'Thie-e-e-e-f. Thie-e-e-e-e-f!'

She ran out of her room and bumped straight into Toadspit. They followed Morg to the kitchen, where they found Pounce cramming dumplings into his mouth and silver spoons into his pockets.

He shrugged when he saw them, and dropped the spoons back on the table, saying, 'I thought they was just rubbish. I was doin' yez a favour, gettin' rid of 'em.'

Then his face changed and he said, 'Listen, ya know Old Lady Skint's in town?'

'Yes,' said Toadspit, expressionless. 'We know.'

'Ya know she's got Mouse and Bonnie?'

'Yes.'

'Well, here's somethin' ya *don't* know. I just seen a new load of prisoners bein' marched down to the slave ship. Not just snotties this time – there was grownups too. I thought one of the blokes looked a bit like someone I knew, so I asked around. Found out 'is name—'

'Na-a-a-ame,' croaked Morg, curling her claws around the back of a chair.

'It was Roth. 'Arken Roth.'

Goldie's skin felt suddenly hot and tight. Her voice, when she spoke, seemed to belong to someone else. 'Harken Roth?' she whispered. '*Pa?*'

'That's it,' said Pounce. ''Arken Roth and 'is wife Grace.'

'Ma *too?*' Goldie was afraid she might fall over.

'And their friends. The Hahns.'

Toadspit shook his head, as if he was trying to make Pounce's words go away. 'No! *No!*'

'Reckon Old Lady Skint's collectin' slaves for the salt mines,' said Pounce, watching Goldie out of the corner of his eye. 'Folk don't last long doin' that sorta work. Reckon she's come to get replacements for all the dead 'uns.'

'De-e-e-e-e-e-ead,' croaked Morg, raising one great claw. 'De-e-e-e-e-e-e-e-e-ead.'

'No,' said Toadspit again. But this time there was such heartbreak in his voice that Goldie could hardly bear it.

'It doesn't change anything,' she said, although her own pain was like an iron band around her chest. 'It just gives us a few more people to rescue.'

'Whaddaya mean?' said Pounce, who had grabbed another dumpling and was edging towards the door.

'We were going in tonight anyway, to get Bonnie and Mouse out. And—' She stopped, not wanting to tell Pounce too much about their plans.

Pounce's mouth fell open. 'You was gunna save Mousie?'

'You don't think we'd leave him there, do you?'

'I dunno. Maybe.' Pounce looked at Goldie, then away again. ''E's just a worthless little snotty. No one cares about 'im 'cept me.'

'He's our friend,' said Goldie. Then she turned back to Toadspit and said, 'We'll do it *exactly* the same way. Except—' A thought struck her and she grabbed Pounce's arm. 'If you had to choose between Mouse and the *Piglet*, which would you choose?'

'Don't be stupid,' said Pounce, pulling away.

'No, I mean it. Would you sacrifice the *Piglet* to save your friend?'

Pounce lifted his shoulder as if he didn't care one way or the other, but Goldie could see that he was struggling to hold back tears, and she knew the answer.

'In that case,' she said, 'you'd better come with us.' She turned to Toadspit. 'I'll go in by myself while you and Pounce get the *Piglet*.'

'No.' Toadspit shook his head vehemently. 'You can't go alone.'

'It makes sense, Toadspit, you know it does. If I get caught you'll still be free to try again. And if I *don't* get caught, the *Piglet* being there at the end might just tip the balance.'

Toadspit glared at her as if he wanted to argue but knew she was right. He chewed his lip, then scowled at Pounce. 'I don't trust him.'

'That's why you're going with him,' said Goldie. 'But I don't think he'll betray us. He's got as much at stake as us, haven't you, Pounce?'

The boy didn't meet her eyes. 'Yeah. Um— Are yez really gunna get Mousie out?'

'If we can,' said Goldie.

'Well,' said Pounce. 'Well.' Then, very quickly and quietly, he muttered, 'Yez had better be careful. Old Lady Skint's no fool and neither's Harrow. They'll be lookin' out for anyone stupid enough to try a rescue.' He reddened. 'They might even have set a – a trap or somethin'!'

Goldie forced a grin. 'Don't worry, Pounce. Trap or not, they won't see me. I promise you they won't see a thing unless I want them to.'

The slave ship perched at its moorings like a huge predatory bird. Its deck was hung with lanterns and its blood-red sails were rolled in bundles around the spars. Somewhere in its hold a hundred children wept with despair.

The sailor with the ruined nose, Mince, was standing guard at the top of the gangway. Goldie drifted towards him. *I am the dust on a moth's wing. I am nothing . . .*

The tide lapped against the hull. Mince cleared his throat and spat into the water. Goldie stepped past him onto the deck of the *Silver Lining*.

Toadspit would be on his way to fetch the *Piglet* by now, with Pounce. He had hugged her when they parted, and said, 'Are you sure you know what you're doing?'

'Of course I'm sure,' Goldie had replied. But she wasn't. Not at all. She hefted the bag in her arms and looked for somewhere to hide it, in case things went wrong.

The *Silver Lining* was much bigger than the *Piglet*, and once she had stowed the bag safely, it took her some time to find her way to the slave hold. She sidled down the narrow ladderways, keeping an eye out for the other sailor, Jangle, and hoping that Double was still sick in her cabin and would not suddenly appear.

But the deeper she went, the less the sailors seemed to matter. Although the ship was new, fear clung to every part of it, and Goldie could hear the echo of a thousand desperate cries. The hair on her neck rose and, by the time she came to the hold, she was running with sweat. In the back of her mind, Princess Frisia cursed the slavers and demanded revenge.

It was dark down there in the bowels of the ship. There were one or two lanterns but they were so far apart that they barely touched the gloom. The air stank of terror and filth, and the weeping was so loud that Goldie had to put her fingers in her ears, or she would not have been able to take another step.

She found Ma and Pa in the very deepest part of the ship. They were sleeping face down in a pile of dirty straw, as were the people on either side of them. Further along that dreadful row, Goldie thought she could see Toadspit's parents. They were sleeping too. A lantern burned above their heads.

There were no children in this section. Goldie wondered where Bonnie and Mouse were, and hoped it would not be too hard to find them.

She took a deep breath and gathered her courage. Then she let go of the Nothingness.

One of the prisoners stared dully at her from the end of the row, but did not speak. Goldie took her picklock and knife from her pocket and crouched beside her parents. They were chained at wrist and ankle, but the locks were simple and she knew that it would only take a minute or two to open them.

'Ma!' she breathed. She touched her mother's shoulder and felt her flinch. 'It's me! Shhh! Don't say anything! Don't move!'

A horrible grunting sound came from the straw, as if Ma was trying to speak and couldn't. At the same time, Pa began to thrash against his chains so violently that he managed to throw himself onto his back.

With a shrinking heart, Goldie saw the gag in his

mouth, and the helpless plea in his eyes. *Run, sweeting! Run!*

But it was too late to run. The 'prisoners' on either side had already thrown off their shackles and leaped up with pistols in their hands.

One of them was the sailor Jangle. The other, dressed in an anonymous brown coat, was Blessed Guardian Hope.

DOUBLE

Double

uardian Hope hissed with triumph. 'You didn't think you'd see *me* again, did you, Golden Roth? Thought you'd got rid of me in Spoke! But now here I am, and here *you* are, walked into my little trap, sweet as pie. And look, you brought your tools with you! I'll have those, thank you very much!'

She snatched the picklock and knife out of Goldie's hands and put them in her pocket. Goldie bit her lip, hardly able to believe that Guardian Hope was still alive. From the floor, Ma gazed up at her with eyes full of pain and sorrow. A bruise was starting up on Pa's cheekbone, above the gag.

Guardian Hope dragged Goldie to her feet. 'So where are your little friends, Toadspit and Bonnie Hahn? I thought I'd have all three of you. Don't they care about their parents?'

She snapped shackles around Goldie's wrists, and laughed. 'Never mind. One is better than none. This reminds me of the old days when you wore the punishment chains. You felt sorry for yourself then, didn't you? But now— Dear me, it's almost worth a trip south to see you in the slave market! Proud Golden Roth, brought to heel at last!'

'Here,' said Jangle, reaching for Goldie's chain. 'I'll put 'er in with the other snotties.'

Goldie couldn't help herself – she stumbled backwards. At the same time, Guardian Hope jerked the chain out of the sailor's reach. 'Oh no, I'm not taking any chances with this one. She's too clever for her own good. When is Old Lady Skint due back?'

'Not till morning,' said Jangle. 'She'll be up to 'er elbows in roast duck by now, along with the rest of the crew.'

'Who's in charge while she's away?'

'That'd be Double. But you won't see 'er. She's green with bellyache. Ain't come out of 'er cabin since we got 'ere.'

The Guardian sniffed. 'Well, she must come out now. This is too important to take any risks.'

'Can't see Double gettin' out of 'er sickbed for a snotty,' said Jangle.

'This *snotty*,' said Guardian Hope, drawing herself up, 'has caused the Fugleman more trouble than you can imagine! If she escapes, I will see that all the force of the peninsula is brought against you and your ship.'

'We've 'ad people chasin' us before.' Jangle laughed. 'They never caught us yet.'

One of the women behind him began to cry, and he kicked her, without bothering to look down. Pa dragged his chained wrists out of the straw and patted the woman's shoulder, and the sailor kicked *him* too. Goldie strained at her shackles, knowing that she could do nothing to help.

'All the same,' said Hope, 'I will see this Double before I leave.'

'It's your funeral,' said Jangle. 'Her cabin's up 'ere.'

Guardian Hope pushed Goldie ahead of her through the stinking hold. The awful reek of the place filled Goldie's throat and lungs until she was sure she was going to be sick. She thought that nothing could add to her horror, but then she saw Favour and her parents, their faces yellow with fear, and realised that they must have been picked up at the same time as Ma and

Pa. She saw Mouse curled up tight as a bug, his eyes squeezed shut as if he was trying to pretend he wasn't there. She saw a hundred children, some of them crying softly in the gloom, others dumb with exhaustion and despair.

They watched her pass, their eyes hopeless. Goldie's stomach churned, and her heart tore at its moorings.

'You're very quiet!' Hope jabbed her in the ribs as they climbed a ladderway. 'I hope you realise this is all your fault. His Honour didn't want to take such drastic action, but he had no choice.'

'That's not true,' said Goldie. Her voice shook with anger. 'There's always a choice.' She glared over her shoulder at Guardian Hope. 'Always!'

'Where's this cabin?' snapped Hope, and she pushed Goldie so hard that she crashed into the wall at the head of the ladderway and almost fell to her knees.

'There,' said the sailor, pointing to a door with a raised sill. He banged his fist on it. 'Hey, Double? Someone wants to see ya.'

Inside the cabin, a voice snarled, 'Go away. I'm sick.'

Hope dragged Goldie over to the door. 'I am Blessed Guardian Hope,' she said, her mouth close to the wood. 'I have something I wish to discuss with you. A special prisoner. A girl.'

Silence from inside the cabin. Then the voice said, 'What about her?'

'You must come out.' Guardian Hope reddened. 'I will not be spoken to through a closed door.'

Goldie heard the creak of a hammock, then the sound of reluctant feet. Her mouth felt as if it was filled with sawdust.

A latch clicked. A dry voice said, 'How about an *open* door?'

Old Lady Skint's second-in-command had blonde hair cropped close to her head and a face tattooed with stripes. Her eyes were red, as if she hadn't slept for several nights.

Guardian Hope pushed Goldie forward so that her shins banged against the sill. 'This girl,' she said, 'is a notorious escaper. She and her friends killed one of the most dangerous men in Spoke.'

Jangle snorted. 'She don't look like a killer.'

Double's eyes flickered across Goldie's face and away again, and for a moment Goldie thought she had seen the slaver somewhere before. But that was impossible. She would have remembered those stripes.

'This girl came here tonight,' continued Hope, 'to free her parents. I want to be sure that she will not get away again. You must keep a constant guard over her. And you had better search her properly. I have already confiscated one device for opening locks. She may well have another.'

'Is that all?' Double scratched her armpit and yawned.

'No, it is not!' snapped Guardian Hope. 'I will be back first thing in the morning with the Fugleman. I expect to find the child and her parents still here!'

'Do you think we're beginners at this trade? We've never had a snotty escape yet!'

'Then make sure this is not the first time!'

The two women glared at one another. Then Guardian Hope thrust the end of Goldie's chain at Jangle and marched away without a backward glance.

Double was yawning again. 'Give Mince a shout,' she said. 'Then put the brat down with the other snotties. I'm going back to bed.' She rubbed her forehead, as if it was hurting as much as her stomach.

'Mince!' bellowed Jangle. Then he turned back to Double and said, 'Don't ya want to search 'er? Skint won't like it if she gets away.'

'Gets *away*?' The stripes on Double's face writhed. 'She's a *snotty!* We've carried hundreds of snotties. Have any of them ever got away?'

'But if she's a famous escaper—'

Double rolled her eyes.

'—then we should search 'er.'

'Oh, for Bald Thoke's sake,' muttered Double. 'All right! Bring her in here where there's a bit of light.'

Goldie heard footsteps, and Mince came up behind her. 'What's goin' on?'

'A fine watch you kept,' said Double, glowering at him. 'Look what got past you!'

Mince peered at Goldie. 'Nah. I woulda seen 'er. She musta snuck on board another way.'

'Just as well for you,' said Jangle. 'She's a killer, she is. If ya'd tried to stop 'er she mighta broke yer neck with 'er little finger.' And both men roared with laughter.

Double's hands were surprisingly gentle. She sorted through Goldie's pockets, and found nothing except a dirty kerchief. She sighed. Then she pulled Goldie's jacket open and inspected the lining.

The blue bird brooch was tucked inside the jacket collar. Double's fingers stumbled across it. A muscle in her cheek twitched.

'Bah!' she said, and with a jerk of her wrist she tore the brooch away from the cloth and held it up for the sailors to see. 'A killer? An escaper? You brought me from my sickbed for this? Look at the trinkets she wears! This is just a stupid little girl playing at heroics!'

'She could maybe use that to pick a lock . . .' mumbled Jangle, peering at the brooch.

DOUBLE

'And you could maybe use your brains for a change,' snarled Double. 'We could have got good money for a *proper* escaper. Could've sold her to a criminal gang. But a girl like this?' She let out her breath in a huff of displeasure. 'She's a waste of space.'

'She might have somethin' else on 'er,' said Jangle, but he no longer sounded sure of himself. 'A knife or somethin'. Hidden more careful like.'

Double didn't seem to hear him. 'I suppose *someone* will buy her,' she muttered, absently dropping Goldie's brooch into the pocket of her own coat and turning away. 'Put her with the other snotties. I'm going to bed.'

Mince dragged Goldie unceremoniously out of the cabin. But before he could shut the door, Double swung back around.

'I thought we only carried snotties this trip.' She nodded at Goldie. 'What are her parents doing on board?'

'It was a trap,' said Jangle. 'That Guardian set it up.'

Double held her stomach as if her bellyache had suddenly grown worse. 'You really got on the wrong side of *her*, girl. Bad luck for you *and* your parents. What's your name?'

Goldie had to fight to keep the despair out of her voice. 'Golden Roth.'

'And your parents? What are their names?'

'Why d'ya want to know that, Double?' said Mince. He chortled. 'Don't matter what their names are. They ain't *got* no names, not once they're on board the *Silver Lining*.'

Double raised her head and sniffed. 'What's that burning smell?'

Both sailors stared at her.

'Oooh,' said Double, mockingly. 'It's *your brain*, Mince, trying to think.'

'I wasn't tryin' to think! I just wondered—'

'Well, don't! If there's any wondering to be done round here, I'm the one who'll do it.' She glared at both men until they looked away. Then she turned back to Goldie. 'Names!' she snarled.

Goldie swallowed. 'Harken. And Grace.'

Double's face, beneath its tattoos, might have been a wall, it was so blank. Then she began to laugh. It was a terrible sound, as harsh as the clash of swords. 'Well, it looks as if Harken, Grace and Golden Roth are going *south* for their holidays this year. *What* a lucky family! Make sure you tuck them in well tonight, Mince. We don't want them complaining about the service, now, do we?'

At that, Mince and Jangle laughed too, their disagreement forgotten. They were still chuckling as they herded Goldie back down the ladderways to the hold.

'She's a rum 'un, that Double,' said Jangle, as he shackled Goldie into place between two sobbing five-year-olds. 'I thought she was goin' soft on us for a minute there.'

'Double? Soft?' said Mince. 'Nah, she's all right. She's clever, she is. Here, shut up, you!' And he kicked the girl on Goldie's right until her sobbing became a terrified whimper.

Goldie bit her lip so hard that she could taste blood. But she said nothing.

'Ya reckon we should keep a watch on this one, like the Guardian told us?' Mince nodded at Goldie.

'Nah, she's not goin' nowhere,' said Jangle.

He tested Goldie's chains, and those of the girls on either side of her. Then he and Mince sauntered off, laughing and chatting as if Goldie and the weeping children no longer existed.

GREAT WOODEN
SAVE US!

Old Lady Skint

uardian Hope sat outside the banquet room, smoothing her brand-new black robes and enjoying the thought of Golden Roth in chains. Her only regret was that she had not been able to capture the Hahn children as well. She felt cheated, and wondered what she could do to make up for it.

Perhaps, she thought, she would have Golden Roth *whipped* before she was taken south to the slave markets. Yes, why not? The brat deserved it, after all!

She chuckled to herself and listened to the sounds coming through the banquet room door. It was clear that most of the *Silver Lining*'s crew had fallen asleep at the table. Their snores were punctuated by Old Lady Skint's cackle as she described an attempted escape by some of her slaves, and the bloody outcome.

Hope leaned back in her chair, sighing happily. The night wore on.

At last, as the sun rose, she heard the scraping of chairs and the whack of a fleshy hand across a score of ears. 'Wake up, ratbags,' bellowed Old Lady Skint. 'Tide'll be on the turn soon and we're headin' south in the barky.'

'I thought you were staying another day, Skint,' said the Fugleman.

'Nah, not me. Got important business elsewhere.'

'But there's another batch of prisoners to load. What sort of business?'

Hope pressed her ear to the door as Old Lady Skint's voice sank to a murmur. 'It's these rumours of plague.'

'Surely you don't believe them? The city is as clean as a washed plate.'

Old Lady Skint laughed. 'How old do you reckon I am?'

'A beauteous young woman like yourself?' said the Fugleman smoothly. 'Why, surely you're not a day over thirty!'

Hope snorted. The slaver laughed again. 'I'm sixty-seven last birthday. And I didn't get to this grand age by takin' chances with somethin' as nasty as plague. It was worth stayin' for a day – that's a good load of cargo you've sold me, and you did us proud last night – but now it's time to go.'

She raised her voice. 'Come on, you lot! Get your pathetic bones out that door before I start breakin' 'em.'

As Hope flattened herself against the wall, the door flew open and the groaning crew members stumbled out of the banquet room, cursing and spitting and rubbing their heads. Their tattoos shone with grease, as if they had been lying face down in their food.

Behind them strode Old Lady Skint, her beetles gnawing at the crumbs that had fallen from her chins. And behind the slaver came the Fugleman, his sword at his side and his uniform as elegant as ever, despite the long night.

'Your Honour!' cried Hope, stepping up beside him. 'You will be pleased to hear that my trap worked. At this moment, Golden Roth lies in the hold of the *Silver Lining*, in chains!'

Oh, it was worth all the trouble Hope had gone to, just to see the slow smile that spread across the Fugleman's face! She hurried on. 'That girl will not interfere with your plans again, Your Honour. All that lies ahead of her is misery. Would you like to see her, and tell her so?'

'Hmm,' said the Fugleman, tapping the hilt of his sword. 'I believe I would.'

There were a dozen street-rigs parked close by for the trip to the docks. Hope squeezed in between two large tattooed men, keeping her face as bland as possible.

But as she stalked up the gangway of the *Silver Lining*, close behind the Fugleman, she whispered, 'Did you sleep well, Golden Roth? Did the chains hurt? Did your mother and father bewail their fate?'

It was a long time since she had been so happy.

Old Lady Skint and her crew were already preparing for departure. Hope beckoned to the sailor with the ruined nose. 'His Honour and I wish to see the special prisoner before you leave. Please escort us to her.'

The lower decks of the *Silver Lining* stank worse than ever. Hope followed the sailor and the Fugleman down the narrow ladderways, grabbing at ropes with one hand and clutching a kerchief to her nose with the other. Mice and spiders skittered past her feet, and she drew her robes closer and muttered a short prayer to the Weeping Lady.

Most of the brats were asleep, their faces hidden in their arms. The few who were awake shrank from the light of the lantern. Their groans and whimpers got on Hope's nerves, and she kicked them as she passed, to punish them for making her suffer. A dirty, whitish-coloured mouse peered up at her, then dashed off into the darkness.

'Vermin,' muttered Hope. 'I cannot abide vermin!'

At last the sailor pointed to a jumble of limbs. 'Told ya she wouldn't escape. She's been tucked up in 'er comfy bed all night.' He laughed, and poked at the miserable figure with his toe. 'Wakey, wakey!'

The girl groaned, but didn't move.

'Golden Roth,' Hope said loudly. 'His Honour the Fugleman has come to see you.'

The answering whisper was so quiet that Hope had to bend over to hear it. 'I— I feel s-sick.'

'*Sick?*' said Hope. She turned to the Fugleman. 'Apparently the prisoner feels *sick*, Your Honour.'

The Fugleman's teeth gleamed. 'She will feel sicker before we are finished with her. Make her sit up.'

Hope gave a little sigh of happiness and kicked the Roth girl into a sitting position. Chains rattled. The brat groaned horribly and looked up, blinking at the light.

For a moment, Hope thought that the sailor must

have led them to the wrong girl. 'Golden?' she said uncertainly.

'G-G-Guardian H-Hope,' the brat whispered. 'I feel s-s-sick.'

Ah, so it *was* Golden Roth. But there was something—

'You, sailor. Bring the lantern closer,' said Hope.

The sailor grumbled, and held the lantern up to the brat's face. 'I don't see what—' he began. Then a horrified gurgle came from his throat. The lantern swayed wildly. 'Her skin!' he hissed. 'Look! And her *neck*! Great Wooden save us!' And he began to flick his fingers frantically and back away.

The Fugleman snatched the lantern from him. 'What is it?' he snapped. 'What are you talking about?'

'Si-i-ick,' groaned Golden Roth. Her chained hands grabbed feebly at Hope's robes. 'And tired. So-o tired. Help me. He-elp!'

And suddenly every child in the hold was awake and wailing. 'Si-i-ck! I'm si-i-i-ick!'

Hope felt as if she had stepped into a nightmare. The wailing and the smell were dreadful enough. But more dreadful still were the black patches on Golden Roth's skin, and the swellings on her neck . . .

'Plague!' shrieked Guardian Hope, as she stumbled towards the ladderway. She could see the black patches on the other brats now, and the swellings on *their* necks. 'There's *plague* on the ship!'

The Fugleman shoved her to one side and ran up the narrow stairs ahead of her. There was no sign of the lantern – he must have dropped it. No, the sailor had it again, and he too was pushing past Hope, shouting, 'Abandon ship! The cargo's got plague! Cap'n, the cargo's got *plague!*'

Hope couldn't bear the thought of being left down there in the darkness with a hundred diseased children. She dragged herself up one ladderway after another, trying not to breathe, her eyes fixed on the rapidly disappearing light of the lantern. 'Wait for me!' she cried.

It was not until she was on deck, and the sailors running all around her in panic, that she remembered how her foot had *touched* the Roth brat. She kicked off her shoes and stumbled whimpering towards the gangway.

But the gangway was blocked. Old Lady Skint stood there, a pistol in each hand, facing the terrified sailors. Her chins quivered with rage. 'Who cried plague?' she roared. 'Who dares say there's disease on my beautiful new ship? Was it you, Mince?'

'It was!' shouted Mince in a high voice. The remains of his nose twitched. His face, beneath the tattoos, was white with terror. 'I seen the black skin and the buboes! The cargo's riddled with it!'

'He's right,' said the Fugleman, who had used his sword to get to the front of the crowd. 'I saw it too. Let me off, Skint. I don't care what you do with the rest of this rabble, but *I* have business to attend to.'

Old Lady Skint didn't seem to hear him. 'How do you know it's plague, Mince? Coulda been dirt and fleabites. It's dark in them holds.'

'I swear it's the sickness, Cap'n!' cried Mince. 'The ship's a goner! And so are we if we don't get outta here quick smart!'

'Yeah, let us go, Cap'n!' cried another sailor.

'Ya can't make us stay 'ere and die!'

'Don't be crool, Cap'n!'

Hope thought she might be able to edge past Skint while the old lady was distracted. But despite the babble of the crew, the captain stood firm, glaring at Mince. 'I'm not abandonin' a new ship on the say-so of a man who can't even keep his nose on his face!' she roared. 'I want to hear from someone with more than half a brain. Where's Double?'

It seemed impossible to Hope that the noise on deck could get louder, but it did. 'Double!' bellowed Old Lady Skint. 'Get out 'ere! Now! And the rest of you *shut up*!'

Astonishingly, the sailors obeyed her, muttering prayers under their breath to Great Wooden and the Weeping Lady, and flicking their fingers in silent terror. Only the Fugleman stood aloof from the panic, but Hope could see the pulse beating above his jaw.

And then Double appeared.

She looked worse than she had last night. *Far* worse. As she staggered across the deck, holding her stomach, she croaked, 'There's something wrong with me, Captain. I feel si-ick.'

She grabbed at one of her crew mates, but the man backed away. Double swayed and clutched her armpit, and her eyes widened in horror, as if she had just found one of the dreaded buboes.

Hope raised her hand and pointed. 'She's got it too!' she screamed. 'She's got *plague*!'

PLAGUE SHIP

Goldie crouched in the shadows of the quarterdeck, her face dark and swollen. She had removed her unlocked shackles and followed Guardian Hope up from the hold as silently as an arrow, hoping to see the crew of the *Silver Lining* in a state of panic.

She hadn't expected Old Lady Skint's reluctance to abandon ship, and her demand for proof. Fear clutched at her and she wished she still had

Mouse

Auntie Praise's blue bird brooch to give her courage. They were so close to freedom! If they should fail now—

But then Double stumbled out. And Guardian Hope screamed.

That was all it took. The rest of the sailors surged towards Old Lady Skint in an unstoppable wave and pushed her down the gangway to the wharf. By then the slaver captain was as white-faced as the rest of them, and she made no attempt to retake her ship. Instead, she aimed her pistols at two of the crew.

'Mince!' she bellowed. 'Get back on board. You too, Jangle. You're goin' back up there with Double.'

'No!' cried Mince and Jangle together. 'Cap'n—'

'You was both there all night,' shouted Skint. 'And I won't 'ave you infectin' the rest of us. Get up that gangway or I'll shoot you.'

But it was not until a dozen more pistols were cocked that Mince and Jangle obeyed their captain.

Goldie crept across to where Mouse was waiting beneath an open skylight, his face as grotesque as hers. In the darkness of below decks, it looked like plague. Up here it was clearly paint and papier-mâché.

'Make sure everyone below stays quiet,' breathed Goldie. She put her finger to her lips. 'No sound except for groans.'

Mouse disappeared. The sailors on the docks scanned the water. '*There's* a ship, Cap'n, right there,' cried one of them. 'It's small, but it'll get us away from this cursed place.'

Goldie heard Guardian Hope say, 'But that's Cord's ship!' No one took any notice of her. The sailors rushed towards the *Piglet*, which was tied up behind the *Silver Lining*.

There was a shout. 'Here, git orf me boat! Whatcha doin'? *Git orf!*' and Pounce, struggling and protesting, was bundled over the rail onto the wharf.

Guardian Hope's voice floated up to the quarterdeck. 'Pounce? What are you doing here? I told you to stay out of sight once you had baited the trap.'

'Yeah, well,' said Pounce. 'I couldn't trap more than one of 'em, so I had to change me plans. Worked out all right though. I got a prisoner for the Foobleman. So how about ya get Mousie off that slave ship like ya promised? And tell that scummy lot to give the *Piglet* back. It's mine.'

'What prisoner?' said the Fugleman, striding forward.

The sailors threw another boy onto the wharf. His hands were trussed with rope, and his face was livid with anger and betrayal.

'It's the Hahn boy!' squawked Guardian Hope. 'Toad-spit! We have him after all!' She smiled triumphantly.

So did the Fugleman.

When Goldie saw those smiles, a deep and terrible hatred surged through her veins. In the back of her mind, Frisia was whispering about—

—*revenge! Kill them! Cut off their ears! Release the wolf-sark*—

'No!' whispered Goldie. 'Not now! Go away!' And she slowed her breath and brought her mind inwards and repeated, 'This is me. This is who I am. This is *me*!' until the deck of the slave ship firmed beneath her.

On the *Piglet*, Old Lady Skint and her crew were preparing for a hasty departure. The Fugleman turned to Pounce. 'You want your friend? And a ship? You can have both. There.' He pointed towards the *Silver Lining*, and the three miserable sailors who stood on her deck, as far from each other as possible. 'It's yours.'

'Nah, that's a plague ship.' Pounce began to edge away, talking rapidly. 'All right, I'll tell yer what. Yer friends can 'ave the *Piglet*, I don't really need it. And you can 'ave the *Silver Linin'*. That's all right, no need to thank me, I'll just take Mousie and go. We'll be outta yer hair before ya know it.'

The Fugleman whipped his sword from its scabbard and pointed it at Pounce's chest. 'It was not an *offer*, boy. It was a *command*.' He smiled again, and the sword sang through the air towards Toadspit. 'As for your prisoner—'

In the shadows of the quarterdeck Goldie prayed to the Seven Gods and flicked her fingers until they were sore. This was the part of their plan that she had been least sure about. 'Don't hurt him,' she whispered.

The tip of the sword pressed against Toadspit's throat. He winced and blood trickled down his neck.

'As for your prisoner,' said the Fugleman, 'I have one or two scores to settle with the Hidden Rock. So—'

Goldie clamped her hands over her mouth. *Don't hurt him!*

'So he will be going with you.'

Toadspit said nothing. But Pounce fell to his knees, his voice high with fright. 'Please, Harrow, don't send me on the plague ship! Ain't I done good work for ya in the past? Didn't I set the trap up, just like old Flense told me? Don't send me to me doom!'

Guardian Hope was hugging herself with delight. The Fugleman bared his teeth at Pounce. 'You are scum, boy. Scum from the gutter. The world is well rid of you.' And he prodded his prisoners towards the *Silver Lining*.

But at the foot of the gangway, Toadspit stopped. 'It was just me and Goldie,' he said over his shoulder. 'All that Hidden Rock stuff. You mustn't blame the other keepers, or the museum. They had no part in it.'

'What nonsense,' scoffed Guardian Hope. 'Of course they—'

The Fugleman held up his hand to silence her. 'I don't blame them in the slightest,' he said.

Even from that distance Goldie could see how Toadspit clenched his bound fists. 'Then you won't use Frow Carrion on the museum?'

The Fugleman smiled a dangerous smile. 'I wouldn't dream of it. Now get up that gangway. If the *Silver Lining* is not gone from here within the quarter hour I will burn it to the waterline, with everyone on board. I don't care where you go to die, as long as it is nowhere near me!'

Thirteen minutes later, the *Silver Lining* chugged out of Jewel Harbour.

Goldie had retreated to Old Lady Skint's cabin, where Mouse was waiting for her. Both of them wanted to unchain the captive children as soon as possible, but they waited, crouching on the captain's desk beneath the skylight, afraid that their ruse might yet be discovered.

Mince stood at the wheel with his back to them. Jangle was below, in the engine room, and Double leaned silently against the rail, watching the city disappear in the distance. If Goldie craned her neck she could see Toadspit and Pounce huddled on the main deck in pretended terror.

Except not all of it was pretended, at least on Toadspit's part. Because the Fugleman had lied when he said that he didn't blame the other keepers for the actions of the Hidden Rock. Goldie had heard it in his voice and seen it in his face. At this very moment he was probably giving the orders that would send Frow Carrion clanking up Old Arsenal Hill.

At that thought, a sense of great urgency took hold of Goldie. 'Bald Thoke, *Glorious* Thoke, god of tricks and disguises,' she whispered. 'You've helped me so far. Please help us to get off this ship and back to the museum as quickly as possible—'

Mouse nudged her. Jewel was out of sight at last, the gas engines had stopped, and Mince and Jangle were frantically lowering one of the ship's dinghies.

Goldie could hear Double pleading with them. 'C'mon, Mince, I'm not as sick as I thought I was. Take me with you.'

Mince ignored her.

'It's not plague,' cried Double. 'I just had a bellyache, that's all.'

'So why did she pretend it *was* plague?' Goldie

whispered to Mouse. 'I don't understand.'

'See?' said Double, holding up her arms. 'No buboes, no nothing. Even my bellyache's gone.'

'I wish they'd take her,' Goldie whispered. 'But they're not going to. We'd better get everyone unchained.' She handed Mouse the keys from the hook by the door. 'Try and get them to stay out of sight until we know what Double's going to do. And keep the plague stuff on their faces.'

Mouse grinned, and the papier-mâché on his skin cracked. In his sleeve, a dozen white mice slept soundly, exhausted by their labours.

It had taken Goldie most of the night to get the captive children painted and dyed convincingly. At first she had been afraid that Mince and Jangle would change their minds and come to check on her. And so she had waited for more than an hour before untaping the knife from her armpit and the picklock from the sole of her foot.

But even when she was freed from her shackles it was not easy. The younger children were so terrified that they would not stop crying. It was not until Goldie unchained Mouse and took him and his pets through the holds with her that the young captives began to listen. The white mice were comforting in a way that nothing else was.

They were quick and silent too, and could run all

over the ship without being noticed. As soon as Goldie had retrieved the hidden package, she set the mice to work. They chewed paper to a pulp and plastered fake sores onto necks and armpits. They smeared black paint over skin, while the children giggled and squirmed.

Goldie was everywhere, checking on the mice, reassuring the captives. She barely had time to talk to Bonnie or Favour. All she could do was say, over and over again, 'Don't be afraid, we're going to get out of here!' and hope that she was right.

She said the same to Toadspit's parents and to Ma and Pa, who went deathly white when they saw her, and then could not stop crying and laughing and holding her hand. But when she explained what she was doing, they let go immediately and promised that they would make sure all the adults knew what to do.

And now at last freedom was in sight. Goldie could hear the splash of oars as Mince and Jangle rowed away from the *Silver Lining*, heading for the distant shore. If only they had taken Double with them!

Old Lady Skint's second-in-command was sitting on the deck with her head in her hands. She did not look particularly frightening – in fact, there was something lost and lonely about her.

'Good!' thought Goldie fiercely. 'I hope she's as miserable as all the slaves she's captured over the years.'

And perhaps she was – because now it was Double's turn to be caught. While Toadspit wriggled free of his ropes, Pounce took out a pistol and aimed it at the slaver. 'Don't you try nothin',' he said. 'This ship's ours now.'

Double shrugged. 'You're welcome to it. Give me the other boat and I'll be gone before you know it.'

Toadspit and Pounce looked at each other. 'All right,' said Pounce, 'ya can 'ave it. Now get out of 'ere.'

'If I could lower it by myself,' said Double in a sarcastic voice, 'I'd be gone already.'

Goldie could hear squeals and cries coming up from below, and she knew that Mouse would not be able to hold the freed children for much longer. She slipped her hands out of the skylight and signalled to Toadspit. *Hurry! Get rid of her!*

Toadspit gave an infinitesimal nod. But it was too late. Before the boat could be loosened from its blocks, a horde of children spilled out onto the deck from every part of the ship. They were filthy and hungry and bruised, and covered in paint and papier-mâché, but it was as clear as could be that they were not diseased.

There was no reason now for Goldie to stay hidden. She wriggled out of the skylight and crossed the deck to Double, who greeted her with a peculiar smile.

'So the Guardian was right about you, Golden Roth,' said the slaver. 'You've bettered Old Lady Skint, and there's not many people who can say that.'

Goldie ignored her. She no longer cared what happened to Double. 'We have to get back to the museum,' she said to Toadspit.

He nodded. *He* had seen the lie in the Fugleman's face too.

'Well then, you can drop me off—' the slaver began.

'Goldie! Sweeting!' It was Ma and Pa. They stumbled across the deck, battered and happy, with Toadspit's parents and Bonnie right behind them. Bonnie threw her arms around her brother's neck, and their parents embraced both of them. Ma and Pa kissed Goldie. Mouse slipped past them all, and he and Pounce hugged each other joyously.

Double chose that moment to dive over the side of the ship into the water.

'Is that one of the slavers?' cried Pa. 'It is? She's getting away!' And with a roar of anger he leaped after Double.

Ma screamed and ran to the rail. 'Harken! Harken, you *can't swim!*'

It was true. Pa sank, then bobbed to the surface, floundering in a frantic circle. Goldie gripped her mother's arm with white fingers. 'Pa!' she whispered.

Everyone was leaning over the rail by now, shouting advice. Ma screamed and wept and begged them to save her husband, but none of them could swim either.

It was Toadspit who thought of the ship's boat. He ran towards it with Pounce and a dozen other children, and began to fumble with the ropes. But his helpers got in each other's way and tied the knots tighter instead of loosening them.

Pa sank, rose, and sank again, his hands clutching the air above his head.

All this time, Double had been swimming towards the shore with a steady rhythm. But now she stopped and trod water, and looked back to see what all the noise was about.

'Pleeeeeease!' wailed Ma, as Pa vanished beneath the waves. 'Save him, please! I beg you!'

She won't, thought Goldie. *She's a slaver. Why should she care about Pa?*

But still she held her breath, and when Double turned back to the ship, thrashing through the water with her powerful arms, Goldie cheered with the rest of them.

The next minute or two seemed like hours. Double found the spot where Pa had disappeared, and dived beneath the surface. Toadspit and Pounce gave up on the boat and slung a rope over the side. Ma sobbed, and prayed aloud to the Seven Gods, and flicked her fingers. Bonnie slipped her hand into Goldie's.

A stream of bubbles rose to the surface of the water and burst, and Goldie felt as if her heart was bursting with them. She closed her eyes, imagining Pa sinking through the darkness, down and down and down . . .

'She's got him!' Toadspit's father, Herro Hahn, banged his fist on the rail. 'She's *got him!*'

Goldie's eyes flew open. Ma squealed with joy. There was Pa, with Double holding his head clear of the water. He was sputtering and coughing and choking – but he was alive.

'Over 'ere!' shouted Pounce, from the top of the rope.

Double swam towards the ship, dragging Pa behind her. When she reached the rope she tried to push him up it, but he clung to her and would not let go.

And so, in the end, with a grunt of annoyance, she climbed the rope herself, dragging him with her.

As they staggered over the rail, Ma and Goldie threw their arms around Pa and wept. 'Thank you!' cried Ma, over her husband's shoulder. 'Thank you! Thank you, thank you, thank you!'

Double ducked her head and turned away. Pa held

Ma and Goldie in his arms as if he would never let them out of his sight again. He was wet and shivering. 'What a fool I am,' he whispered. 'Trying to play the hero like that.'

Goldie kissed his cheek. 'You have to learn to think before you act, Pa.'

'*I* thought you were brave.' Ma laughed shakily. 'But perhaps just a little forgetful.'

'Well,' said Pa, after a moment, 'I am still alive despite my foolishness. So let us get on with it.'

He tapped the slaver on the shoulder. 'I promised myself that you would not escape, and you will not.'

'Harken!' said Ma. 'She saved your life!'

'And I am truly grateful,' said Pa. 'But she must pay for what she tried to do to these people. And for what she has done to others in the past.'

Double said nothing. Her shoulders were hunched and she stared at the deck as if she did not want anyone to see her face.

'Listen, we have to get back to Jewel,' said Toadspit, pushing to the front of the crowd. 'The Fugleman's going to bombard the Museum of Dunt. We have to stop him.'

Adults and children gazed at him in dismay. Many of them had taken shelter in the museum during last year's Great Storm, and although they did not understand its true nature, and what would happen if it was attacked, they did not want to see it destroyed.

'Then this woman must come with us,' said Pa, looking sternly at Double.

'We'll need her anyway,' said Goldie, 'to get us to shore. We don't know how to work this ship.'

'You think *I* can work it with a handful of landsmen and a hundred useless snotties?' mumbled Double, without raising her head.

At the sound of the slaver's voice, Ma flinched.

'In that case,' said Pa, 'we will chain you in the slave hold and be done with it. I am sure we can manage—'

'No!' cried Ma. 'No more chains, not for anyone.'

'If we don't chain her,' said Pa, 'she will jump over-board again.'

Everyone within earshot murmured agreement.

'No, I don't think she will,' said Ma, and with a trembling hand she touched the slaver's arm.

Double froze.

'Grace?' said Pa. 'What are you doing?'

Ma ignored him. 'You have a good heart,' she whispered, so quietly that Goldie had to lean forward to hear her. 'I know you do.'

'I have no heart,' mumbled Double.

'If that was true, you would have let my husband drown.'

Double laughed angrily. 'Perhaps I had a heart once. But if I did, it wore out long ago and I threw the useless

235

thing overboard.'

Except for a few small children, the ship had fallen quiet. It seemed to Goldie that something important was happening, although she did not know what it was. She wished she could see the slaver more clearly, but Double would not raise her head.

'Please help us,' said Ma. 'My daughter is one of the museum's keepers and the other keepers are like a family to her. And family is—' Her voice broke. 'Family is more important than anything.'

'You don't know what you're asking,' whispered Double.

'I do.' A tear rolled down Ma's face. 'I know exactly what I'm asking.' And she raised her hand and stroked the slaver's cheek.

'*Ma?*' said Goldie, shocked beyond belief.

'Grace, what on earth—?' said Pa.

'Shhh!' whispered Ma.

By now, even the smallest child had fallen silent. The only sound Goldie could hear was water lapping against the hull, and the constant creaking of the ship.

Something was happening to the slaver. A tear ran down *her* cheek and fell to the deck. Slowly – oh, so slowly – she raised her head.

Goldie looked from Double to Ma, and from Ma to Double, and a dreadful knowledge uncoiled within her.

Now that they stood side by side, the likeness between the two women could not be hidden, not even by slaver tattoos. Old Lady Skint's second-in-command was—

'Auntie Praise,' whispered Goldie, staring at the slaver in horror. 'You're my long-lost Auntie Praise!'

BOLD AUNTIE
PRAISE

Double

Every plank and nail of the *Silver
Lining* seemed to vibrate with the
shock of it. The adults gaped their
disbelief. Favour and Bonnie cried out in
dismay. The smallest children burst into tears,
as if their world had been turned upside down
yet again.

Goldie felt like bursting into tears with
them. She could see the appalled judgement
in people's eyes, and knew that her own face
carried the same expression.

Ma was the only one who didn't seem
to notice. She took her sister's hands in

hers. 'I have missed you every day since you disappeared,' she whispered. 'What happened to you? How did you— How *could* you have become a slaver?'

Everyone on the ship craned to hear the answer.

'Won't you tell me?' said Ma.

Double shook her head, but the words burst out of her anyway, as if they had been stuck inside her all these years, like an abscess waiting for the knife. 'It— It was the day after my Separation,' she mumbled. 'They— They grabbed me off the streets and were going to sell me. But Old Lady Skint took a liking to me for some reason and decided to keep me as a sort of pet.'

She grimaced. 'I was still a captive, of course, and couldn't escape, though I tried. I tried many times, and whenever I was brought back, Skint would laugh and say I had spirit. After six months she asked me to join her crew. I refused.'

Herro Hahn grunted in disbelief. 'Shhh!' said Ma with a glare.

'She asked me again three months later,' continued Double. 'Again I refused, and again and again. But some time in the second year I began to wonder *why* I was refusing. They were not cruel to me, you see. They were kind, in a rough sort of way. And after a while, what they did began to seem normal. They gave me another name and I forgot who I was. Kindness can do that to you, quicker than cruelty.'

Her mouth twisted. 'You want my advice, people? Watch out for kindness! In the wrong hands, it can be deadlier than a gun and far more subtle. I'm witness to that. Remember what happened to Praise Koch and hold to your true self, no matter how sweetly those around you talk.'

She fell silent for a moment or two. Then she muttered, 'So there you are. The not-so-grand story of my downfall. It was only when we sailed into Jewel that I truly remembered . . .'

Ever since she was small, Goldie had used the thought of her bold aunt to give herself courage. In times of danger she had clutched the blue bird brooch and whispered her aunt's name. She had tried to be *like* her. She had been proud when Ma said she *was* like her!

Now the very idea made Goldie feel sick.

A warm hand gripped hers, and Toadspit put his lips to her ear. 'I'm jealous,' he murmured. 'All my relatives are so boring.'

Goldie knew he was trying to comfort her, but nothing could make her feel better. 'She's not really Auntie Praise,' she whispered fiercely. 'She's *Double* and that's what I'm going to call her.'

She turned away from the awful sight of Ma embracing the slaver, and raised her voice above the hubbub. 'We must get back to Jewel as quickly as possible,' she cried. 'We must stop the Fugleman destroying the museum.'

Everyone stared at her in confusion, as if the revelations of the past few minutes had driven the museum from their minds.

'*Can* we stop him?' asked a girl's voice from the back of the crowd.

'Not likely,' muttered the boy beside her. 'He'd turn Frow Carrion on *us*!'

There was a murmur of agreement from those around him. Feeling a certain gratitude to the museum for sheltering them was one thing, but standing up to Frow Carrion was a different matter altogether.

'What's the matter with yez?' demanded Pounce, jumping up onto the rail. 'We fooled Old Lady Skint, didn't we? I reckon that means we can do anythin' we like.' He raised his eyebrows. 'Unless, of course, yez are gunna lie down like a bunch of idjits and let the Foobleman walk all over yez?'

Goldie jumped up beside him. 'Pounce is right. If we want our city back, we have to fight for it.'

Another murmur ran through the crowd. 'But we don't know how to make this ship go,' said Toadspit's mother.

'*She* is going to show us.' Goldie pointed at Double, who stood stiff and silent in the circle of Ma's arms, clearly regretting her public confession.

'She's going to take us to a safe landing,' continued Goldie. 'She owes it to us.'

She glared at the slaver. *You're not my aunt!*

Double pushed Ma to one side. 'You want to get to shore? I'll take you there. But I won't go to prison.'

'And neither you should,' said Ma in a tremulous voice. 'You didn't choose to be a slaver. It could have happened to any of us.'

Disbelief rustled through the crowd. Pa shook his head. 'We make no promises. But if you help us now it will count in your favour.'

Double stared at him for a long moment. Then she said, 'That's something, I suppose.' And she shoved her way through the crowd and leaped up onto the quarterdeck. 'Who knows a bit about gas engines?'

She didn't really look like Ma, thought Goldie. Ma was all sweetness and warmth, whereas the slaver's face showed nothing but hardness.

'Me!' cried Pounce, jumping down from the rail.

'And me!' shouted Toadspit.

'Get below, then, and see if you can restart the engines. I'll give you ten minutes, and then I'll come after you with a belaying pin!'

Toadspit and Pounce raced off. Everyone else milled around, glancing first up at the quarterdeck and then at Ma and Pa, who stood in silence with their arms around each other. Ma was glowing with confused happiness. Pa just looked grim.

Goldie had lost sight of Bonnie and Mouse, but now they wriggled through the crowd to stand beside her. Mouse patted her arm and hummed, as if he knew how miserable she was feeling.

Bonnie whispered, 'I bet Old Lady Skint wouldn't have saved your pa. There must be nice slavers as well as nasty ones.'

She was wrong, thought Goldie. And so was Ma. Auntie Praise was lost for good. The best thing to do was forget about her, and concentrate on stopping the Fugleman and Frow Carrion.

It was nine minutes, by Goldie's calculation, before the gas engines rumbled to life. Nearly everyone on deck let out a shriek of delight.

Double pointed to a group of older boys and girls, and shouted above the noise, 'You lot! Get over by the anchor. What do you mean, where? *There*, of course! What are you, blind? No, don't touch anything until I say so. And you!' She pointed to Bonnie. 'You're my runner. Go and tell those two snotties I want quarter-speed ahead, nothing more. If they try anything fancy I'll sling 'em over the rail and whip 'em. Understand?'

Bonnie nodded and ran for the hatchway. 'Come back as soon as you've told 'em,' shouted Double.

Then she pointed to Mouse and Goldie. 'Up here. Now.'

Goldie didn't move.

'I said *now*! Or don't you care about your precious museum as much as your ma thinks you do?'

Mouse grabbed Goldie's hand, and she let him drag her towards the quarterdeck. Double's voice rose to a bellow. 'The rest of you stay out of the way until you're told different. And *get those snotties out of my rigging!*'

As Goldie and Mouse mounted the steps to the quarterdeck, the engines rumbled louder. Double swung the great wheel as if it were no heavier than a child's hoop, and the *Silver Lining* began to turn.

'This is a bad coast for ships this size,' said the slaver. 'I need to know how much water we've got under the keel. You two are going to take soundings.'

She pointed to the bow of the ship and explained what she wanted. Without a word, Goldie spun on her heel. She could feel Double's eyes on her back, but she did not turn around.

The shore was not as far away as it looked. With

everyone following instructions as best they could, Double brought the *Silver Lining* safely into the middle of a rocky cove. The engines cut off abruptly. A moment later, Toadspit and Pounce reappeared on deck, looking pleased with themselves.

As the anchor chain began to unwind, Double drew Goldie and Toadspit to one side. 'It'll take a while to disembark everyone,' she said, 'seeing as we've only got the one boat. And then you've got to get them all across country to Jewel. In that time, the Fugleman could bombard a dozen museums.'

'He has to get Frow Carrion up Old Arsenal Hill,' said Toadspit. 'That'll slow him down.'

'It won't take all day,' said Double. She eyed the two children. 'If this was my expedition, I'd pick out my best crew – the useful ones, the fighters and the thinkers – to take with me. And I'd leave the rest of this mob to follow later.'

Goldie didn't want to admit it, but it made sense. She studied the people around her. 'Pounce,' she called. 'We want you. And Mouse too.'

Double raised an eyebrow as Mouse stepped forward. 'He's a mite small and tender for battle, isn't he?'

Goldie glared at her. 'He's not too small and tender for the salt mines!'

'Dearling—' protested Ma.

But Double merely smiled, as if nothing Goldie said could touch her.

'And Bonnie,' said Toadspit. 'You'd better come with us.'

His sister beamed.

'A bunch of snotties?' said Double. 'Is that the best you can do?'

Pounce puffed out his chest. 'We is as good as an army, the five of us. Ain't no one else 'ere as useful as we is.'

'He's right,' said Ma. 'These children put the rest of us to shame. But—' She brushed the papier-mâché sores from Goldie's neck. 'But dearling, I'd like to make a suggestion. I have no idea how you are going to stop Frow Carrion, but if anyone can do it, it will be you and your friends. There's just one thing. I think you should take your aunt with you.'

'*What?*' said Goldie.

'I'm sure she'll be useful,' said Ma.

In the back of Goldie's mind, Princess Frisia whispered, *In the midst of battle, a strong arm counts for more than a kind face.*

Still Goldie hesitated. 'Pa?'

She could see that her father loathed the slaver as much as she did. But he said, 'Lives are at stake here, and so is the future of Jewel. *If* your aunt will go with you and *if* she can be trusted—' he looked doubtful

246

'—then we must put our prejudices aside for a while at least. She is clearly a formidable woman.'

Double made a sarcastic little bow. 'Thank you, Harken Roth. I will return the compliment. Your death-defying leap into the ocean was one of the silliest things I have ever seen—'

Pa flushed bright red.

'—but it was also one of the bravest. Every expedition should have a brave fool in its company. Someone who will, if needed, sacrifice themselves in a blaze of idiotic glory.'

Now Goldie hated her more than ever. She turned her back on the slaver and said loudly to Toadspit, 'I'd like to take Pa. I don't want to take Double, but I think we must. Every expedition should have a slaver in its company. Someone who can, if needed, be used as cannon fodder.'

Double snorted with laughter. Ma linked her arm through Pa's on one side and Double's on the other, and said, 'You needn't think you're going without me. Because you're not.'

'I was about to say the same thing,' said Frow Hahn, and she and her husband would not be dissuaded, however much Toadspit argued with them.

As the ship's boat was lowered into the water under Double's instruction, Ma watched the slaver, and Pa watched Ma. Goldie tried not to watch any of them, but she couldn't tear her eyes away. Her mind kept slipping back to last night, on board the *Silver Lining*, when she had been captured and brought before Old Lady Skint's second-in-command.

And suddenly it struck her that Double *had known who she was*, almost from the beginning. The Slaver had recognised the blue bird brooch. She had stopped the two sailors from searching Goldie properly.

And this morning, when Old Lady Skint had refused to believe that there was indeed plague on her ship, it was Double who had tipped the balance.

As if she could read Goldie's thoughts, the slaver dipped her hand into her pocket and held out the brooch. 'Here,' she said, 'you can have this back.'

Goldie shook her head and walked away. She never wanted to touch that brooch again! It meant nothing to her. The fact that Double had helped them escape meant *nothing* to her. All Goldie cared about now was getting back to the museum in time to stop the bombardment.

She wiped an angry tear from her cheek. 'Bald Thoke,' she whispered. 'Please help us to get there in time. And help us to stop Frow Carrion. I don't care how we do it. Just show us the way. I'll do anything. *Anything*—'

BOMBARDMENT

It was late afternoon by the time the small group reached Jewel. They managed to slip into the city without being seen by either Blessed Guardians or mercenaries, which raised their spirits a little. But as they began to climb Old Arsenal Hill, Goldie heard the dreadful grinding roar of a gas tractor somewhere ahead of them, and felt the ground quake beneath her feet.

Frow Carrion

Frow Carrion was almost in position.

Up until that point, Goldie had believed that they would be able to stop the great gun. According to Double, a cannon could be disabled by driving an iron spike down the touch hole, and they had brought such a spike from the ship's carpentry store, and a hammer as well.

'It won't be easy for them, getting Frow Carrion up that hill,' Goldie had said as they left the *Silver Lining* behind and rowed towards the shore. 'There'll be mercenaries all over the place and lots of noise and confusion. If we Conceal ourselves, either Toadspit or I should be able to get close enough to do some damage.'

'Conceal yourselves? What are you talking about?' said Double, peering over her shoulder as she rowed.

Goldie pretended she hadn't heard. *We can do it,* she told herself. *We CAN do it!*

But by the time they reached Frow Carrion, the great gun had come to a halt in Swindler's Plaza, which was as close as the gas tractor could get to the museum. A dozen mercenaries were turfing people out of their homes and sending them weeping down the hill to find shelter wherever they could. Another dozen were winching the monstrous iron barrel towards its target. And in a wide circle around Frow Carrion's base, three score of armed, watchful men stood shoulder to shoulder, so close to each other that not even a thief from the Museum of Dunt could get past them.

The Fugleman had learned his lesson at last.

When she saw that impenetrable circle, Goldie's heart sank to her boots. Toadspit frowned, and she knew that he too was scanning for weak points and finding none.

'How do you stop a gun like that if you can't get near it?' she whispered.

Toadspit didn't answer. The smell of cold iron drifted past their hiding place at the edge of the plaza, and Goldie shivered. 'Do you think Herro Dan knows it's here?'

Toadspit nodded, his lower lip raw from chewing. 'The museum must be tearing itself apart by now. He'll know, all right. And he'll need us.'

The two children looked at each other. They were both battered and worn by the events of the last twenty-four hours. They wanted baths and hot food, and comfortable beds to crawl into. More than that, they wanted to run as far away from Frow Carrion as possible.

But they could not run. They were keepers of the Museum of Dunt, and they were needed.

They crept back to where the others were waiting. 'It's no use,' Toadspit said to the expectant faces. 'It's too well guarded.'

There was a murmur of dismay. 'So what do we do now?' asked Herro Hahn.

'Any sensible person would dive for cover,' muttered Double. 'A museum is only a museum after all.'

'Not this one!' snapped Goldie. She turned to the two sets of parents. 'Toadspit and I have to go and help the other keepers, but the rest of you—'

'Don't say it,' interrupted Frow Hahn. 'If *you're* going into the museum—' her voice wobbled, but her mind was clearly made up '—then so are we.'

'No!' said Toadspit.

'That's *all* of us,' said Herro Hahn, looking as stubborn as his wife. 'We've discussed it.'

'There might be something we can do,' said Ma.

Pa, Pounce, Mouse and Bonnie nodded agreement, even though fear whitened their faces and made their shadows tremble.

Double blew out an irritated breath. 'You're all mad! You're going to die in there, you realise?'

'You can leave if you want to,' said Pa stiffly.

'Never said I was leaving.' And Double followed the others towards the museum, only slowing to make sure that Ma wasn't left behind.

The Fugleman had not bothered to set a guard on the cul de sac. Toadspit led them down it at a run, with Goldie bringing up the rear. As she tore up the front steps of the museum, she heard the rumble of cannonballs being rolled across Swindler's Plaza towards Frow Carrion.

In front of her, Double skidded to a halt. 'What *is* this place?'

Goldie ran past her without answering. Unlike the slaver, the two sets of parents could not feel the violent *shifting*, but even they looked shocked. This was not the peaceful museum they remembered. A claw of black water was crawling across the entrance hall towards them. Spider webs half-filled the doorways, as thick as rope. The air was heavy with dust, and the dust was heavy with malice.

'Come *on*!' said Goldie, and she and Toadspit dragged their parents around the water, under the spider webs and through the front rooms as quickly as they could. Behind them, Pounce kept up a constant stream of complaint about the stupidity of anyone who thought they could beat the Foobleman. But he did not falter, and when the small group burst into the back rooms, he was there with them, helping Bonnie when she tripped and urging Mouse to run faster.

They found Morg, Broo and the older keepers gathered deep inside the museum, in the room called the Tench. The Protector was there too, propped up on a mattress, with a pile of solid wooden tables around her, and the cat at her side. She cried out when she saw them, and Olga Ciavolga, Herro Dan and Sinew swung around, their tired faces lit up with momentary relief. Then they went back to singing and playing the First Song.

Broo bounded over to the children, his eyes sparking like fireworks. He licked Goldie's face with his huge tongue, and did the same to Bonnie, Toadspit and Mouse. Then he stuck his nose inside Mouse's jacket and said anxiously, 'Are you still there, small people?'

The mice ran across the top of the brizzlehound's head, squeaking their hellos. Pounce groaned with amazement. Then he pulled himself together with a visible effort and said, 'Hey, old Black Ox. Remember me?'

Double turned to Ma and said, 'I thought I was beyond surprise. I was wrong. What *is* this place?'

'Pla-a-a-ace,' croaked Morg from the top of one of the cell doors.

Goldie had always hated the Tench. It stank of misery, and its cramped cells made her shiver. Now, with the museum in ferment around her, she thought she could hear the creak of a treadmill, and the clank of chains, and the sound of someone crying for mercy that would never come.

In the back of her mind, Princess Frisia berated her for leading her family and friends into such danger, with no plan and no way out.

Goldie grabbed Toadspit's hand. 'What are we going to *do*?'

'I don't know,' said Toadspit. 'We'll think of something.'

'You'll have to think quick,' said Double, coming up behind them. 'Or we'll all be mincemeat. How about you start by introducing me to your friends?' And she nodded at the Protector and at the older keepers.

It was clear from Herro Dan's expression that he was not pleased to have a slaver in the museum. But when Double questioned him about the walls, and how they would stand up to cannon fire, he said, 'They're strong enough to hold for a while, even against a great gun. There's five hundred years of wildness in this stone, and it won't fall easily.'

'The problem is,' said Sinew, his fingers plucking a tired note from the strings of his harp, 'it won't lie quiet either. It'll fight back. And that'll be worse than anything the Fugleman can throw at us. The plague rooms are already on the move.'

'*Plague* rooms?' said Double.

But before Sinew could explain, the bombardment began.

The roar of Frow Carrion as she launched her first cannonball almost lifted Goldie off her feet. Morg squawked and threw herself upwards. Ma screamed. As the long rolling explosion died away, Goldie heard a howling like the approach of a hurricane – and something crashed into the ancient stone walls.

The impact sucked all the air out of the museum, then blew it back, so that first Goldie had no breath and then she had too much. The museum shook with outrage. Dust cascaded from the high ceilings. In the front rooms, jars cracked open and the mummified snakes inside them fell to the floor and slithered away. Somewhere below Goldie's feet, the waters of Old Scratch rose as high as a tidal wave.

Choking with dust and shock, Goldie crawled to the wall and placed her hand flat against it. The wild music hit her, as hot as lava, and she cried out in pain. Her blood boiled. Her head swam. She dragged the notes of the First Song from her throat, and heard the strings of Sinew's harp nearby. Then Olga Ciavolga joined in, and Toadspit, and Herro Dan and Mouse, their voices no more than a whisper against the deep crash of the wild music.

Out of the corner of her eye, Goldie saw Double arguing with Ma. Pa and the others were frantically building the tables into a shelter. Broo stalked the length

of the Tench and back, growling out the notes of the
First Song.

Mouse sang louder, his high sweet voice sliding
like a note of grace through the chaos. The wild music
began to settle a little—

Frow Carrion launched her second cannonball.

When it hit, Broo bellowed with rage, and so did
the museum. Its bluestone walls stood firm, but inside
them, cabinets crashed to the floor and the rooms *shifted*
and *shifted* again. The wild music rode the keepers
like a nightmare.

The third cannonball hit the Museum of Dunt.

Goldie felt as if she was drowning. Her ears rang.
Her head ached. She could feel the wildness surging
around her like a pack of wolves howling outside a
broken window. Deep inside her, Princess Frisia howled
too, demanding to be let loose.

She had no idea how long they all crouched there,
singing desperately. It seemed like hours – it might have
been no more than minutes. In that time, mantraps
clattered down the stairs of Harry Mount like mortal
creatures. The wild music swelled like an incoming tide.
Death and destruction hurled themselves at the Dirty
Gate . . .

And then, as suddenly as it had begun, the
bombardment stopped.

There was a moment of ringing silence, then Pounce poked his head out from under the tables, banged his hand against his ear and said, "Ave they run outta cannonballs?'

Olga Ciavolga wiped the grit from her eyes. 'I fear they are only playing with us. They will start again soon.'

'Half a dozen more hits like that last one,' said Herro Dan, 'and we're done for.'

'Half a dozen more hits,' cried Double, 'and we'll all be as flat as a flounder! I say we get out now, while we can!' She turned to Ma, who still had her hands over her ears. 'Grace, you have to come!'

'No.' Ma shook her head, and for a moment she looked as fierce as her sister. 'I'm not leaving without my daughter!'

It took all Goldie's will to say, '*I* can't leave.' She felt bruised from head to toe, and so frightened that all she wanted to do was crawl into a hole somewhere. But the museum was on the brink of explosion, like a balloon that had been blown up beyond all commonsense. Half a dozen more hits and everything in it would burst out into the streets of Jewel. Without Mouse and his ability to tame the untameable, it would surely have done so already.

'For Bald Thoke's sake, *why* can't you leave?' Double's face was stark white beneath its tattoos. 'It's the only sensible thing to do!'

Just then, the museum *shifted*. 'That's why,' said Sinew, and his fingers struck his harp strings. Goldie and the other keepers began to sing again. Despite the pause in the bombardment, the wild music was growing stronger, so that even when it settled a little, Herro Dan and Olga Ciavolga kept their hands on the wall and sang under their breath.

Sinew lowered his harp. 'If we leave,' he said to Double, 'then everything is lost. The city and everyone in it. We can't let it happen. We have to stop it somehow.'

Double looked as if she was about to burst with anger and frustration. 'But you haven't even got a plan!'

'I have a plan,' growled Broo. 'I will KILL the Fugleman. I will GRRRRRIND his bones to SMITHERRRRREENS!'

'Well, that's a start,' said Double. 'We could—'

'He's surrounded by mercenaries,' interrupted Toadspit. 'Goldie and I could barely see the top of his head. No one can get to the gun, and no one can get to him. Not even you, Broo.'

'He's no fool,' muttered Herro Dan, with a bitter note in his voice.

'Hey,' said Pounce. 'Where's Mousie got to?'

Goldie looked around. The little boy had been right beside Herro Dan, but now he was gone.

'Mouse!' shouted Pounce with a note of panic in his voice. 'Where are ya? Mousie?'

He began to drag at one of the fallen cabinets, but Pa stopped him. 'He's not there. I saw him run out of the room a minute ago.'

'Where did 'e go?' demanded Pounce. He looked around wildly. 'Do any of yez know where 'e went?'

Broo snuffed the air. His black coat was covered in dust and his eyes glowed like fire. 'He is in the kitchen. I will bring him.' And he loped out of the room.

'You 'urry!' shouted Pounce after him. 'Don't you lose 'im!'

Goldie crawled over to the pile of tables, where Bonnie and the Protector were wiping the grit from their faces with trembling hands. 'Are you two all right?'

'It's like drowning in noise,' whispered Bonnie.

'It is indeed,' said the Protector, dragging herself up to a sitting position. 'Goldie, can you call the other keepers, please? Before the bombardment starts again?'

The keepers gathered around her in a silent circle. Sinew sat beside her and offered her his shoulder, and she leaned against him and said, 'The museum must not fall. We are all agreed on that, are we not?'

Everyone except Double nodded. The slaver folded her arms and snorted in frustration.

The Protector pushed her eyeglasses up her nose.

'And no one has any suggestions as to how we can stop the Fugleman? *Practical* suggestions?'

Silence. Goldie felt as if her brain had been forced through a sieve, until there was not a single idea left whole and sensible.

The Protector leaned more heavily against Sinew. 'As far as I can see,' she said, 'there is only one solution. We must bargain with him, and quickly.'

'But we can't get near him—' began Toadspit.

'We can't attack him, that's true,' said the Protector. 'But if we approach him under a white parley flag the mercenaries should let us through. We must offer him something of great value, but only if he agrees to leave the museum alone.'

'Bah,' said Olga Ciavolga. 'Do you think he would keep the agreement? Treachery is in his nature.'

A bead of sweat ran down the Protector's forehead, cutting through the dust. 'Of course. But it will buy us time. And that is what we need.'

Another *shift*. Goldie's voice was as crackly as old paper, but she sang, as did the other keepers, all of them thinking hard.

When they came back together at last, Herro Dan tapped the Protector's arm with a stubby finger. 'Nope, you ain't gunna do it. It wouldn't buy much time anyway.'

'What isn't she going to do?' whispered Bonnie, who had crept around to stand close to Goldie.

'She wants to give herself up,' whispered Goldie.

The Protector closed her eyes, then opened them again. 'I would certainly prefer *not* to hand myself over to my brother's tender care. He thinks I am dead and once he discovers I am not, he will do his best to rectify the matter. But I am the Protector, and that position is not misnamed. I have a duty to the city.'

Toadspit shook his head. 'Herro Dan's right. It wouldn't buy enough time to make a difference.' He had that focused expression on his face again, that made him look older than his years. 'We need something more . . .'

There was a rattle of claws in the doorway behind Goldie, and Pounce leaped to his feet. 'Did ya find 'im?' he demanded, as Broo bounded into the room. 'Where is 'e?'

'He is here,' rumbled Broo, and he stepped aside to reveal Mouse.

The little boy looked as if he had been burrowing through piles of lathe and plaster. His face was covered in dust and his white hair was matted, but he smiled shakily at Pounce, and dragged the baby's bath, still filled with scraps of paper, into the room behind him.

Goldie felt a flurry of hope. 'A fortune!' she said.

'That's what we need!' And she sprang to her feet and helped Mouse pull the bath under the shelter.

'A *fortune*?' said Double. 'I can think of a dozen things we need more than a fortune!'

Goldie ignored her. She ignored Ma and Pa, and Herro and Frow Hahn too, who were all looking as doubtful as the slaver. 'Go on,' she said to Mouse. 'Quick!'

The boy whistled, and his mice crept out from inside his jacket. But their white bodies trembled, and they clung to Mouse and would not go into the bath.

'Poor little sprats are scared silly,' said Pounce. 'Try again, Mousie.'

The boy whistled a second time, and crooned softly, but his pets were too frightened to leave the safety of his body.

Goldie thought of the way the mice and the cat had worked together on board the *Piglet*, when the children were trying to escape from Cord. 'Cat?' she said. 'Can you help?'

The cat, which had been lying silently beside the Protector all this time, raised its battered head. 'Moooooouses?' Then it dragged itself to its feet and limped to the bath.

Double muttered, 'It seems that children were not enough. Now I find myself allied with small furry animals.'

The cat was clearly in pain. But it blinked reassuringly at the mice, and purred so loudly that Goldie could feel the vibration in her chest. The mice squeaked. Their trembling eased a little. The cat waved a regal paw and said, 'Dooooown!'

The mice squeaked again. Then, in a flood of white fur and pink ears, they disappeared into the bath.

The scraps of paper rustled. The museum *shifted*. Goldie scrambled to the nearest wall and sang, all the while keeping her eyes on the bath and the white-haired boy.

As soon as she could, she dived back into the shelter. 'What does it say, Mouse?'

She scanned the bits of paper that lay on the floor, her spine prickling. 'It's the same as last time! Exactly the same! *Of gold. This journey will. Last chance to win. Beast.* And a picture of a road.'

Herro Dan closed his eyes. His brown face was racked with grief, and Goldie shivered, as if someone had walked across her grave. 'What does it mean, Herro Dan? Please tell me. Where am I going?'

But before the old man could answer there was an awful roar and Frow Carrion renewed her assault.

As the cannonballs pounded against the walls, the museum seemed to swell with rage. The air was already hot, but now it grew feverish, and as thick as porridge.

Whale bones splintered and cracked. Old military uniforms lashed out with tattered arms and legs, smashing the glass of their cabinets. In the room called Vermin, teeth chattered in anticipation.

Goldie could no longer hear Mouse or Toadspit or even her own voice. The wild music swept everything before it. The Lady's Mile rampaged from one side of the museum to the other. The ground in Old Mine Shafts split like a crevasse and the neighbouring room of Lost Children tumbled into it.

The Dirty Gate swung open.

'Sing!' roared Herro Dan, and the keepers sang their throats raw. But the Museum of Dunt had had enough, and now it was taking matters into its own hands. The wildness was fighting back.

Even as she sang so desperately, Goldie could feel the disaster that was upon them. Black water poured into the lower rooms, followed by the unnameable creature that lived in Old Scratch. Famine crept through Early Settlers. Somewhere a siege engine rumbled into action.

But that was only the beginning. To Goldie's horror, a column of soldiers in ancient costumes was marching out of the war rooms and through the Dirty Gate. And behind the soldiers, pouring out of the plague rooms in numberless hordes, came the rats.

'What is it?' Double cried in Goldie's ear. 'I felt something! What's happening?'

The slaver's voice jolted Goldie out of her shock. Beside her, Olga Ciavolga was shouting, 'Dan, tell Goldie about the Beast Road! It might yet reverse this! It is our only hope!'

The old man let out a dreadful groan. 'There's no time to get her there! This bombardment's drivin' things too fast!'

'He is RRRRIGHT!' snarled Broo. 'The end of EVERRRRYTHING is almost upon us!'

Another cannonball crashed overhead. As the reverberations died away, the Protector dragged herself out from under the tables. 'Is it time you need?'

'Yes!' cried Herro Dan. 'If we could just slow everythin' down a bit—'

'But while this bombardment lasts,' said Olga Ciavolga, 'we cannot!'

'Then I will give you time,' said the Protector in a grim voice. 'Herro Roth, help me out to my brother.'

'No, wait!' Toadspit raced across to Bonnie and muttered something in her ear. Then he ran out of the room.

'Where's he gone?' cried his mother. 'Bonnie? What's he *doing*?'

Bonnie crouched beneath the tables, mute with fright. A cannonball hit the museum, directly overhead. Chips of wood and stone plummeted down around Goldie, and she put her arms over her face and cowered as close to the wall as she could. She could feel death's relentless advance through the dusty corridors. She forced herself to keep singing, knowing that it was no use, and that the city and everyone in it was as good as lost.

There was one final crashing roar – and the bombardment stopped again.

The silence this time was so terrible that Goldie could hardly bear it. Her ears would not stop ringing. She felt the soldiers slow their headlong pace, and the rats with them, as if the force that drove them had lessened.

'Bonnie!' she shouted. She didn't think she would hear herself otherwise. 'Where's Toadspit gone?'

The pile of tables in the middle of the room trembled. Herro Hahn emerged, then Bonnie. She was crying, the tears cutting deep runnels in the plaster that covered her skin.

'He said—' she began, then grief overtook her.

Her father wrapped his arms around her. 'It's going to be all right, sweeting,' he said.

'No, it's not!' Bonnie threw off his arms and marched over to Goldie. 'I don't know—' She stopped and took a snuffly breath. 'I don't know what the Beast Road is, or how you're going to walk it. But you'd better hurry. Because Toadspit's gone to buy you some time.'

'How?' said Goldie, although she was afraid that she already knew.

'He's— He's going out under a parley flag. He's going to challenge the Fugleman to a duel!' More tears flooded Bonnie's eyes, and this time she did not try to stop them. 'A duel at sunset. A duel to the death!'

NATIVE AND STRANGER

Toadspit

From the moment Frow Carrion had ground to a halt in Swindler's Plaza, the Fugleman had been expecting tricks from his enemies. He had warned Brace to be on the alert, and had surrounded himself with armed men. If anything nasty came out of the museum, it would be shot down before it advanced more than a few paces.

What he *wasn't* expecting was to see a boy clamber out of the smoke and rubble, waving a white flag and carrying a sword.

To the Fugleman's dismay, the roar of Frow Carrion stopped immediately. He rubbed his ears, which felt as if they were filled with sand, and shouted at the field marshal. 'What's the matter? *I said, what's the matter?* You assured me you would keep firing until the place was flattened!'

Brace pointed to the boy, who was picking his way carefully towards the troops. 'Parley flag.'

'Nonsense,' said the Fugleman, shading his eyes. 'It's just an old tablecloth.'

'Doesn't matter,' said Brace. 'It's white and that's what counts. Rules of war. Both sides of a conflict must respect the parley flag.' He shrugged. 'Besides, they might want to surrender.'

The Fugleman stared at him in astonishment. 'But I don't want them to surrender! I want them destroyed. Shoot the brat before he gets any closer!'

Now it was the field marshal's turn to stare. 'Are you mad? It's a *parley flag*!' He spoke loudly and clearly, as if the Fugleman was an idiot. 'Which means *he* can't shoot us and *we* can't shoot him. Rules. Of. War!'

The Fugleman was not the least bit interested in the rules of war, and said so, vehemently. Then he put his hand on his sword and repeated his order to shoot.

'I will not!' said the field marshal, puffing up his cheeks in outrage.

'Remember who's paying you!'

'What I remember,' snapped Brace, 'is how hard it was to *get* that payment!' And with a great wagging of his moustache he turned away from the Fugleman and cried, 'Let the boy through! We'll see what he has to say.'

The brat was so covered in plaster dust that he looked like a walking statue. Only his eyes showed clearly, white around the rim as if it took all the courage he possessed to walk so steadily towards Frow Carrion, knowing that with each step he might be blown to pieces.

The Fugleman didn't recognise him until the very last minute. And even then it was only due to the squawk of horror from Guardian Hope. 'It's Toadspit Hahn! But he's got *pla*—'

'Be *quiet*!' roared the Fugleman, cutting her off in mid-wail. His temper was rising; why did he always have to be surrounded by fools? First Brace with his ridiculous 'rules of war'. Now Guardian Hope, who had no more sense than to cry *plague* at a time like this!

He glared at the approaching figure, wondering how the brat had escaped from the *Silver Lining*. Was he infected? The Fugleman was tempted to run the boy through with his sword and burn the body, just in case.

Brace would protest, of course, and bleat about the parley flag, but if it was done quickly enough . . .

The boy, however, stopped a dozen paces away and raised the white flag above his head. 'I bring—' His voice slipped and wobbled, and he started again. 'I bring a challenge!'

The Fugleman could not help himself. His mouth fell open and he laughed out loud at the absurdity of it. Some of the mercenaries began to chortle too, but they soon fell silent. There was something about the way the boy stood; the look in his eyes; his air of deadly seriousness.

Guardian Hope tugged at the Fugleman's elbow, her face contorted with fright. 'Your Honour!' she whispered. 'That boy! He has pl—'

The Fugleman's glare made her swallow the offending word. But she would not be silenced, not entirely. '*You know what is wrong with him!*' she hissed. 'Kill him! Now! Save your people from a terrible death!'

The Fugleman would have liked nothing better than to kill the boy, but Field Marshal Brace was in his way. And besides, the whole plague ship episode was beginning to stink like week-old fish. It had been too convenient. Too . . . *clever*.

'In fact,' he muttered, 'it reeks of the ridiculous tricks practised by the Hidden Rock.'

'Tricks, Your Honour?' said Hope, still flapping around him.

'The ship, you fool! And this little charade too, probably.' The Fugleman shoved Hope out of the way and raised his voice. 'It's nothing but a trick, Brace, and we should treat it as such! Shoot him. Get rid of him. The museum is playing games with us.'

The field marshal ignored him. 'What is this challenge, boy?' he asked.

Smudge, who had found a place of sorts in the mercenary ranks, nudged his companions and said loudly, 'That's Toadspit he's talking to. I know Toadspit.'

The brat took a visible breath. 'I— I challenge the Fugleman to a duel!'

'*What?*' said the Fugleman. 'Are you deranged, Toadspit Hahn? Has the bombardment knocked a hole in your stupid skull? You want to fight *me*?'

'A— A duel at sunset.' The brat's voice wobbled, then grew stronger. 'To the death!'

'Pah!' said the Fugleman, turning away. 'I would not waste my time!'

Field Marshal Brace glared at him in disapproval. 'Can't turn down a challenge, not when it's issued under a parley flag. Rules of war.'

The Fugleman found himself sputtering. 'He's a mere boy! I'm not going to fight a *boy*!'

There were hostile murmurs from the men around him. 'A challenge is a challenge,' said Brace, smiling through his teeth.

'But it's a delaying tactic, can't you see that? There are dangerous things inside that museum and you are giving the keepers time to rally them. You're supposed to be a soldier, Brace. I suggest you act like one. Resume the bombardment!'

But the more the Fugleman protested, the more the field marshal dug in his heels. He placed a guard on the boy, in case it *was* nothing but a trick, and set a number of his men to watch the museum. The rest of the mercenaries began to clear a suitable space for the duel and to build a ring of fires around it.

The Fugleman ground his teeth until they hurt. 'Guardian Hope,' he said, in deceptively mild tones. 'It seems that, if we wish to keep our allies, I have no choice but to take part in this ridiculous game.' He lowered his voice so that only Hope and the brat could hear him. 'But I will do it on my own terms. Do you still have your little pistol?'

'Yes, Your Honour!'

'Good,' murmured the Fugleman. 'Keep an eye out for anyone trying to escape from the museum. The mercenaries will not fire on children. But if you see the boy's sister, you have my permission to shoot her.'

The boy grew white under the plaster dust, but said nothing.

Hope smiled. 'With pleasure, Your Honour.'

The Fugleman turned back to Brace. 'Very well, Field Marshal, I accept the challenge. I will fight this boy in a duel to the death. And when I have beaten him – when I have *killed* him – then we will destroy the Museum of Dunt!'

The thought of Toadspit in the hands of the Fugleman was so dreadful that Goldie could hardly breathe. For a moment it eclipsed everything else. She looked at the faces around her and saw her own horror reflected in them.

But then Olga Ciavolga drew herself up, like an old warrior who knows that nothing must distract her from her purpose. 'It is not yet sunset,' she said, 'and Toadspit is no fool. He will be able to hold the Fugleman off for a while—'

'But then the Fugleman will kill him!' wailed Bonnie.

Frow Hahn sobbed, and Herro Hahn muttered, 'I'll go and get him. I'll bring him back.'

'No, *I'll* go,' said the Protector. 'We can't let him sacrifice himself like this.'

'Be quiet, all of you!' commanded Olga Ciavolga. Her eyes flashed. 'The Dirty Gate is open and war and plague are stalking these corridors, searching for the front door that will release them into the city. Thanks to Toadspit's challenge, they are moving far more slowly, but they *are* moving. Our only hope now is if Goldie can walk the Beast Road.'

'But what *is* the Beast Road?' cried Ma. 'Is it dangerous?'

'Will it stop these soldiers you're talking about?' said Pa. 'Will it stop the rats?'

'What about the Fugleman?' said Double. 'And Frow Carrion. Will it stop them?'

'Will it save Toadspit?' whispered Frow Hahn.

Herro Dan stepped forward, his face solemn. 'We don't know for sure what it'll do. Maybe all of that. Maybe none. But we gotta give it a try.'

A babble of questions rose around Goldie. Her own mind was blank, as she tried to ready herself for whatever was coming. She heard Double's voice rise above the rest.

'All right, say Goldie *does* walk this Beast Road. What do the rest of us do in the meantime? Sit here and make polite conversation? Can't we slow these rats and soldiers down a bit more? I'll have a go if no one else will.'

'Me too!' said Bonnie.

'Good,' said Olga Ciavolga. 'Where is your bow, child?'

Herro Hahn's face grew paler than ever. 'Surely you're not involving the younger children in this! Isn't it enough that my son—'

'The children are involved whether we want them to be or not,' interrupted Olga Ciavolga. 'Have you ever seen a city stricken by plague, Herro, or torn apart by a marauding army?'

'N-no, but—'

'I have. And I tell you, we must all do *whatever we can* to stop it from happening here. Do you understand me?'

Herro Hahn swallowed – and nodded. Olga Ciavolga turned back to Bonnie and raised an eyebrow. 'Your bow?'

'In the office.'

'Please fetch it, Sinew,' said the old woman. 'Bring a bow for me also, and a tinderbox, and cloth for wrapping around arrow heads. Pistols too, if you can find them.' To Bonnie she said, 'We will shoot flaming arrows in front of the rats, yes? We cannot turn them back with such feeble weapons – there are too many of them. But Double is right; perhaps we can slow them down a little more.' She turned to Mouse and Pounce. 'Are you two with us? Good. You have your own skills. Do what you can.'

Goldie was listening to the museum. Deep in the back rooms, the floors shook under the weight of a thousand booted feet. Rats swarmed, slick and dirty, down staircases and under floorboards. The museum raged, and Broo raged with it, his whole body trembling with the desire to fight.

'Sinew, go quickly,' said Olga Ciavolga. 'We do not have much time. Dan, tell Goldie about the Beast Road.'

Herro Dan nodded, slow and sad. Then, in a voice that came from the mists of his childhood, he began to chant.

'Who can walk the Beast Road?
There must be three.
Two mortal enemies,
with one between them
who is both friend and enemy,
native and stranger.'

That's me, thought Goldie with a shock of recognition. *Me and Princess Frisia! Native and stranger!*

'Where does the Beast Road go?' chanted Herro Dan.

'To a timeless place
from which no one
has ever returned.'

'What?' said Pa, looking horrified. *'No one?'*

'And you're going to send *our daughter?*' squeaked Ma.

278

'*What does the Beast Road hold?*' continued Herro Dan.

'Terror for those who hurry.
Death for those who linger.
But for Furuuna
it holds salvation.'

He stopped and blinked. Goldie cleared her throat. She felt as if she was being dragged towards something so big and frightening that she could hardly bear to think about it.

Terror.

Death.

. . . And salvation.

'F-Furuuna?' she said in a shaky voice. 'There *is* no Furuuna, not any longer. Is there?'

'If the ancient land of my people still exists anywhere,' said Herro Dan, 'it's here in the Museum of Dunt.'

'But what's the salvation?'

'Don't know, lass. The old folk always said it was somethin' you had to find and bring back, but no one knew for sure.'

Goldie's whole body ached, and all she wanted to do was fall into bed and sleep for days on end. But she swallowed the gritty lump in her throat and said, 'Two mortal enemies. That's Broo and the cat.'

The brizzlehound pricked up his ears. '*I* am going? Good. If there is terror I will BITE it!'

'Hoooouuund,' muttered the cat in disgusted tones, but at the same time it staggered to its feet and came to stand beside Goldie. Somewhere in the distance, kettle drums began to beat.

'And one who is both native and stranger. That's me—' Goldie hesitated, but this was no time for secrets. She must tell them. 'With the voice of Princess Frisia inside me.'

'What?' said Double.

'*Really?*' said Bonnie, briefly distracted from her worry about Toadspit. 'You lucky thing!'

But Herro Dan and Olga Ciavolga glanced at each other, and Olga Ciavolga murmured, 'We suspected as much. Does that mean you have the wolf-sark as well?'

Goldie nodded, and for a moment everyone except the two old keepers seemed to fade into the background. 'You— You don't think I'm mad, do you?' she whispered.

'You?' said Herro Dan. 'I never met a saner person. Seems you're strong enough even for this.' He hugged her. 'But what a burden you've been carryin', lass.'

Goldie buried her face in the old man's shoulder, speechless. They *did* understand after all. She should have told them long ago. She should have trusted them.

'You are afraid of the wolf-sark, are you not?' said Olga Ciavolga softly.

'Yes!' Goldie raised her head. 'I nearly killed Mouse when we came out of the Big Lie. And I nearly killed Favour too!' That was just yesterday, she realised with a shock. It felt like weeks ago.

'But you did *not* kill them, child. Remember that, when the wolf-sark next takes hold of you. Remember that *you* are still there, deep inside.' The old woman gripped Goldie's arm with a steady hand. 'Even Frisia did not find the wolf-sark an easy thing to live with. But it is a weapon, nothing more, and like all weapons it is up to you how you use it. Remember, there is always a choice.'

Warmth and strength flooded through Goldie. *They trust me,* she thought. *They believe in me.*

She stepped out of Herro Dan's embrace and the world swam back into focus. Somewhere not too far away a bugle sounded, and thousands of hairless tails dragged – *hisss hisss* – through dusty corridors. The air in the Tench sizzled at the thought of what was coming.

'Where do I start, Herro Dan?' said Goldie. 'Where do I find the Beast Road?'

The old man's reply was cut off by Sinew, who came trotting through the door carrying two bows with their quivers, and several pistols. 'Nearly didn't make it,' he said cheerfully. 'The roof of the office fell in just as I was leaving. Here, Bonnie, your bow is unharmed, which is more than can be said for my nerves.'

He winked at Goldie. 'Got the Beast Road sorted out? I thought you might have. What can I do to help?'

'Not you,' said Goldie. 'Ma and Pa.' And she gave her parents and the Protector brief instructions.

'We trust you will come back to us, sweeting,' said Pa, sombrely brushing the hair out of her eyes.

Ma bit her lip. 'We're proud of you. You know that, don't you?'

Goldie nodded, unable to speak.

'We're cutting it fine,' said Sinew, handing one pistol to Double, and offering the others to Bonnie's parents. Herro and Frow Hahn took them gingerly, their faces a picture of confusion, fear and determination.

'Yes,' said Olga Ciavolga. 'We had better go. Dan will follow as soon as he can.' As she spoke, she slung her bow over her shoulder, took out her kerchief and began to untie all but the biggest knots.

Immediately, a dozen winds blustered through the Tench, raising a storm of plaster dust and rattling the cell doors as they passed. Above the noise, Goldie could hear Sinew's voice as he hurried out of the room.

'Looks like it's just us few brave folk, eh, Bonnie? Plus Olga Ciavolga's breezes, which should never be underestimated. Still, it's a challenge, isn't it, Mouse? Let's hope my playing is bad enough to stop an army!' He struck a cheerful note on his harp. 'Come on, Pounce, Morg. Come on, Frow Hahn, Herro Hahn, keep up or we'll never see you again! Come on, Double . . .'

Morg flew after him with a screech, and the Hahns ran to join Olga Ciavolga. But Double did not move. Instead, she took the blue bird brooch from her pocket and pressed it into Goldie's hand. 'You might not want an aunt who has been a slaver,' she said quickly. 'Yes, I've seen the way you look at me, and I deserve every bit of it. I've done things that'll haunt me for the rest of my life. But I'm not going to see my niece lost, with no one to save her. If you don't return from wherever you're going, why then, I'll come after you!'

With those words, she drew Goldie into a fierce embrace. Goldie found herself hugging her aunt in return, and gaining unexpected comfort from those strong arms. Then the slaver too was gone.

'Quickly now,' said Herro Dan. 'You'll have to carry the cat. She's very weak still.'

Broo growled. '*I* would not let myself be carried like a milk-fed pup! Can we not leave the creature behind?'

'Hush, Broo,' said Goldie. 'I need both of you.'

Then she scooped the cat up in her arms, turned to Herro Dan and said, 'I'm ready.'

A TIMELESS PLACE . . .

The Beast Road began in the very heart of the museum, deep inside the hill called Devil's Kitchen. Goldie stood on its threshold with the cat in her arms and Broo breathing down her neck. Her lantern created a small circle of light, but everything else was darkness. The air in the tunnel was dry, and the rock walls were sharp with crystals.

She had been here before. Or at least, she had passed the entrance to this tunnel without knowing what it was. Somewhere

Broo

below her was the Place of Remembering, with its ancient bones and whispering skulls.

Herro Dan stepped forward, his own lantern swaying as he dug in his pocket. 'We don't know where you're goin', lass, or what you'll find when you get there. So take these. Just in case.'

He dropped a pile of silver coins into Goldie's hand. Then he patted her shoulder. 'Go on, now. It's nearly sunset. There's no time to waste.'

Goldie's arms tightened around the cat. 'Broo?' she said.

The brizzlehound's breath was hot on her cheek. 'I will lead the way,' he growled. 'Stay close.' And he strode into the tunnel.

It was not until Goldie followed him that she realised the true weight of darkness. It pressed upon her from every side, filling her ears and nostrils. The light of her lantern shrank almost to nothing.

She crouched down with the cat on her knees and tried to turn the wick of the lantern up. But instead of growing, the flame shrank further and further, until at last it flickered and died.

There was no sign of Herro Dan's lantern. It should have been only a few paces behind her, but the old keeper had disappeared so completely that he might never have existed.

'Broo?' said Goldie, in sudden fright. 'Are you there?'

'I am here,' rumbled the brizzlehound, his wet nose nudging her forehead.

'Something's wrong with the lantern,' she said, and she dropped the coins into her pocket and fumbled for the tinderbox.

'We must not linger,' said Broo.

'I know. But I can't see.' She tried to re-kindle the wick, but now there was something wrong with the tinderbox as well, and it would not give her so much as a spark.

'Maybe we should go back and get another lantern,' she said. 'For safety. We don't know what might be ahead of us.'

'Death comes to those who linger.'

'But I can't *see!*' Goldie's breath was sharp and shallow in her throat. The darkness was crawling into her head now, and she found it almost impossible to think.

She clutched the warm body of the cat. 'Cat? Can *you* see?'

'Of course not,' said Broo scornfully. '*I* will go first. My nose is better than any lantern.'

The cat stiffened in Goldie's arms. 'Doooown,' it demanded.

'No, you can't walk,' said Goldie.

'Cccccan!' spat the cat, and it tumbled out of her arms onto the hard ground. 'Firssssst!' it said, and Goldie heard a scuffle as it tried to limp past Broo.

The brizzlehound's growl came from the very depths of his soul. '*I* am first! Get out of my way, useless cat, or I will KILL you!'

'No!' said Goldie, and she wrapped her arms around Broo's neck. She could feel the tension vibrating through his body, and she knew that, although they squabbled like small children, the hatred between the two creatures was real. Her journey was on the brink of failing before it ever began.

'Listen to me,' she said quickly. She felt a little calmer now that there was something to do. 'We don't know where the danger will come from, so I want Broo to walk behind me and protect our rear.'

The brizzlehound began to protest, but she drew him closer and whispered in his ear, 'The cat is very weak. I need it in front of me in case it falls over. And I need your strength at my back.'

Aloud, she said, 'Cat, are you sure you can walk? We can't afford to go too slowly.'

She felt the cat rub against her knee. 'Firrrrst,' it purred. It twitched its tail. 'Hoooold.'

They set off again in darkness so thick that Goldie wondered if she had gone blind. She shuffled along with Broo at her shoulder and the cat's tail between her fingers – a tail that dipped and jerked as its owner's poor battered body fought to stay upright. But Olga Ciavolga was right, the descendants of idlecats were tough, and the trio made good time through that first part of the tunnel.

Herro Dan's words echoed inside Goldie's head. *Terror for those who hurry. Death for those who linger.* Were they going too fast? she wondered. Or not fast enough? She had no idea. All she could do was press on in total darkness and try not to think about what might be happening to her friends.

It was easy to lose track of time. But Goldie thought they had been travelling for no more than a few minutes when she heard Broo rumble at her shoulder. 'I can see—'

And then, as suddenly and completely as if a wall had fallen in front of him, his voice was cut off. At the same time, the cat's tail vanished from between Goldie's fingers.

Something told Goldie that she must not make a sound, so she stifled the gasp that came to her throat and did not call out to either animal. Instead she stopped and fumbled all around, searching for their warm, reassuring bodies.

She could not find them.

She ran her hand over the wall of the tunnel, trying not to panic. A moment ago it had been as dry as old bone. Now it was wet, and she could hear water dripping close by. She could hear her own breath too, and somewhere inside her a knot of terror was growing bigger by the second. What had happened? Where was she? Where were her companions? Should she keep going or turn back and look for them?

She thought of the other keepers, trying to slow the approach of death and destruction. And Toadspit who, if he was still alive, would be getting ready to fight the Fugleman. And she knew that she must keep going, no matter what. She slid one shaky foot forward – and felt a hard edge, as if the path ended right there in front of her.

No. No, it didn't end, she realised. It just became very narrow. A ledge, nothing more. Goldie shuffled forward, pressing herself against the wall. Wherever she was, it was cold. Water dripped from above and trickled down her neck. She had the sense that there was a great wide space on her left, like a cavern with a low ceiling.

The distant splash, when it came, froze her in her tracks. It sounded big. But even worse, it sounded horribly familiar. A moment later, just as she had feared, water rose and lapped hungrily at her feet.

She was in Old Scratch.

She had no idea how she had got there, but it was the last place she wanted to be. Her breath grew sharper. She took a too-hasty step forward, and her foot slipped. She heard the splash again, closer now, and knew that the creature that lived beneath the water could smell her fear.

And was hunting her.

She had never been so afraid. Terror gripped her, and for a dozen heartbeats she could not think or move. The darkness lay like a blanket over her face.

But then she remembered Toadspit and all the other people who were relying on her. And she knew that she *must not fail.*

She took her terror in both hands, like a spiky, shivering, ugly ball that she could hardly bear to hold. She greeted it politely, the way Herro Dan had taught her so long ago. Then she did what she had to do, in spite of it.

She ran.

She ran along the ledge in the pitch dark, with her feet quick and clever on the slimy bricks, and the wall to guide her. She ran with the dreadful splashing sound growing closer and closer and the water leaping up in front of her and grasping at her ankles and knees. She ran until her desperate fingers found a wooden door set into the wall. She pushed it open and fell through it, slamming it shut behind her and tumbling to the ground with her eyes closed.

When she opened her eyes again, there were two men standing over her.

She couldn't see them properly at first. The light was too bright and her eyes rebelled against it. She blinked and jammed them shut and blinked again. She put her hand on the ground to steady herself and felt grass between her fingers.

'Is a leedle gel,' said one of the men in an unmistakable accent – and the terror struck Goldie all over again.

She was on the wrong side of the Dirty Gate. In the war rooms.

It's not real, she thought frantically. *The Dirty Gate is open, so these men probably aren't even here any more. The Beast Road is just trying to frighten me. It's not real! It's a sort of dream!*

One of the men grabbed her by the wrist and hauled her to her feet. Goldie blinked up at him. He wore a grey coat and knee breeches and had only one arm.

His companion had a terrible scar that arced across his face, ending in an empty eye socket. His single blue eye glared at Goldie as if his wounds were her fault. 'Is de *same* leedle gel,' he growled.

With a gasp, Goldie realised that these were the two men who had captured her and Toadspit months ago, when they went through the Dirty Gate searching for Herro Dan. The children had come close to death on that occasion. Only Goldie's cleverness, and the ferocity of Broo and Morg, had saved them.

Goldie could see now what that ferocity had done.

Her knees were as soft as jelly. *It's not real!* she told herself again.

But the soldier's grip on her wrist was real enough, and so was the bayonet that his friend was fixing purposefully to the barrel of his musket. The rank smell of the army camp drifted past, and Goldie knew that it was not a dream at all, but one of the museum's mysteries, and that if she died here she would really die. There would be no one to find salvation. No one to stop the Fugleman killing Toadspit. No one to save the museum and Jewel.

In desperation she slipped her free hand into her pocket. She had nothing that would save her, only the silver coins, and there were not nearly enough of them to buy her life, not from these men. But perhaps there were enough to distract the two soldiers for a while . . .

She flexed her fingers. Then, with her heart in her mouth, she reached past the one-armed man and plucked a silver coin out of the air. 'Thank you, Herro,' she said.

The soldiers gaped at her, and at the coin. Goldie put the silver piece in her pocket.

'Oh, there's more?' she said, hoping that her voice wasn't trembling as much as she thought it was. And she reached out a second time and plucked another piece of silver out of nowhere.

She put that one in her pocket too. Or at least she appeared to. Really she palmed it, and when she reached out a third time, it was the same coin that snapped into her fingers, looking for all the world as if someone who could not be seen had given it to her.

But then she held up her hand. 'No more,' she said. 'It's a waste of your good money.' She pointed to the bayonet. 'I won't be able to use it, you see. But thank you anyway.'

And she dropped the coin into her pocket and closed her eyes as if she was ready to die.

'Who yoo talkink to?' The voice was so close to her ear that she could feel the soldier's breath on her cheek.

'That man there,' she said, and without opening her eyes she pointed. 'With the big leather purse.'

'Is no one dere,' said the soldier.

Goldie shrugged. 'If you say so.'

Silence. It was almost more than she could bear to keep her eyes shut.

The soldier grabbed her again. 'Where dat money come from?' he growled.

With an expression of great puzzlement on her face, Goldie opened her eyes. 'He's right there. Beside you.'

Both men stared at the spot she was pointing to.

'Can't you see him? Maybe he's a ghost,' said Goldie. She took one of the coins from her pocket and held it up so that the sunlight caught the silver. 'Though his money seems real.'

The one-eyed soldier snatched the coin out of her hand, and bit the edge of it. Greed warred with superstition on his ravaged face. He turned to the spot where no one stood and held out his own hand. 'Yoo gif me money,' he said.

Nothing happened.

Goldie slid her fingers into her pocket and palmed another coin. There were nine, now that the soldier had taken one. She could see the faint shimmer of the Dirty Gate fifty paces to her left. In the world that she had left behind it stood wide open, but here it was closed. Would nine coins be enough to get her there?

'I could ask for more money,' she said. 'But only if you promise not to kill me.'

The men leered at her. 'We promise, leedle gel,' said the one with the bayonet. 'Yoo get us lots of money and yoo go free.' And he laughed a hungry laugh and winked at his friend.

Goldie nodded as if she believed him. Then she reached out and plucked the coin from the air. She gave that one to the one-eyed man, and the next to his friend.

Seven coins remained.

Goldie let her eyes drift to the left. 'Where are you going, Herro?'

'He is goink?' said the one-eyed man. 'Tell him to stay!'

'He won't stay,' said Goldie, 'but we could go with him.' And without waiting for permission, she began to walk away from the soldiers. She heard them growling behind her, and the skin on her back tightened. Quickly she made another coin appear, and handed it over.

Six remained.

Goldie led the men through the grass as quickly as she dared. It cost her two more coins. But by then she was standing right next to the Dirty Gate, and safety was only a breath away.

The Dirty Gate was not solid; its iron strips were welded into a giant honeycomb, and it shimmered so quietly in the long grass that it was barely visible, unless you knew where to look. Goldie had once seen Broo wriggle through one of those honeycomb holes. The soldiers could not escape that way, not when the Gate was closed, and neither could the rats from the plague rooms. But Goldie was Fifth Keeper . . .

The two men were watching her closely. She braced herself. She would only get one chance at this.

With her heart in her mouth, she raised her hand and pointed. 'Oh no,' she cried. 'He's going, and he's— *Look!*'

The soldiers could not help themselves. Their heads swivelled in the direction she was pointing. Goldie grabbed the last four coins from her pocket and threw them high in the air. They fell into the grass some distance away, as if the ghost had tossed out a parting gift. The soldiers leaped after them, elbowing each other aside in their greed.

Goldie dived through one of the holes in the Dirty Gate.

It was a tight squeeze, and she had no idea what she would find on the other side. It was clear by now that the Beast Road was testing her, and she thought she was ready for anything.

But then she saw the high glass dome over her head, and she knew that she was in the Great Hall of Jewel, a building that no longer existed. Guardian Hope was there too, with crowds of parents and children, and gazetteers scribbling in their notebooks. The Fugleman, his face streaked with ash and blood, stood at the front of the stage, making an announcement.

Goldie looked down at the white silk ribbon on her wrist – the ribbon that tied her to Ma. And just before her memories of the museum and everything about it vanished, and the past closed over her as cold and deep as the waters of Old Scratch, she realised that the Beast Road had taken her all the way back to Separation Day . . .

. . . and it was to be cancelled! The day she had been waiting for all her life! It wasn't possible! It couldn't be cancelled! It *couldn't*!

But Ma was already urging her towards the whitesmith, to have the silver cuff fastened around her wrist once more, and the silver guardchain attached to it. Pa was patting her shoulder and whispering, 'It's too dangerous, dearling. Perhaps the Protector will try again next year.'

'Or the year after,' said Ma, trying to cuddle Goldie and push her closer to the whitesmith at the same time.

'No, I can't wait that long!' said Goldie. The words seemed to burst out of her. 'I have to Separate today!'

Her voice rang across the Great Hall. Guardian Hope turned around, her plump face creased with sympathy. 'Poor child, you were looking forward to your freedom, weren't you?'

For some reason, Goldie had not expected Guardian Hope to react like that. It made her forget what she had been about to say.

The Guardian heaved herself up onto the stage. 'You'll see,' she said, 'the time will pass quickly.'

At that, Goldie's voice came back to her. 'But they promised we could Separate today!'

'Hush, sweeting,' said Ma. 'Don't excite yourself.'

'It's the shock.' Guardian Hope put her hand on Goldie's forehead. 'She's a little upset, that's all. She'll feel better soon.'

Goldie brushed the Guardian's hand away. 'I won't feel better! They *promised*!'

'My poor dear child,' said Guardian Hope, in the kindest of tones. 'I know how hard it is to be unselfish at times like this.'

And Goldie could see from the look in her eyes that she *did* know, that *she* had had disappointments too, as dreadful as this one, and that she had borne them bravely.

The Guardian lowered her voice to a whisper. 'But if you make a fuss you will hurt your parents. You will hurt me too. Most dreadfully.'

With those words, a splinter of shame lodged in Goldie's heart. She loved Guardian Hope almost as much as she loved Ma and Pa, and the idea of hurting her—

No! Wait! There was something wrong with that thought. It grated on Goldie like a discord from a badly

299

tuned harp and, for a moment, darkness seemed to close in on her, pitch-black darkness, and the sensation of fur between her fingers.

But then it was gone, and Guardian Hope's kind voice was wrapping around her like cotton wool. 'Dear child. Dear, *dear* child. Everyone here loves you, you know. You mustn't disappoint them. Be patient and it will all turn out for the best.'

Tears sprang to Goldie's eyes, and she shoved her hand into her pocket. She did *so* want to be free!

But maybe Guardian Hope's right, she thought reluctantly. *Maybe I'm being selfish and ungrateful and making things hard for everyone else.*

Something pricked her finger, and she winced. It was the pin of her brooch, the little blue bird with the outstretched wings. She wrapped her hand around it, and the discord grated on her ears again. Only this time it seemed to trail a word behind it.

Kindness.

A window creaked open in Goldie's mind, and she knew that someone had said something to her once, about kindness. Something important. What was it?

Ma kissed her cheek, and pushed her closer to the whitesmith. 'Not long now, sweeting. Look, we're third in line.'

'You'll be glad to get home, I expect,' said Guardian Hope, still smiling. 'After such a disappointing day.'

What was it? thought Goldie. She could hear the *clink clink* of the whitesmith's hammer as he refastened Jube's cuff around his wrist, and attached the silver guardchain. Now there was just Favour in front of her.

She squeezed the brooch, and still the memory would not come. But the blue bird's wings seemed to flutter in her hand, as if they were making a desperate bid for freedom.

A sense of dread took hold of Goldie. There was something at stake here that she didn't understand.

What WAS it?

'There now,' said Ma. 'Favour's almost done. That was quick, wasn't it? Be ready, sweeting. You're next.'

Goldie gripped the brooch in bloodless fingers. The sense of dread was growing, and there was no time left. She took a deep breath and jammed the pin into the end of her thumb.

Somewhere in her past – or perhaps it was her future – a voice said, 'Remember what happened to Praise Koch and hold to your true self, no matter how sweetly those around you talk.'

Goldie's eyes widened. The shame was still there, as sharp as grief inside her. But the voice was sharper. 'Hold to your true self!'

I don't want to wear the guardchain again, thought Goldie, and suddenly she knew that *that* was the truest thing about her. *I WON'T wear the guardchain again!*

As if in response, she felt the brooch grow hot. The pin lengthened and twisted. The blue wings transformed into scissor blades.

Goldie leaned against Pa's broad chest and whispered words of love. She kissed Ma's cheek. With a mixture of terror and joy, she slid the scissors out of her pocket and cut through the white silk ribbon with a single snip.

Then, before anyone could stop her, she ran off the stage and out the back door of the Great Hall . . .

. . . and found herself in total darkness, with the cat's tail between her fingers, and Broo leaning over her shoulder, just finishing the sentence he had begun half a lifetime ago.

'—a light ahead of us.'

THE BEAST ROAD

As the sun slid below the western horizon, the Fugleman threw off his cloak and rolled up his shirtsleeves. His temper had cooled and he was almost looking forward to this absurd challenge. After all, his sister was dead, the city was cowed, and soon the last remnants of the Hidden Rock would be crushed to rubble.

He swung his arms in a circle and stared at the boy in front of him.

The Cat

'So,' he said, in a mocking voice. 'This is my mighty adversary.'

The boy did not react. He merely stood with his sword loose in his hand.

The Fugleman slid his own blade from its scabbard, and tested its balance, as if he had no thought of starting the duel for another five minutes or so. 'Are you ready to entertain these troops with your death, boy? Or do you think that your friends inside the museum will come and save you? Let me tell you, by the time they arrive, it will be too late.'

And without further warning he leaped forward.

But the boy was no longer in his path. He had darted away and was on the other side of the circle.

The Fugleman snorted. 'Do you expect me to chase you? I am quite comfortable here, I assure you.' And he leaped a second time, driving his sword through the air towards the brat's neck.

Again the boy ran. And again and again, as if his only desire was to draw out the proceedings for as long as possible.

The Fugleman shook his head in disgust. 'I thought I was supposed to be fighting a duel. Instead it seems I am on a rabbit hunt!'

The mercenaries and the Blessed Guardians laughed. Field Marshal Brace nodded. 'You must engage, lad,' he said. 'If you don't, your challenge is forfeit.'

For once, it seemed, the rules of war were on the Fugleman's side. He turned back to the boy, who had gone very still. 'Come here, little rabbit,' said the Fugleman, beckoning. 'It is time to fight.'

The boy took a step forward, as if hypnotised. The Fugleman looked into his eyes, expecting to see blank terror.

Instead, an unexpected smile crossed the brat's face, as if he was thinking of someone or something he loved. He fixed his gaze on the Fugleman and said in a calm, clear voice, 'If I have to die tonight, I will make it count for something.'

Then *he* leaped forward. The duel had begun at last.

Goldie sat down very suddenly on the rock floor of the tunnel. Broo hadn't noticed her absence, and neither had the cat. She must have been gone for no more than the blink of an eye.

A timeless place . . .

'Why have you stopped?' growled the brizzlehound.

'I've been—' began Goldie. But *where* she had been was so enormous that she could not explain it. She ran her finger over the unmarked ball of her thumb and wondered what would have happened if she had failed any one of the three tests.

But she had *not* failed them. And now they were over. She scrambled to her feet again. The cat pressed against her. 'Liiiight,' it purred.

'I have told her that already,' snapped Broo. 'There is no need for you to say it.'

Goldie blinked. The darkness pressed upon her as heavily as ever. 'A light? Where?'

And then she saw it, growing on the rock walls like moss, so faint that she might have been imagining it.

'Broo,' she whispered. 'Do you know what it is?'

'A plant,' rumbled the brizzlehound. 'It will not harm us.'

The further they went, the more the moss light spread. Before long Goldie was able to let go of the cat's tail and walk unaided, peering around uneasily. The tunnel was opening up now into a series of caves, and she thought of the Place of Remembering and wondered what lay ahead.

'Salvation,' she whispered.

Behind her, Broo growled. At exactly the same moment, the cat stopped in its tracks, the hackles on its back so rigid that its scrawny body seemed to double in size.

'What is it?' breathed Goldie.

'There is something ahead,' growled Broo.

'Croooowd,' agreed the cat in an angry wail. It was not as lame as it had been, and Goldie no longer felt the least bit tired. She wondered if there was something in the air of the caves, some healing quality.

Then she realised what the cat had said, and she whispered, 'What sort of crowd? Is it dangerous?'

For once the two creatures were in agreement.

'Yessssss!'

'GRRRRREAT danger!'

Goldie's legs trembled. She had thought the tests were over.

As the three of them crept forward, the path widened, and huge boulders began to appear on every side, with bones scattered between them.

Human bones.

'I can hear water,' whispered Goldie. Her mouth was so dry that she could hardly get the words out. 'No, it's wind!'

The wind seemed to come from all around them, sighing and moaning like a living thing. It blew one way and then the other, scooping between the boulders and running invisible fingers across Goldie's arms. Broo's lip drew back from his teeth in a snarl. The cat's spine curved like a bow, and its tail bristled. Both of them glared up at the towering boulders, as if *they* were the enemy. As if *they* were the danger.

And then Goldie saw it.

Every part of her shrank from the sight. She wanted to run, but she dared not move. She dug her fingernails into the palms of her hands and swallowed her scream.

The boulders were not boulders.

They were brizzlehounds. And idlecats.

Real idlecats!

They towered above Goldie, their fangs as long as her hand. Their massive paws rested on well-chewed bones. Their grey-spotted coats rippled with muscle, their tails switched to and fro in their sleep, and they smelled like slow-stalking death.

The brizzlehounds were no better. Every single one of them was as black as night, but there the resemblance to Broo ended. Their skulls were brutal, and some dream had set them all to snarling and grinding their teeth. There were at least a hundred of them – no, more! *Five* hundred, stretching to every corner of the cave, and five hundred idlecats as well. Their sleeping breath moaned in and out, as if they might wake at any moment.

Goldie cowered in the very middle of the path, her own teeth chattering with fright. Broo and the cat pressed against her. Every hair on their bodies stood on end and, for the moment at least, their hatred of each other was forgotten.

'We must not LINGERRRRR!' growled Broo.

'Shhhh!' hissed Goldie.

But the beasts around them did not stir, and after a minute or two she found the courage to whisper, 'Keep going!'

The path took them to the very centre of the cave. And there they stopped, breathless. Directly in front of them was the biggest idlecat of all. Its eyes were closed. Its ears flicked back and forth, as if it was dreaming. Tucked between its front paws was a small iron casket.

'Is that it?' breathed Goldie. 'Is that what we have to bring back?'

The cat crouched beside her. Its lameness was completely gone now, and the bandage had fallen from its ribs. 'Dooooon't knoooow.'

'It *must* be,' whispered Goldie, although she did not understand how salvation could lie inside an iron casket. 'There's nothing else here. I'll have to steal it.'

The thought filled her with horror, but she could see no alternative. With her heart stuttering inside her, she crept towards the idlecat. The closer she came, the bigger it looked until, by the time she was an arm's length away, it loomed above her like a cliff face. She glanced over her shoulder at Broo and the cat, but they seemed a hundred miles away, and she knew they could not help her.

She thought of the ancient armies of soldiers and rats that were marching through the museum at this very moment. She thought of her friends, harrying them from every side with harp, wind, bow, pistol and beak, trying to slow them down so that she, Goldie, would have time to walk the Beast Road and save the city. She thought of Toadspit.

She swallowed the fear that was trying to clamber up her throat, and focused her mind until all she could see was the casket, and the paws on either side of it. *I can do this*, she told herself. *I'm a thief. I'm Fifth Keeper.*

Her fingers were as soft as velvet, as quiet as a wish. As she wrapped them around the top of the casket, the idlecat grunted in its sleep. Goldie froze. But the great beast did not wake, and she lifted the casket and sidled away with her prize held tight in her arms.

Broo and the cat were waiting for her. 'What is inside the box?' asked Broo.

'I don't know.' Goldie hesitated. Every instinct told her that they should leave this place as quickly as possible. But what if she was mistaken? What if the casket wasn't what they were seeking?

She placed it carefully on the ground, took out her knife and began to pry at the lid. It was stiff and rusty, as if it had not been opened for hundreds of years. She wiggled the knife all around the edge and back again, and the rust fell away and the lid creaked open. Full of hope and expectation, the three companions peered inside.

The iron casket was empty.

Goldie rocked back on her heels, stricken with disappointment. She could have wept. She could have lain down on the rocky path and cried like a baby. She had failed. She had failed her friends and everyone in Jewel.

That last thought was enough to drag her to her feet again. She *mustn't* fail! Too much depended upon her. She gazed around the great cavern, wondering where it was hidden, the *thing* that she was supposed to bring back. The sighing breath of the idlecats curled around her ears, as regular as waves on a beach.

And suddenly all her tiredness returned and she found herself yawning.

'Frooooown,' said the cat, gazing up at her.

Goldie yawned again, and this time Broo yawned with her. She pinched her hand. It didn't help. The breath of the sleeping beasts seemed to spin around her like a cocoon, and her eyes grew heavy. She was so tired . . .

'Ooooout!' said the cat, nudging her sharply. 'Oooout noooow!' But then *its* mouth opened, and *it* began to yawn.

With a groan, Broo sank to his haunches. Goldie took a step towards him and her foot kicked against a naked skull.

Death comes to those who linger.

'Broo, wake up.' She had to force the words out. 'Wake up!'

But instead of waking, the brizzlehound sighed and closed his eyes.

'Hhhhound!' spat the cat, in between yawns, and the disgust in its voice was so deep that Broo's eyes opened and he lurched to his feet again.

'We must not – LINGERRRRRR!' he growled, wobbling from side to side.

'No,' whispered Goldie. But her own desire for sleep was overwhelming. It fogged her mind and crept into her heart. She gazed stupidly at the nearest idlecat and wondered why she had been afraid of it.

Its paws looked as soft as pillows . . .

She leaned against the idlecat's flank. It was so warm and comforting that her legs folded and she slid to her knees again.

'Ooooout!' wailed the cat in her ear.

'Mmmm,' mumbled Goldie, her eyelids fluttering. 'In a minute.' She felt as if she was asleep already, and dreaming. She fumbled for her pillow. It was furrier than she had expected, but she was too tired to care. She lay down and closed her eyes.

There was a moment of blissful silence then, somewhere nearby, Broo grunted. 'Leave me alone, useless cat. I am – sleeping.'

'Sssstupid!' hissed the cat. 'Sssstupid hhhhhound!'

'I am – not stupid. Be quiet—' the brizzlehound yawned hugely '—or I will – kill you.'

'Pupppp!' spat the cat. 'Sssstupid pupppp!'

Broo growled deep in his throat, as if this new insult had stung him. 'I am not a pup!'

'Ffffeeble pupppp!'

'I am NOT A PUP!'

Goldie forced her eyes open. The brizzlehound was struggling to his feet, his lips drawn back from his teeth. She thought that she should probably do something before the two animals came to blows, but her limbs were so heavy she couldn't move.

'Cat,' she whispered. 'Leave him alone.'

The cat responded by flattening its ears against its skull and hissing even louder. 'Puuuuny pupppp! Crrrrringing mmmmilk-fed pupp!'

Such an insult from his mortal enemy was too much for Broo. He growled furiously, 'I will KILL you!' and launched himself at his tormentor.

The cat sprang out of the way. But it lashed out as it did so, and its claws raked across the brizzlehound's tender muzzle.

As if in a dream, Goldie heard Broo howl with rage. She saw a line of pink flesh open up on his nose, as neatly as if the cat had drawn it with a pen. A single drop of blood welled up from it.

The pillow under Goldie's cheek twitched.

The blood seemed to take a lifetime to fall. It hung suspended from Broo's jowls, as bright as a ruby in the gloom. The cat crouched, unmoving. The whole cavern seemed to hold its breath.

Broo snorted and shook his head. The drop of blood flew from his nose in a great arc – and splashed onto the floor of the cave.

Goldie woke up suddenly and completely. Her pillow pitched sideways, and she rolled away from it and stumbled to her feet. Broo was beside her in an instant, and the cat too. They pressed against each other, their hearts beating wildly. Goldie stared in horror at the spot where her head had rested just seconds before.

The idlecat was waking.

Muscles stretched and flexed beneath the grey-spotted coat. Claws slid out of their sheaths and scraped against the floor of the cave. Enormous jaws opened in a yawn.

Goldie edged backwards, trying not to tread on the scattered bones. They had to get out of here. Now!

But when she turned around she saw another idlecat

waking up, and another, and another. The brizzle-hounds were stirring too. All over the cave, enormous beasts shook their heads and licked their lips and stretched their long legs out before them.

Then they opened their eyes and, in a single wave of motion, rose to their feet.

Goldie stuffed her knuckles into her mouth. She was going to die here, she knew that now. In a moment, a thousand pairs of eyes would turn to look at her . . .

Broo growled and stepped forward.

'No!' hissed Goldie. 'There are too many of them! You can't fight them all!'

'I can fight ANYTHING,' rumbled Broo. His eyes burned; his coat was as black as cinder. 'I am a BRRRRIZZLEHOUND!'

His roar was a challenge to every creature in the cavern. Their heads swivelled and they glared at the intruder. Broo growled again. Beside him, the cat wailed. It was tiny in comparison with the idlecats, but it did not seem to notice. It's tail thrashed and it stood poised, ready to attack.

Goldie groaned aloud. Her companions – her foolish, mad, beautiful friends – were about to throw themselves against a foe so great that they would be dead within seconds. She would have to watch it happen – and then she too would die.

In the back of her mind, Princess Frisia whispered, *If you must die, die with pride! Die fighting!*

All around the cavern, the hissing and growling was building to a crescendo. Enormous paws padded in ever-diminishing circles. Brizzlehounds threw back their heads and roared so loudly that pebbles fell from the roof above them. In front of Goldie, Broo and the cat stood four-square and courageous, ready to fight for their lives.

I'm a part of this, thought Goldie, *whether I want to be or not*. And before she could change her mind, she stepped forward to stand beside her companions.

The nearest idlecat turned its yellow eyes towards her and hissed. Goldie flinched. How she wished she had a weapon! How she wished she had Frisia's sword in her hand!

The idlecat stretched out its enormous paw. Goldie was on the brink of panic and, in a desperate attempt to contain it, she told herself that she *did* have a sword. It was right there by her side! Look, she could wrap her fingers around the smooth hilt, like this! She could loosen it in its sheath! If the idlecat came any closer she would draw it— No, she would draw it anyway!

As the weight of the imaginary sword fell into her hand, she felt a sudden heat in her belly.

The wolf-sark.

It rose up inside her, huge and fierce. Briefly, instinctively, she tried to push it down. But then she realised. *This* was her weapon!

'Yes!' she whispered. 'Yes!'

A blaze of heat surged from her toes to her head, like molten silver, and the fear burned away to nothing. A red mist filled her . . .

'Yes!' cried the warrior princess, and she bared her teeth and snarled. She did not need a sword! She would pick up these foolish creatures and tear them apart with her bare hands!

With the wolf-sark *roaring* in her chest, she screamed a battlecry – and threw herself at the idlecat.

SALVATION

I n the cleared space in front of the museum, the Fugleman and the boy were fighting. The firelight danced on their faces as they drove one way and then the other, grunting with effort.

The Fugleman watched the boy's eyes, anticipating the next blow. W h e n it came – a vicious thrust to the stomach – he blocked and parried, then launched a series

Brizzlehound and Idlecat

of return thrusts.

But the boy darted under his blade and drew first blood. 'That's for Bonnie!' he cried, as the Fugleman stared in disbelief at his torn shoulder.

With a scream of fury, the Fugleman threw himself at the brat, driving him back and back until Frow Carrion was behind him and there was nowhere left to run.

The Fugleman smiled and raised his sword, sure that this was the end. But as his blade fell, the boy dived beneath it and skipped to the other side of the circle.

The duel was not over yet.

'Victory to the Wolf!' screamed the warrior princess, launching herself at the idlecat. Her hands were swords. Her voice was a knife, honed to a lethal point. 'Victory to the Wolf!'

But instead of fighting her, the idlecat leaped out of her way with a snarl.

Disappointed, the warrior spun around. There were enemies on every side of her, roaring like a thunderstorm. They surged towards her in a mass, their teeth slavering, their backs ridged with fury. But when she challenged them— 'The Wolf! *The Wolf!* —they fell back. And when she stalked towards them, burning for a fight, they fell back even further, as if the ferocious energy of the wolf-sark was a shield that they could not break through.

The warrior princess stood in the middle of the cavern and howled with frustration. Her eyes fell on the one creature that had not backed away. It was a brizzlehound, and it watched her with a curious look on its face, as if it knew something about her that she had forgotten.

The red mist was like a dreadful thirst inside her. '*Blood!*' it whispered. '*Blood and death!*'

The princess picked up a shattered leg bone. It was as sharp as a sword, and she held it before her as she strode towards the brizzlehound.

'Blood!' she roared. 'Blood and death!'

The brizzlehound did not move. 'Goldie,' it said.

The warrior princess raised her sword.

'Goldie,' said the brizzlehound again, cocking its head to one side. 'It's me.'

The words meant nothing. The sword slashed down, and the great hound leaped out of the way just in time. The princess shouted with rage and dived after it. But before she could attack, a burning pain sliced across the calf of her leg.

She turned, as quick as a wink, and saw a cat growling up at her. 'Oooouuut,' wailed the cat. 'Oooouuut nooooow!'

There was something about *those* words that struck her. She had heard them before, and they meant something. Something important . . .

No! Nothing was important except blood! She raised her sword and dashed at the cat.

'Goldie!' roared the brizzlehound behind her. 'Remember your TRRRRUE enemy!'

Her true enemy? The red mist cared *nothing* for truth! Her enemy was anyone who stood in front of her!

She expected the cat to run. Instead, it stood its ground. As her sword slashed towards it, it glared up at her and hissed, 'Ffffugleman! Harrooooow!'

The two names, spat out with such hatred, stopped her in her tracks. Her sword came to a halt no more than a whisker from the cat's head. Her arm trembled with the effort of keeping it there, but she did not let it fall.

Fugleman. Harrow. Her TRUE enemy.

It was like a bugle call in the darkness. The red mist parted a little, and the warrior princess knew what she must do.

It was not easy to turn away from the monsters in front of her. Every part of her was tuned to the madness of battle. Her muscles twitched. The blood raced through her veins in a torrent. She felt as if she was trying to harness a great ravening beast, only the beast was inside her, gnawing at her bones and demanding slaughter.

She almost gave in to it. But . . .

Fugleman.

The very sound of the word filled her with loathing. It drew her through the cavern with her sword raised like a banner, and the idlecats and brizzlehounds fell in on either side of her, as if they too had caught a glimpse of their true enemy.

It was the strangest of passages, that march through the cavern and the tunnels beyond. The wolf-sark rode the warrior princess every inch of the way, making it almost impossible to think. But somewhere in the depths of her mind she saw herself as a fire ship, sailing into the middle of an unsuspecting fleet and burning everything around her, at the same time as she herself was reduced to ashes.

And somewhere even deeper, where a shred of sanity still lurked, she knew that the wolf-sark was the only thing that kept her safe from the monsters that stalked beside her, and that she must not let go of it, on pain of death.

The cat trotted in front of her, unafraid. One of the brizzlehounds was there too, and every now and again he looked over his shoulder and addressed her as 'Goldie'. She ignored him. A single word drummed inside her, drawing her onwards through the tunnels.

Fugleman.

The Fugleman was tiring. As he ducked a two-handed blow that would have taken his head off, his mind raced, trying to work out how to turn the tables before he grew so weary that he made a fatal mistake. He must get in closer, where his strength would count. What he needed—

There was a hoot of laughter from the mercenaries as he stumbled on a pile of rubble. He caught himself just in time, and jumped sideways. The boy's sword whistled past him, so close that it shaved the skin from his ear. His Guardians hissed with anger.

What he needed, he thought savagely, was something that would shake the brat's concentration! Just for a second or two . . .

He gathered his strength and lunged forward. At the same time, his eyes flickered to one side and back again, as if he had seen something unexpected in the firelight. Out of the corner of his mouth he rasped, 'Guardian Hope, there's the sister! Quick, shoot her!'

It worked. The brat yelped, 'Bonnie!' and broke away. Hope, who was looking around in bewilderment, waggled her pistol at him. The boy stalled, just for an instant, and the Fugleman struck a glancing blow that wounded him in the leg. Then, with a second blow, he disarmed the boy and knocked him to the ground.

Field Marshal Brace nodded bleakly. But the Blessed Guardians cheered, and the mercenaries stamped their feet in a frenzy of approval. Guardian Hope's face shone red with delight.

The Fugleman rested the tip of his sword on the boy's chest, just above the heart. His ear burned, his shoulder was beginning to hurt, and his mood was growing more vindictive by the second.

But even as his muscles tensed for the death blow, someone shouted a warning. The Fugleman spun around. What he saw, advancing through the firelight towards him, was so astonishing that the weapon almost fell from his hand.

Marching out of the museum in old-fashioned costumes came rank upon rank of soldiers. They carried flaming torches and muskets and swords and pikes. Their feet shook the ground. Their eyes glittered murderously.

In the space between one choked breath and the next,

the Fugleman realised who they were. *The barbarians from behind the Dirty Gate!* Had the keepers released them, to protect the museum? Whatever their purpose, they did not look as if they would be easily turned from it. But surely *he* could reason with them? Surely he could charm them, persuade them . . . *use* them?

With a smile of welcome, he strode towards the flaming torches – and stopped. The ground beneath those torches was moving. All around the barbarians, scuttling over walls, streaming between their feet and on every side of them, it heaved and surged like a grotesque living carpet. A carpet made of – the Fugleman took an involuntary step backwards – of *rats*! Of enormous rats, grey and black and filthy brown!

A huge bird was diving at them, trying to drive them back. A little girl and an old woman shot fiery arrows in front of them. But their efforts were in vain. There were too many of the creatures, just as there were too many barbarians for the pathetic figures who were trying to slow them down with harp, pistol and song.

For only the second time in his life, the Fugleman found himself at a loss. What use was charm against a horde of vermin?

He heard a bellow from Field Marshal Brace. 'Shoulder your rifles, men! Ready! Steady! Fire!'

The guns stuttered out their deadly song, and

the first row of barbarians fell in a heap. But another row took their place immediately, and barbarians and rats surged forward as if they were one creature. Rifles *snapped*. Muskets *crackled*. With a roar, the two armies met.

It was only then, as blood began to spill across the ruined ground, that the Fugleman saw what else had come out of the museum.

It was a procession of sorts. But such a procession! A girl strode at the head of it, clutching a human leg bone. Her face was as grim as death. And on each side of her, stretching far back into the darkness of the museum, stalked the stuff of nightmares.

The Fugleman's skin crawled. He opened his mouth to shout, then closed it again. He clenched his fists and saw the moment when the soldiers from both armies realised what was behind them.

Between one heartbeat and the next, the fighting stalled. Shocked faces turned towards the monstrous beasts.

'Stand firm, you scoundrels,' bellowed Field Marshal Brace, 'or I'll shoot you myself! Ready! Steady! Fire!'

This time, rifles and muskets spat together, with a common purpose. But the beasts did not even flinch. Instead, they roared, as if the bullets had merely angered them.

The sound was so terrifying that many men broke and ran, and the brizzlehounds chased after them on silent paws, herding the mercenaries one way and the barbarians from behind the Dirty Gate the other. The rats dashed hither and thither between them, squealing with fright as the idlecats snapped at their tails.

'Your Honour!' screamed Guardian Hope. The Fugleman turned in time to see one of the idlecats stalking towards him with death in its eyes.

He shuddered and forced himself into action. 'Ho!' he cried at the top of his voice. 'A hundred silver thalers for every soldier who kills a beast!' And he swung his sword at the head of the idlecat.

It went straight through.

The Fugleman almost fell over with shock and disbelief. His sword clattered against the pavement and he dragged it up to shoulder height and struck another blow. The idlecat opened its terrible jaws and roared at him, so close that he could see the old blood on its teeth and smell its foul breath.

But the sword slid through it as if there was nothing there.

'It's a phantasm!' the Fugleman croaked. He looked around wildly. 'They're all phantasms!'

No one seemed to hear him. Guardian Hope had tucked herself between Frow Carrion's wheels and was babbling, 'Mercy! Mercy!' The rest of the Guardians had run away. Field Marshal Brace was rallying his mercenaries as best he could.

'They are ghosts, Brace,' shouted the Fugleman. 'Nothing but ghosts from the long-dead past! Tell your men not to be afraid, they can't hurt us!'

Smudge, who had stood firm up till now, stared at him in horror. Then the stupid man shrieked, 'Demons! *Demons!*' and he and his nearest companions threw down their rifles and ran.

With that, a red-hot fury gripped the Fugleman. Once again, the Museum of Dunt had torn his careful plans to shreds! He ground his teeth and looked around for someone on whom he could vent his rage.

The boy was lying helpless on the ground nearby. On every side of him, the phantasms prowled, lashing out with ghostly claws.

But the Fugleman was not afraid of ghosts. 'You!' he snarled, striding over to the boy and raising his sword. 'You and your keeper friends. This is all your fault!'

And he swept the sword down in a deadly arc.

THE FINAL BATTLE

The warrior princess heard the cries of 'Ghosts!' and 'Demons!' as if through a dream. The wolf-sark burned inside her, as hot as a furnace, and she clutched her leg-bone sword and strode through the flickering firelight, searching for the man she had come to kill.

The brizzlehounds and the idlecats peeled away on either side, hunting singly and in packs. They passed through walls without hesitating; their ghostly paws swiped harmlessly at the

The Fugleman

rats and soldiers, and the rats and soldiers ran for their lives.

The princess studied them, wondering which of them was her true enemy.

And then she saw him, no more than five paces away, near the great gun.

Fugleman.

His face was flushed with rage and he stood over someone – a boy – holding a sword high in the air. Even as she watched, he shouted words that she didn't catch. And the sword began to fall.

Something deep inside her cried out in horror. She threw herself across the space, thrusting the leg bone out at arm's length. There came a shriek from between the wheels of the great gun. And her enemy's sword hit the leg bone.

The shock of it went right through her, and the bone shattered into a dozen pieces. But the sword was turned aside, and her sudden intervention left the Fugleman stunned and gaping. Quickly she scanned the ground for another weapon.

'There!' shouted the boy, pointing to a sword that lay just beyond his reach.

The warrior princess snatched it up. As her fingers wrapped around the hilt – the *familiar* hilt – the wolf-sark howled with joy. The red mist thickened and she threw herself at the Fugleman with murder in her heart.

But this time he was ready for her. His sword clattered against hers and forced it to one side. He screamed in her face. 'A *girl*? A *girl* has brought me down? I will slice you to pieces, Golden Roth, for what you have done!'

'The Wolf! The Wolf!' cried the warrior, and she struck again, in a flurry of blows that stripped the words from the Fugleman's throat and drove him backwards, away from the boy.

All around them, brizzlehounds herded men like cattle. The mercenaries were sent running down the hill in a panic, but the soldiers from behind the Dirty Gate were driven back up the steps of the museum and along its dusty corridors. Idlecats pursued rats through every drain and gutter, winkling them out with ghostly claws, until they too scuttled back the way they had come. The air stank of gunpowder and fear.

The warrior princess knew all this, and cared nothing for it. The only thing that mattered was the duel. She slashed at her opponent's head, and when he fought back she stepped out of the line of attack and lunged at his legs. The wolf-sark gave her a strength beyond anything she would otherwise have had; her warrior training kept her muscles loose and her body balanced.

After only a minute or two her enemy was breathing heavily. He showed his teeth and snarled, 'You will be sorry you were ever born!'

The words did not touch her. She drove in harder, and harder, as quick as firelight and as impossible to catch. She struck at her opponent's face and thrust at his stomach. She turned him so that the fire was in his eyes, and he winced and cried out, 'Shoot her, Hope! *Shoot her, you fool!*'

But there was no shot, just a whimper of terror from beneath the great gun, and the screams of the soldiers as they fled from the phantasms.

The warrior fought on. The wounded boy cried encouragement, but it meant nothing. The phantasms and the small group of mercenaries who still held out against them; the girl with the bow who came running with her parents to stand guard over the boy; the woman with the slaver tattoos; the man with the harp and the boys who accompanied him; the two old keepers who watched the duel with their hearts in their mouths – none of them meant a thing to the warrior. There was only the fight.

And then a moment arrived when the battle-rage and the training slotted together so perfectly that she *became* the wolf, and her sword was the wolf's claw. She growled, and leaped at her prey with such force that his weapon flew from his hand and he crashed to the ground, kicking like a rabbit.

As the wolf stood over him, the past unfurled behind her eyes. A great black hound fell wounded to the floor. An ancient army sprang into action, threatening everyone she loved. A longbow lay abandoned on the cobblestones, and next to it, an arrow stained with blood. Four children crouched in a sewer with the water rising.

A terrified city . . . A good woman thrown into the canals like rubbish . . . A slave ship . . .

Mist descended on the wolf – a great howling red mist. She raised her claw for the killing blow.

'No!' screamed the rabbit. 'You can't kill me! I'm the *Fugleman*!'

'Blood and death!' howled the wolf.

'No! I surrender! Listen to me, I *surrender*! We— We *all* surrender! Brace! Lay down your weapons, you and your men! Quickly! *Quickly!* I surrender, I swear! *I give my word!*'

'Blood and *death*!' The wolf's voice was hoarse with fury. But somewhere inside her, a last skerrick of sanity whispered, '*Remember, there is always a choice.*'

She did not want to listen. The wolf-sark rode her so strongly that she could feel the fur on her head and the hot saliva dripping from her jaws. 'No choice!' she growled. 'Revenge!'

333

'Goldie!' shouted the boy lying on the ground. 'Stop! They've surrendered!'

'No choice!' she growled again, but the boy's voice was like a wind that pierced the wolf-mist, and the speck of sanity grew larger.

'. . . *always a choice* . . .'

More voices joined in – voices she loved. 'Goldie! Goldie!'

She could have turned away from them even then, and let the battle-rage do what it hungered to do. But she had fought too hard to be the person she was and to live the life that she wanted to live. And she would not give it up now, not even for revenge.

With a great shudder, she forced the wolf-sark down. She forced the warrior princess down too, until the person standing over the Fugleman, sword in hand, was Goldie Roth. No more, no less.

She looked up and saw Herro Dan and Olga Ciavolga watching her, with Auntie Praise, Sinew, Mouse and Pounce beside them. Bonnie and her parents were crouched next to Toadspit. Guardian Hope still whimpered between the wheels of Frow Carrion, and Field Marshal Brace and his few remaining mercenaries stood back to back, with their guns on the ground at their feet and a score of brizzlehounds padding around them in a silent, threatening circle.

There was no sign now of the rats, or of the ancient soldiers who had come so close to invading the city. They were gone, driven back to where they had come from.

Goldie was suddenly so tired that she could hardly think. Where was Broo? She looked at the prowling phantasms and realised that he might be any one of them, and that she could no longer tell him apart.

Where was the cat? It had been with her when she came out of the museum, at the head of that strange procession.

She shifted her weight—

—and the Fugleman, who was not a rabbit after all, but a fox of infinite cunning, kicked her legs out from underneath her, grabbed her sword and leaped to his feet.

'No one move or the girl dies!' he shouted, holding the sword to Goldie's throat.

Bonnie froze in the act of raising her bow. So did Auntie Praise, her hand on the pistol in her belt. Toadspit groaned, and Herro Dan cried out in anger.

But Guardian Hope opened her eyes and crawled from between the wheels of Frow Carrion. Her great fear of a moment ago had given way to an even greater viciousness, and she kicked Toadspit as she passed him, and slapped Auntie Praise's face. Then she snatched their weapons and held them all at gunpoint, saying, 'Did you think you would win? What fools you are!'

Goldie lay on the ground, burning with fury. She should never have taken her eyes off the Fugleman, not even for a second! She should have known—

Without shifting the sword from her throat, the Fugleman glanced towards the mercenaries. 'Pick up your guns, Brace! I need you.'

The field marshal and his men did not move. The brizzlehounds snarled silently at them.

'There's nothing to fear from a few phantasms!' cried the Fugleman. 'Come, I need you here. There is *rubbish* to be disposed of.'

The firelight leaped and flickered. Field Marshal Brace nodded to his soldiers, who picked up their rifles and edged past the brizzlehounds. Herro Dan and Olga Ciavolga gripped each other's hands, their gaze fixed on Goldie.

'The prisoners are all yours,' said the Fugleman, when at last the mercenaries stood before him. He waved his free hand in a generous arc. 'Shoot them, bayonet them, I don't mind, as long as they are dead.' He looked down at Goldie and his teeth gleamed. 'Except for this one. I will take care of her myself.'

The field marshal coughed into his fist. 'You surrendered,' he said.

'I did indeed,' laughed the Fugleman. 'A fine trick, was it not?'

'Mm.' Brace sucked on his teeth. 'You told *us* to surrender, and we did so.'

'All part of the ruse, my dear Brace. It does not bother you, does it? Why, I imagine that you and your men must surrender all the time, then stab your enemy in the back when they are no longer expecting it. That is war, is it not?'

Goldie heard the mercenaries hiss under their breath, as if they had been insulted.

Brace's eyes were like pewter. 'But you gave your word.'

'And I would give it again, a hundred times over if necessary,' said the Fugleman with his most charming smile. 'Now, shall we get on with it? Once these scum are dead there is a bonus waiting in the Treasury for you and your brave men. A *considerable* bonus. We will break out the very best wine tonight, I think, to celebrate the end of the Hidden Rock. What a partnership we have, Brace! And remember, this is only the beginning—'

'You. Gave. Your. *Word*,' said the field marshal. His fists clenched and unclenched as if he wanted to hit someone.

The Fugleman stared at him, puzzled. 'Are you quite well, Field Marshal? Did you take a wound in the fighting?'

'You surrendered. *We* surrendered.'

'A head wound, perhaps? You are repeating yourself, man!'

Field Marshal Brace's face twitched. 'Then I will repeat myself one last time. You surrendered. We surrendered. We can do nothing more here. This alliance is finished.'

'*What?*' said the Fugleman, realising too late that the other man was serious. His sword hand spasmed, and blood ran down Goldie's neck. She lay as still as stone.

The field marshal took three steps towards Frow Carrion, then swung back. 'You have no honour,' he said in a voice as quiet and deadly as the plague. 'You have no *idea* of honour. You think that because we are mercenaries you have bought us completely. But there are rules in this business. Rules of war. And you have broken them one by one.'

The Fugleman began to protest but Brace continued over the top of him. 'Oh yes, you want us to stay! No doubt you will promise us anything if we stay.' His face twisted in disgust. 'No doubt you will give us *your word*!'

He signalled, and all but two of his men stepped away from the Fugleman and swarmed towards Frow Carrion, loading cannonballs onto a cart and hitching up the gas tractor.

It took them ten minutes to ready the great gun for departure. In that time, no one else moved or spoke. The Fugleman might have been a statue. A muscle in his jaw flickered, nothing more.

But Goldie could feel the dreadful eagerness in the sword that rested at her throat, and she knew that, as soon as the soldiers left, the Fugleman would kill her.

She slipped her hand into her pocket and wrapped her fingers around the blue bird brooch.

The moment came more quickly than she had expected. The gas tractor rumbled to life and lurched away into the darkness, dragging Frow Carrion behind it. The cobblestones shook. All around the open space, walls and chimneys that had been weakened by the bombardment tumbled to the ground in a cloud of dust.

Without looking back, Field Marshal Brace raised his hand. The two men who had been standing on either side of the Fugleman jogged away.

The Fugleman's grip tightened on the hilt of his sword. But before he could thrust it downwards, Pounce began to beg for mercy in a whiny, irritating voice. The Fugleman glanced up at him . . .

And in that split second of distraction, Goldie whipped the blue bird brooch out of her pocket and plunged its pin deep into the calf of his leg.

The Fugleman screamed with pain. Goldie threw herself sideways, trying to scramble to her feet. She could hear Guardian Hope shouting, and several pistol shots. She looked around for help, but the Fugleman had already wrenched the brooch from his flesh and was advancing on her, sword in hand.

There was only one thing left to do. 'Pa!' screamed Goldie at the top of her voice. 'Now! *Now!*'

The Fugleman laughed grimly. 'No more tricks, girl!' he snarled. 'This time you are mine!'

He raised the sword. Behind him, a quiet voice said, 'Hello, brother.'

The Fugleman spun around so quickly that he lost his footing. Auntie Praise leaped out of the shadows and wrenched the sword from his fingers. Guardian Hope rushed to the rescue, raising her pistol, but Toadspit stuck out his good leg, and she tripped over him and fell to the ground, where Bonnie and Pounce sat on her.

The Fugleman hardly seemed to notice. He was staring at the Protector, who stood firm and unforgiving in front of him, supported by Ma and Pa.

'You—' said the Fugleman. 'You're dead!'

'I am alive,' said the Protector. 'And you are beaten.'

'Never!' snarled the Fugleman, and before anyone could stop him he jumped to his feet and scrambled away across the broken ground.

Herro Hahn and Sinew would have gone after him,

but Olga Ciavolga halted them with a gesture. 'He will not get far,' she said. 'Look.'

All this while, a small pack of brizzlehounds had been pacing silently in the background. Now they surged forward to block the Fugleman's escape, their teeth so dreadful and their eyes so savage that the Fugleman hesitated.

But then he drew himself up and cried, 'You do not frighten me! You are nothing but phantasms! You cannot hurt me!'

He walked right through the first great beast, and the second, and all they could do was snarl.

The Fugleman laughed a bitter laugh. 'You are dust!' he shouted, in the face of the third brizzlehound. 'Ancient dust, and no more powerful than a dead leaf on the ground! I will escape you all, and one day I will return and destroy what you are so keen to protect. Try and stop me! Try and kill me! Go on, do your worst!'

He laughed again.

And in the middle of his laughter, the third brizzlehound, who had one white ear and was not a phantasm after all, opened his great jaws and snapped the Fugleman's neck.

SALVATION IS A
DOUBLE-EDGED
SWORD

Goldie Roth

inew found some rope that
the mercenaries had left
behind, and bound Guardian
Hope tightly. Olga Ciavolga stitched
Toadspit's leg while he bit his lip
and tried hard not to cry out, and
Bonnie and her parents winced
until the stitching was done.

Goldie sat on the remains of a
chimney, stunned by what had just
happened. Pa wrapped his arms around
her and she leaned against his chest,
unable to speak.

'You know there's not a prison that could've held him,' murmured Ma, nodding towards the Fugleman's corpse, which Herro Dan had covered with the parley flag. 'He would've charmed the bars themselves into stepping aside and letting him through.'

Goldie knew that Ma was right. But the stunned feeling would not go away. She felt as if all her nerve endings were laid bare, so that the city and the museum wrapped around her as tightly as Pa's arms. If she closed her eyes, she could almost see Frow Carrion rumbling across Old Arsenal Bridge on its way out of Jewel. She saw the last soldier and the last rat dive through the Dirty Gate. She felt the Gate slam shut behind them.

It's finished, she told herself. *It's over.*

And yet somehow it wasn't. The museum was still restless, and all around her the air crackled, as if something important hung in the balance.

Perhaps it was to do with the phantasms, which were gathering in the plaza once more, stiff-legged and snarling. Goldie thought she was too weary to care.

But then the cat rubbed against her leg, and Morg flew down to join them. A moment later, Broo loped towards them with his breath huffing out in clouds.

'The mercenaries and the Guardians are gone,' rumbled Broo. 'They will not return. But now—'

'That's good,' said Goldie, trying not to notice the blood on Broo's jaws. She forced herself to smile, knowing that the brizzlehound had only done what was in his nature, and that she was not sorry. The Fugleman had brought his fate upon himself. Justice had been done.

'But now,' continued Broo, 'there is a problem.'

Behind him, five hundred phantom brizzlehounds raised their hackles and growled on such a deep note that Goldie could feel it vibrating in her chest.

'Prrrrrroblem,' said the cat, and five hundred idlecats wailed in angry agreement.

Auntie Praise strode through them, looking as if phantasms were something she dealt with every day of her life. 'Am I imagining things,' she said, 'or are these brutes about to declare war on each other? Goldie, can you stop them?'

Toadspit hopped over to the ruined chimney, with Bonnie supporting him. And the next minute everyone was gathered in front of Goldie, expecting her to do something.

'They're mortal enemies,' Goldie said slowly, trying to collect her wits. 'I— I think they only came together to save the museum.'

'And now *that* threat's gone they're ready to turn on each other,' said Herro Dan. He eyed the great beasts warily. 'They might only be phantasms, but they've got *me* scared. You'd best send 'em back where they came from, lass, as quick as you can.'

Goldie nodded and beckoned to Broo and the cat. 'Will they talk to me?' she whispered.

'We will ask them,' said Broo. And he and the cat trotted across the space that separated them from the phantasms.

When they returned, they brought a single brizzlehound with them. He was bigger than his companions, and his ghostly frame seemed to blot out half the night sky. Close by – but not *too* close – stalked an equally big idlecat, its tail twitching like knotted rope.

The two creatures were so ancient and wild and terrible that the words Goldie had been planning to say dried up in her throat. Even Auntie Praise blanched when she saw them, and Guardian Hope, who was tied up nearby, began to sob with fear, great fat tears oozing down her cheeks like treacle. Only Mouse edged forward, an expression of awe on his face.

The brizzlehound bent his massive head towards Goldie. 'We have done what we were summoned to do.' His voice rumbled across the cobblestones and out into the listening night. 'What more do you want from us, human?'

Goldie gulped. 'W-will you go back now?'

The idlecat's ears flattened. The brizzlehound sniffed Goldie's hair. 'You are the one who brought us out of the deep caves?'

'Yes,' whispered Goldie.

'But now you are different.'

'Um— Yes.' The terrors of the Beast Road, the wolf-sark that had saved her, the mad frenzy of the sword fight – Goldie felt as if they had happened to someone else.

She fought down her fear and asked again. 'Will you go?'

The brizzlehound shook his head. 'The one—'

'You must,' interrupted Olga Ciavolga sharply. 'This is no place for you.'

But the brizzlehound had not finished. 'The one who leads us out of the deep caves must lead us back again. That is the nature of the Beast Road.'

Goldie sighed inwardly. Her whole body ached, and she wasn't sure if she could walk anywhere, much less as far as the Devil's Kitchen. Nonetheless she began to rise.

Herro Dan's big hand came down on her shoulder. 'Exactly how *far* does she have to lead you?' he said in a suspicious voice. 'To the beginnin' of the tunnel, where the Beast Road starts?'

'Fuuurrrther,' said the idlecat. 'Mmmuch furrrr-ther.'

Goldie felt as if someone had kicked her in the stomach. 'You mean, I have to go back along the Beast Road?'

'No!' cried Ma.

'Definitely not!' said Sinew.

'They want you to walk it *again*?' cried Pa incredulously. 'Is *that* what the creature is saying?'

'Not a chance,' said Herro Dan.

Olga Ciavolga's voice rose hard and sharp above the others. 'She survived the Beast Road once, and that was miracle enough. She would not survive it a second time.'

'Then we will stay here,' said the brizzlehound in a cavernous voice. 'It makes no difference to us.'

Behind him, the great hounds stirred, like the beginnings of a forest fire. The idlecats spat at them, and they growled back and bunched their great muscles. The city held its breath, and so did the museum.

Goldie struggled free of Pa's arms. 'No, wait! Don't fight! You'll terrify people! You *must* go back!'

'*I* will take them,' said Broo.

The cat pushed in front of him. 'Meeeee!'

'Not yooouu,' said the idlecat, glowering down at its small relation. It raised a ghostly paw and swiped at Goldie's cheek. 'Sheeee is the one.'

Ma clamped her hand over her mouth and stifled a sob. Pa grabbed hold of Goldie again and said, very loudly, 'I won't allow it! My girl is *not* going back there!'

'I agree,' said Auntie Praise. She glared at the other keepers. 'You lot sort something out. But don't expect Goldie to fix this. She's done enough.'

Herro Dan shook his head. 'We don't expect her to fix it, lass. Like you say, she's done enough already, and Toadspit too. But—'

He and Olga Ciavolga caught each other's eye. Something passed between them.

'But what?' whispered Goldie. No one spoke. 'But *what*?'

Olga Ciavolga turned to the two great beasts, her face pale. 'You are flesh and blood in the deep caves, are you not?'

'Fleeesh and blooood,' agreed the idlecat.

'And out here you are phantasms?'

'Yesssss.'

'So what is this?' And the old woman pointed at the rubble-strewn ground.

At first all Goldie could see were boot marks and the tracks of Frow Carrion, and she did not understand what Olga Ciavolga was talking about.

But then she saw the *new* indents – the ones with the slash of claws around them and pads the size of dinner plates. The ones that were appearing right before her eyes.

She went cold with horror. *This* was the thing that still hung in the balance, the thing that made the air crackle and the chimney shake beneath her.

The brizzlehounds and the idlecats were becoming real.

'Herro Dan?' she whispered. 'Why are they—'

'Dunno, lass.' The old man sounded as tired as Goldie. 'Maybe they've stayed out here too long. Maybe it's somethin' in the air, or somethin' else that we can't even begin to guess at. These are old, old mysteries.' His voice cracked. 'We don't expect— Not you. Not again.'

Goldie could not speak. She knew what she *should* say, for the sake of everyone in the city, but the words would not form on her tongue.

I've done enough, she thought. *I've done enough!*

With that she found her voice and said, 'I— I don't think I can—'

But the city was listening to her. She could feel it, every bridge and canal and cobblestone waiting on her decision. And almost before she knew it, she found herself saying, 'Maybe— Maybe it wouldn't be so bad, going back a second time. At least I'd know what to expect.'

'No,' said Pa, his eyes fixed on those awful paw prints. 'You're not going and that's the end of it.'

The *thing* that hung in the balance shifted to one side. The idlecats raised their heads as if they could smell blood. Flesh clothed their paws and slid up their legs as smooth as silk.

Goldie clutched Pa's hand, thinking of the past year and how much she had grown up in that time. Was this what it had all been leading to? She didn't want it to end here. She wanted to see more of life. She wanted to be Fifth Keeper, and help put the museum back together. She wanted . . .

But it was no use thinking like that. Something had to be done. And she was the only one who could do it.

It seemed that salvation was a double-edged sword.

She squeezed Pa's hand, then let it go. 'I'll take them,' she said. Her voice cracked around the edges. 'I— I *have* to take them.'

The balance swung the other way. The city listened more closely than ever. The Bridge of Beasts seemed to strain towards Old Arsenal Hill, like a dog on a leash. The House of Repentance, which had served such a cruel and twisted purpose under the Blessed Guardians, sniffed the air, as if it could smell change coming.

Ma's mouth twisted in pain. 'No! Why does it always have to be *you*?' She looked around wildly. 'Why can't someone *else* do it?'

350

'I'm sorry, Ma,' said Goldie, holding her close. She could see the devastation in her mother's eyes, and in her father's too. 'I— I'll come back. Wait for me!'

Toadspit's face was grey. 'You'd *better* come back!' he hissed in her ear. Sinew said more or less the same thing, though much of it was lost under the sobbing of his harp strings. Olga Ciavolga, Herro Dan and Bonnie hugged her. Pounce and Frow Hahn offered her their pistols.

But Mouse—

Mouse was edging towards the brizzlehound. He looked so small that Goldie put out her hand to pull him away. But then he began to croon and whistle, and the brizzlehound and the idlecat turned their terrifying eyes towards him.

'Mousie?' hissed Pounce. 'Whatcha *doin*'?'

Mouse didn't answer. His voice wove a wordless story in the air. His face shone with effort.

The brizzlehound grunted, as if he had learned something interesting. He bent his head again, and breathed on Goldie's forehead. She felt a sudden heat inside her, as if the wolf-sark had woken up and pricked its ears.

'The white-haired pup is right,' rumbled the brizzlehound. He seemed to grow several inches. 'It was the wolf that led us here, and the warrior, not this girl—'

Goldie stood very still, hardly daring to hope. She could feel the balance sitting firmly in the centre, and the city murmuring all around her, *Yes, this is it.*

'—and the wolf and the warrior can take us back again,' said the brizzlehound. 'If the girl will give them to us.'

The unexpected reprieve was almost too much. Goldie gasped – great heaving gulps of precious air – and shook all over. Beside her, Ma and Pa were weeping.

Toadspit wiped his eyes with his sleeve, then made a shooing gesture, as if telling Goldie to get on with it. She felt a strong urge to stick her tongue out at him.

Instead, she said to the two great beasts, 'H-how do I give you the wolf? And the warrior?'

They surged forward to stand on either side of her. 'Put your hands on us,' rumbled the brizzlehound.

Goldie raised her hands and placed them high in the air where the creatures' necks appeared to be. It was the strangest sensation. Their paws and their legs were already flesh and bone, but high on their withers there was only a faint warmth, like a memory of something from long, long ago.

Deep inside Goldie, the wolf-sark's lip drew back from its sharp white teeth.

'W-what now?' she said.

The brizzlehound said nothing. Herro Dan nudged Sinew. 'Reckon it's up to us.'

Sinew touched his harp strings. Toadspit and Olga Ciavolga stepped forward to stand beside him, and Mouse wriggled between them, his mice clinging to his jacket. They began to sing – and play – the First Song. '*Ho oh oh-oh,*' they sang. '*Mm mm oh oh oh-oh oh.*'

As the familiar notes wrapped around her, Goldie had a moment of extreme terror. What would she be when this was finished? Would she lose something she did not want to lose? Would she still recognise herself?

But then the terror passed, and she too began to sing in a firm voice, '*Mm mm ho oh oh-oh,*' she sang. '*Oh oh oh-oh oh.*'

Morg flew up to perch on a nearby wall, and raised and lowered her wings in the same ancient rhythm. The mice squeaked in unison. The cat closed its eyes and crooned, '*Rrrow rrow ow ow ow-ow.*'

And then, with a great shudder, the museum joined in. The ships in Rough Tom, the portraits that hung from the walls of the Lady's Mile, the whale skeletons and the suits of armour and the dreadful *thing* that lived beneath the waters of Old Scratch – they all sang with voices that had not been heard in Jewel for hundreds of years. Their song swept through the streets like a Great Wind, and the wild music surged up from the centre of the earth to meet them.

'*MM MM HO OH OH-OH*,' sang the museum and the city and the wild music. '*OH OH OH-OH OH.*'

Something prickled beneath Goldie's fingers. Broo threw back his head and howled, and deep inside Goldie the wolf-sark howled with him. It was rising up to meet the singing, more powerful than she had ever felt it before. She gasped. On either side of her, she could feel the two great beasts, feel their ghostly hearts begin to beat in their chests, feel their breath on her face and the fur on their backs.

The red mist filled her. She opened her mouth and howled with Broo and the wolf. She saw a great brightness all around . . .

And then it was gone. The brizzlehound and the idlecat stood beside her, as solid as she was. She could smell them, touch them, feel them.

But inside Goldie, there was an emptiness.

The wolf-sark had left her.

And so had the warrior princess.

When Guardian Hope realised that the two great beasts had become flesh and blood, she began to weep again. No one took any notice of her. A procession was forming. Broo and the cat stood at the front of it, bristling with pride. Behind them were the two great beasts who carried the wolf-sark and the spirit of the warrior princess. And behind *them* were the phantasms,

354

bigger and wilder than ever, as if the wolf-sark had touched them too.

At an invisible signal they surged forward across the broken ground, their enmity forgotten for now. Goldie could feel every step they took. Into the museum and through the ruined front rooms. Through the Staff Only door, which was dangling from its hinges. Up Harry Mount and down again. Through the Vacant Block, where the old tree burst into blossom as they passed. Through Broken Bones and Dark Nights and Stony Heart. Across the razor steepness of Knife Edge, and past the Tench's stinking cells.

Until, in the heart of the museum, they came to the place where the Beast Road began. Broo and the cat peeled away, and the other creatures strode alone into the darkness – and disappeared.

With a start, Goldie found herself back in the city and realised that a considerable amount of time had passed. Behind her, Sinew was throwing wood on the fire, and talking to Pounce. 'We could use you and Mouse,' he said. 'There's always room for a couple more keepers, and I think you'd be good.'

'Nah,' said Pounce, 'we's off to sail the seas in the *Silver Lining*, isn't we, Mousie?' He paused. 'Mousie?'

Goldie glanced over her shoulder. Mouse was standing beside Sinew, shaking his head as if nothing would move him.

Pounce groaned. Then his face brightened and he turned to the Protector, who was resting with Frow and Herro Hahn on a pile of rugs. 'Want to buy a nice ship?' he said. 'I'll give ya a good price.'

On the other side of the fire, Pa seemed to have reached an uncomfortable truce with Auntie Praise, and the two of them were talking seriously, with Ma joining in now and again. When Goldie caught their attention, Pa blew a kiss. Ma waved and wiped a tear from her eye. Auntie Praise winked, then turned to Bonnie, who was tugging at her arm.

'I want to hunt down Old Lady Skint,' said Bonnie, 'and put her in prison. Will you help me?'

Pa raised an eyebrow. 'Were you listening to our conversation, Bonnie?'

'No,' said Bonnie. 'I thought of it myself.'

Auntie Praise rolled her eyes and said, 'Some snotties do not seem to understand that they are only snotties! What will you set out to do next, rid the whole world of slavery?'

'Does that mean yes or no?' said Bonnie.

'It means yes, you insolent brat, if you can persuade your parents . . . and if *I* survive prison, where my sister's good man is determined to send me. Now go away. We are talking.'

Goldie looked around for Olga Ciavolga and Herro

Dan, and found them sitting nearby, gazing into the darkness at the battered walls of the museum. 'Well, that's that,' said the old woman. She slipped her boots off and began to rub her feet. 'What do we do now?'

'We rebuild,' said Herro Dan. 'With a bit of work, the walls of the museum'll be strong enough to hold for another five hundred years.' He nodded towards the other keepers. 'And we'll have plenty of help. Here, lass, I'll do that.' And he lifted Olga Ciavolga's feet onto his lap.

Everything was so different – and yet so ordinary – that Goldie found herself smiling.

Someone draped a casual arm around her neck. It was Toadspit, with Morg on his shoulder and a makeshift crutch holding him upright. 'So who are you now?' he said. 'A princess? A mad wolf-girl? Queen of the idlecats?'

Goldie laughed. 'I'm me, that's all.'

As she said it, she realised it was true. The feeling of emptiness was gone and she was completely herself, more so than she had ever been in her life.

She heard a *yip* and Broo, back in his little-white-dog shape, raced towards her with his curly tail held high and the cat gambolling at his side.

Goldie scooped them both up in her arms and kissed them. Broo wagged his tail. The cat scowled at her, just for the sake of it, then began to purr so loudly that Goldie could feel it from her scalp to her toes.

She could feel too, that something had changed in Jewel. Hardly anyone knew it yet. Not the prisoners in the House of Repentance, who had just found their cell doors mysteriously open and their guards gone; nor the children who had been saved from the *Silver Lining* and who were only now trickling back to their homes; nor their heartbroken parents, shuffling to answer an unexpected knock on the door.

None of them knew that the Fugleman was dead. None of them knew that there was something rising up through the cobblestones like the first wild flower of spring.

But it was there. Goldie could sense it.

She wasn't entirely sure what it was. All she knew was that it carried with it the promise of vacant blocks, and dogs and cats and birds. And secret places for children to hide when they wanted to escape from the eyes of adults. And the freedom for those same children to become who they really were.

Even the ones like Goldie Roth, and Toadspit and Bonnie Hahn, who were impatient. And bold.

ACKNOWLEDGEMENTS

I continue to be blessed with wonderful editors, who have pushed me to make this book (and this trilogy) far better than it would have been without them. Many many thanks to Eva Mills and Susannah Chambers at Allen & Unwin, and to Michelle Poploff at Delacorte Press (who came up with the perfect title for Book 3).

Also at Allen & Unwin, I'd like to thank Jyy-Wei Ip, Julia Imogen, Liz Bray and Angela Namoi. The covers created by Design by Committee and Sebastian Ciaffaglione are big favourites, and Seb's wonderful character drawings are adored by everyone who sees them.

I remain indebted to Peter Matheson for his insight and feedback on the various drafts, and to my most excellent agent Margaret Connolly for all her work on my behalf, as well as her enthusiasm and support.

Finally, I wish to thank the ancient Chinese general Sun Tzu, whose book *The Art of War* was the inspiration for Princess Frisia's military wisdom, and Peter Sharpe, who would like to be a character in one of the books, but will have to settle for being the world's best masseur.

ABOUT THE AUTHOR

LIAN TANNER is a children's author and playwright. She has worked as a teacher in Australia and Papua New Guinea, as well as a tourist-bus driver, a freelance journalist, a juggler, a community arts worker, an editor and a professional actor. It took her a while to realise that all of these jobs were really just preparation for being a writer. Nowadays she lives by the beach in southern Tasmania, with a small tabby cat and lots of friendly neighbourhood dogs. She has not yet mastered the art of Concealment by the Imitation of Nothingness, but she is quite good at Camouflage.